The Scarlet Nightingale

Other novels by Alan Titchmarsh

Mr MacGregor
The Last Lighthouse Keeper
Animal Instincts
Only Dad
Rosie
Love and Dr Devon
Folly
The Haunting
Bring Me Home
Mr Gandy's Grand Tour

Alan Titchmarsh
The Scarlet Nightingale

HODDER

First published in Great Britain in 2018 by Hodder & Stoughton
An Hachette UK company

This paperback edition published in 2019

8

A CIP catalogue record for this title is available from the British Library

Paperback ISBN 978 1 473 65834 9
eBook ISBN 978 1 473 65833 2

Typeset in Sabon by Palimpsest Book Production Ltd,
Falkirk, Stirlingshire

Printed and bound in Great Britain by Clays Ltd, Elcograf S.p.A.

Hodder & Stoughton policy is to use papers that are natural,
renewable and recyclable products and made from wood grown in sustainable forests.
The logging and manufacturing processes are expected to conform to the
environmental regulations of the country of origin.

Hodder & Stoughton Ltd
Carmelite House
50 Victoria Embankment
London EC4Y 0DZ

www.hodder.co.uk

For Jilly Cooper
who, twenty years ago, encouraged me
to write my first novel.

And in memory of
Mary Ellis
1917–2018
the last surviving member of the
Air Transport Auxiliary
whose delightful company
provided inspiration for
The Scarlet Nightingale

ACKNOWLEDGEMENTS

I am enormously grateful to Sara Kinsella, Sharona Selby and Rowena Webb whose editorial guidance has been of great help and encouragement. Thanks also to Dee Tyler who recommended that I visit Wanborough Manor, near Guildford, to Stephen Callender who arranged my visit and Richard Suchard and Richard Lansdowne who showed me around the building that is now their home. The signs of its wartime role are still very much in evidence. Patrick Yarnold's *Wanborough Manor – School for Secret Agents* was immensely helpful in providing information of the house's role in training those who were sent on missions into occupied France. Anyone anxious to know more about the men and women who passed through its doors – and their extraordinary courage – should read it.

PROLOGUE

Rosamund Hawksmoor (formerly Hanbury) died peacefully in her ninety-third year in the tall-windowed bedroom overlooking the azure sea at Saint-Jean-Cap-Ferrat. She was discovered by her butler as he delivered her morning tea, her face set in a gentle smile, and the pure white gauze curtains that framed the open windows were rising and falling in the gentle breeze almost as though they were the wings of an angel, wafting the old lady's unencumbered soul to heaven.

At the foot of her bed, resting on a chintz-covered ottoman, lay the manuscript of her final novel. It was tied with red ribbon, as was her custom, and it was to become, as had her previous twenty-two works of romantic fiction, an immediate bestseller. Her literary agent would make sure of that.

Her butler, Jonathan Finch, also passed to Rosamund's executors a large manila envelope that he had discovered in the ormolu-encrusted cabinet at her bedside. It was old and worn and upon it, in stylish italic script, were written the words: 'Only to be opened in the event of my death.'

Rosamund's wishes were adhered to, not least because until the old lady's demise, nobody actually knew it was there. It revealed to her executors – none of whom were blood relations – tantalising clues about her early life. Rosamund – the hospitable old lady who lived a life of luxury in the south of France – had told no one about her childhood, of her experiences as a girl and her exploits as a young woman during the war. The few contemporaries who had managed to survive her had slipped from view, content to live in the past. Rosamund found far more stimulation in the company of younger folk who, like her, found more pleasure and excitement in the present.

It seemed, to those who had entered her orbit within recent times, that Rosamund had always been old and wise, with a zest for life, delighting in the company of anyone with a spark of enthusiasm who could hold their own at the dinner table. She dispensed her worldly wisdom only when it was solicited, and listened with the attention of the genuinely curious when regaled with the convoluted or confusing emotions of the young and inexperienced. She would nod and smile – not the patronising smile of those who have seen it all before and know all the answers, but the understanding smile of those whose experiences of life have taught them that although they may have been there before, nothing is certain when it comes to human nature. Concerned though she would be for the welfare of the young who fluttered around her like moths drawn to a flame, little seemed to worry Rosamund for long; the years had taught her much about the futility of fretting over things that could not be changed.

The contents of the ragged envelope told quite a different story. Assorted fragments, letters and luggage labels gave clues to a path through life that had been anything but smooth. They were all neatly contained in a buff folder, even more frayed at the edges than the envelope itself. Like the manuscript of her novels, the folder was tied around the middle with a length of bright red ribbon. It was of such an age that it should have been faded; the brilliance of its colour bleached by the sun of the Côte d'Azur. But since it had not seen the light of day for many years, it was as vivid as the day it had been woven. At the top of the folder, in black letters, a printed instruction gave an indication of its vintage:

TOP SECRET
EYES ONLY

And below that, in red italic script, were just three words:

THE SCARLET NIGHTINGALE

At first glance the reader might have thought that the contents were snippets of inspiration for yet another love story, popped into a file appropriated after the war by a relation employed in some obscure branch of the Civil Service. They would have been wrong. The folder itself had a more interesting story to tell, and there was nothing fictitious about the fragments it contained. They were the souvenirs and accretions of a life that had most certainly had its share of romance – both on the page and off – but which had also put a young woman in danger. Rosamund might have come from a privileged background, but it was something that she had been quite prepared to sacrifice in the name of love and duty. This is her story.

ROSAMUND HAWKSMOOR

The notes which were the foundation of these recollections were penned somewhat erratically during and just after the war when I started to keep a journal. Some are exactly as they were written; others I have adjusted with the benefit of hindsight. I have not written an in-depth chronicle. My jottings are fragmentary and far from comprehensive. As a writer I have come to appreciate the value – and wisdom – of editing. I have simply touched on one or two matters that might interest, and I have left others to the imagination of those who come after. There are some moments I cannot bear to recall, still, and on occasion I may have skipped episodes which I would prefer to forget, but there are no real untruths here – perhaps just one or two 'economies'. As Dame Edith Sitwell famously said: 'There is no truth; only points of view.' Through these few pages, perhaps my godson Archie will come to know a little more of my earlier life and, I hope, not judge me too harshly.

My earliest recollection is that of sand between my toes. But is that really my first memory or simply the one I choose to cling to? A comfort blanket of sorts? Whatever the case, the feeling of those fine grains, smooth as silk against my infant skin, and the change in feeling when hardened into glistening ribs by waves at the water's edge, nurtured within me a fascination for the sea and a love of coastal life which I have never lost.

Despite this secure and cosy image, it is not a wholly comforting memory, for there is a rawness about the seashore. At any given moment it may be calm and serene, bathed in golden sunlight, the sky as pale as a forget-me-not. Then, when one's back is turned for a moment – making a sandcastle or digging for a razor shell – lumbering clouds as purple as a ripe damson will push up on the horizon. In the space of minutes, the scene will be transformed from that Dorothea Sharp idyll into something redolent of John Piper on a bad day. The thunder cracks, the once-calm sea becomes a turbulent cauldron, and the sudden and violent wind whips up those grains of sand and hurls them into your eyes, blinding you as you stumble for shelter.

To make one's life on the coast is a constant reminder that we are all, quite literally, living on the edge – not just at the mercy of the elements, but also at the mercy of the whims and temperament of others. Somehow the sea is predictable in its capriciousness. Whatever may happen, and however violent the storm or tempest, one knows in one's heart that eventually it will pass; that the tide will go out and the sky will clear. Calm will invariably follow storm. Alas, one cannot say the same of people . . .

But I am racing ahead. When one is young the summers seem to last forever and the memory of dark clouds passes more rapidly than they do when old age causes us to brood upon them. As a young person of my acquaintance sagely remarked: 'When you are seven, a year is a seventh of your life; when you are eighty it is an eightieth, and an eightieth of anything is so much smaller than a seventh.' It is a trite analogy, but I have come to realise that it is a universal truth. As you age, the years fly past with ever-increasing speed. When I was young it seemed as though the halcyon days would never end . . .

Chapter 1

DEVONSHIRE

1928

'Kindness bestowed upon children is a long-term
investment.'

Alicia de Bournanville, *The Waves of Time*, 1919

The water felt cold. Very cold. At first Rosamund thought that
her toes might actually fall off, but gradually they became
accustomed to the temperature of the sea and the wavelets as
they lapped about her feet. The skirt of her floral-patterned
dress was tucked into her knickers, the better to preserve it from
a soaking. Her governess would not be best pleased if she
returned from her excursion with a dress soaked in seawater
and peppered with salt and sand. She did quite like 'Semolina'
– the name she called her even if Celine de Rossignol did get
cross and threaten to wallop her playfully whenever she heard
her charge utter the nickname. But Celine de Rossignol was
such a devil of a name for a seven-year-old girl to get her tongue
around – and for her pen to master, come to that. Her lessons
in the nursery, gazing up at the blackboard at Semolina's italic

script and endeavouring to copy it, almost always ended in disaster, with the white-aproned nanny-cum-tutor standing over Rosamund at the vast porcelain sink under the nursery window and trying, with the aid of a stiff-bristled brush and a bar of stinking carbolic soap, to remove the stubborn black Stephens' ink from her fingers. It was usually to no avail and resulted only in stray wisps of raven hair escaping one after the other from the hairgrips that fastened it close to Celine's head. When Celine could no longer see Rosamund's hands for her own wayward locks she would abandon the job as a bad one, throw the brush into the sink with a muttered 'Zut!' and toss a rough-textured hand towel in Rosamund's direction. It was, the child knew, only a matter of time during one of these personal hygiene sessions before her governess's patience ran out. Released from Semolina's grip, Rosamund would look up at her pleadingly, knowing that she, too, would prefer to be out in the sunshine, heading towards the beach on the sandy path that snaked down between the dunes. One smile and a raised eyebrow would, she knew, be all that was necessary for Celine to say 'Go on then; but walk quietly downstairs, go out of the back door and do not run!' Very occasionally the instruction was delivered in English, but more frequently it came in French.

Whatever the language, the instruction was always in vain. How could one not run when one knew where the sandy path led? Especially when the tide was half in or half out and there was a decent strip of beach to run along and razor shells and whelks and dogfish eggs to prise out of its wave-flattened surface. They would be brought back, cradled in the front of her dress, and arranged on the table that stood outside the back porch of Daneway, its pale paint peeling away like old skin to reveal timbers bleached by years of sun and rain and sand-laden winds. It bore a glittering array of smooth buttons of glass, turned from broken bottle shards into jewels by the sea, along with shells of every shape and pastel shade. They were Rosamund's treasures, though passed unnoticed by every other member of the household.

While Rosamund chased the waves and scoured the sand for its hidden riches, Celine sat above the tide line on a tuft of marram grass, examining in detail a letter that had been sent to her by her beau. That was what she called him; not boyfriend or man friend or anything quite so straightforward, but 'beau', which sounded so much more romantic. So very French. Celine's father – born and raised in Dijon – had made sure that his daughter was brought up to be bilingual, for although he had married an Englishwoman and lived for the greater part of his adult life in her country, he was determined that his daughter would reflect her joint parentage. Celine was eighteen now – just over ten years older than Rosamund. For much of the time they were more like sisters than a governess and her charge, though Celine knew her responsibilities and did her best to let Rosamund know them, too.

It seemed odd to Rosamund that her governess should have a man friend. She had never seen him. She wondered how Celine managed to find time to have what she would call a 'tryst', when all she had off was one afternoon a week and one Sunday a month. But she always knew when Celine had met him. Nothing could be clearer. She would return with a pink face and an unusual air of dreaminess about her. Rosamund would ask questions: 'Who is he, Semolina? What is a "beau"? Why do you like him? Is he tall? Does he have a moustache? Is he as handsome as . . . the grocer?' None of which would receive a proper answer, just a hum and an absentminded instruction to get ready for bed, or wash her face and hands or some other vague instruction that was seldom followed through. Only when

Rosamund asked 'Has he kissed you?' would Celine chase her around the bedroom wielding a slipper, threatening to 'wallop her' again. Though she never did. Rosamund liked it when Celine had been with her beau, for it produced in her an altogether different demeanour to the usual matter-of-fact and no-nonsense approach which brooked no argument. She knew that on such days she could get away, if not with murder, then with more than was the norm in the Hanbury household.

Daneway was a large, solid, stone-built house, not especially grand and more accurately described as handsome rather than beautiful. A series of hipped roofs leaned together in a complex undulation of slate and granite that had withstood many an autumn gale and winter storm and would, with any luck, stand a few more yet. It sat – almost crouched – in a sheltered Devon combe; a grassy valley, fringed by thorn and sycamore trees that had been blown into lop-sided clouds by centuries of salt-laden winds. It was a house of many windows, with one particular dormer that faced southwards towards the sea. This was the one that Rosamund gazed out of most, for it was in her bedroom, right at the top of the house, and had a window seat on which were arranged a doll and two boats – a small wooden rowing boat, a three-master with cotton sails, and 'Raggedy Ann', a yarn-headed doll whose voyages were many and various on the deep blue chintz-covered cushion that passed as their sea.

It was a quiet house as a rule, and she the only child, as had been the case since she was born. There had once been a brother, but she had never known him. Her parents seldom spoke of Robert, a nineteen-year-old who had died in the Great War before she was born. To Rosamund he was a shadowy figure – a ghost almost – and she had learned not to ask too many questions, for whenever she did, her father changed the subject and her mother left the room. Just occasionally she heard mention of the Battle of Arras, and it conjured up in her mind a medieval scene of knights in shining armour and heroic battles with lances and longbows, for to a child's ear Arras sounded very much like arrows.

It would be several years before she learned the full story from Celine, who had picked up snippets from the locals and pieced them together, turning them into a romance of sorts.

'Have you never asked them yourself?' asked Celine one winter evening as she brushed out Rosamund's hair by the nursery fire.

'No. I couldn't possibly.'

Celine shook her head and another hairpin somersaulted on to the nursery floor. 'Well, your father, Valentine Hanbury . . .' she used the full names of her employers as though she were relating a work of fiction, 'was about thirty, I suppose. He was the only son of a Devon landowner and he was rather taken with this beautiful eighteen-year-old called Edith Tempest.'

'The same age as you are?'

'Don't interrupt.' Celine carried on with her brushing. 'He swept her off her feet and married her in spite of the discouragement of his family.

'Did they all hate her?'

'They didn't hate her – disapproving isn't the same as hating, you know. And his sister – your Aunt Venetia – was the only one to encourage him.'

'I like Aunt Venetia.'

'Yes, me too,' murmured Celine, lapsing into reverie for a moment before clearing her throat, putting on her teaching voice and taking up the story once more.

'Valentine and Edith moved into Daneway almost immediately. The master's mother and father were in their seventies and they soon came round, once they realised that Edith, who was the daughter of a local shipping agent, might be just what their son needed to moderate his impulsive nature.'

'What is "impulsive"?'

'It is what you are – doing things on the spur of the moment without thinking of the consequences.' Celine tugged at a particularly stubborn knot in Rosamund's blonde curls.

'Ow.'

'Sit still and stop squirming and it will soon be over.'

'Were you here then?'

'Don't be silly. I'm eighteen, not eighty. With the house, they inherited a cook-housekeeper, a general maid and a chauffeur-gardener, as well as an estate manager and enough agricultural workers to manage 800 acres devoted to arable crops and livestock.'

'You sound like a book.'

'Do you want to hear this story or not?'

'Yes. I like stories. Especially when I know the people in them.'

Celine continued with the tale of how Valentine had taken to the role of gentleman farmer like a duck to water. How the Hanburys were a happy couple and became an established part of the country set – riding to hounds, wining and dining their landed neighbours and treating their staff with a respect born of local tradition. She explained how Robert was born a year after their marriage and that as his father settled into running the estate, there grew in the son a sense of adventure counter to the now more conservative ways of his father. Valentine took his new-found responsibilities seriously – both to the land and to his family. It was not long before the 800-acre estate – tired and unproductive on his inheritance – began to thrive under his stewardship.

But as the father became more conscientious, so the son's

impetuous nature grew ever more pronounced. Robert was possessed of an eagerness and a lust for life that his father found inspiring – a reflection of his former self, perhaps – and his mother exhausting.

'He was a human whirlwind, you see,' explained Celine, 'following first one passion and then another – learning to sail, learning to ride – and if you ever met him, he was passionate and enthusiastic; everybody said so. A bit like you,' she added under her breath. 'Then when he was sixteen the war came. And like a lot of his friends, he longed to join up and fight to save the land he loved. "Your Country Needs You" – that's what General Kitchener said on the recruiting poster – and Robert was determined not to let his country down. But he had to wait until he was eighteen before he could join up, and then it was another year before he could serve on the front line.'

'Did Mother and Father try to stop him?'

'Oh yes. They did their best to put him off, and explained as much as they dared about the other members of the family who had fought in the Crimea and the first Boer War. But it was the eyes, you see.'

'The eyes?'

'Blue eyes just like yours. They shone out at his mother and father under the mop of fair hair and had a way of pleading that was impossible to resist. He'd been away just three months – twelve weeks – when he was killed at the Battle of Arras in 1917. His body never came home.'

Celine stopped brushing and gazed wistfully at the flickering embers of the fire.

Rosamund sat silently for a few moments before asking, 'Were Mother and Father very sad?'

'Of course they were.'

Even Celine was at a loss to conjure up the true depth of

grief that pervaded Daneway after Robert's death. The sadness was of a scale that few outside the household could comprehend. The father became introspective and taciturn, the mother tearful and prone to bouts of hysteria. The estate ticked along under the stewardship of those men of the land too old or too young to fight, but the atmosphere in the house was of impenetrable gloom. It was as if Valentine and Edith were both marooned in separate worlds with little hope of reconciling themselves to their circumstances and to each other. Whenever Valentine would steel himself and make an approach to Edith, attempting to talk about their loss and rekindle any kind of mutual affection or empathy, she would wring her hands and dissolve into tears before turning from him and shutting herself away. Since Robert's death, they had slept in separate rooms, and their joint encounters at meals were for the main part silent and introspective.

It was many months before the dark clouds lifted and the Devon landscape gradually began to work its magic. They would never get over the loss of their only son, but the intensity of their grief gradually eased sufficiently for them to become companionable and to share a bed once more. Four years after Robert's death, their daughter Rosamund was born.

The event came as a surprise to them both, for Valentine was now fifty-four and Edith forty-two. There was no question of Edith being a hands-on mother. Her own parents had engaged a governess to look after her when she was small, and being an older mother, she would do the same. Valentine could not argue; the prospect of being a father to a daughter made him uneasy. He was glad, of course, for the child would ease the mother's pain, but when it came to girls, their upbringing would remain a puzzle to him. And so, within a few days of Rosamund's arrival, Celine was engaged – first of all as a companion –

recommended by Valentine's sister Venetia as having been a good appointment for daughters of her friends in Belgravia who no longer required her. It would also mean that Rosamund would grow up to be bi-lingual, which, as Venetia pointed out, was always a good thing in 'a lady'.

'Do you think I made them less sad?' asked Rosamund as Celine tucked her into bed.

'Of course you did. Most of the time. Though you can be a trial on occasion.'

'Will you stay?'

'That depends.'

'What do you mean?'

'If anything better turns up.'

The look on Rosamund's face told Celine that she had gone too far. 'Of course I will stay. Who else will brush your hair and sort out your clothes and take you to the beach and teach you French and keep you out of trouble?'

'Do you . . . do you love me?'

'What a ridiculous question.'

'But I want to know.'

'I look after you, don't I?'

'That's not the same.'

'Too many questions . . .'

'No. Just one.'

Celine frowned and shook her head. 'I suppose I must do.' Then she smiled. 'That or something like. Now go to sleep or the angels will decide you are not worth a centime.'

By rights Celine should have been moved on to other, more junior charges, but she had become so much a part of the household they didn't even consider it. The prospect of change appealed to neither Valentine nor Edith, who had come to rely on her ministrations as unofficial arbiter in the home – soothing the cook when a tantrum seemed imminent, or gently persuading the chauffeur-gardener that his clothes really did need cleaning with greater regularity than he seemed to believe. And so Celine remained, becoming something of a part-time companion to Edith and a confidante of Rosamund, somehow managing to juggle her two loyalties with tact and grace.

From Rosamund's point of view, learning French seemed pretty pointless. She could not imagine ever wanting to leave 'Devonshire', as she called it. But the lessons never seemed like lessons, and when you have been speaking French since you learned to talk (in the same way that Celine had done), there was little effort involved. Indeed, Edith would occasionally ask them to speak in English when they prattled on rapidly and gaily in the Gallic tongue which, to her, forever remained a mystery.

As she grew into her teens, Rosamund's relationship with her father grew, if anything, more distant. He was puzzled by his daughter's character and found her impossible to fathom. She veered, it seemed, from being a headstrong tomboy to a flighty flibbertigibbet. She and Celine would for the most part behave as though they were sisters; the ten-year age gap seemed to shrink with the passing of the years. On ever more frequent occasions he had to have words with Celine, explaining that perhaps she had gone too far in acceding to the will of his daughter, whether it was being complicit in some activity involving a gallop along the sands on a horse known to be uncontrollable, or in turning a blind eye to an assignation with a local youth.

While Valentine was exasperated and bemused by his daughter's capricious nature, to Edith she was a total mystery: a curiosity deposited on them from another planet. While the mother was down to earth and steady, the daughter had something of her late brother Robert's passionate nature about her. How Edith would have loved her daughter to be calm and biddable, steady and reliable, but it was not to be. Rosamund was headstrong, passionate, enthusiastic. Edith felt she had seen it all before, and something within her shrank back at the thought of history repeating itself.

It was, I suppose, an idyllic childhood – growing up in Devonshire with the sea in front of me and the rolling green hills to left and right of our own particular combe. I've always loved that word – the implication that the valleys of Devonshire have their own character, which of course they do. And I have always referred to it as Devonshire, as in the days of old. Not Devon, which seems too staccato for such a lush and fluid landscape. Of all the shires it remains my favourite, but then it is a county replete with memories.

I suppose I was what you might call a tomboy. I liked nothing more than riding bareback along the sands of our own particular bay, and staying out until it got dark, not that there was anything sinister about that, or anything that Celine de Rossignol would have called 'inapproprie'. Oh, I did love her; more so as the years went by and our relationship changed from that of a governess and her charge to one more akin to that enjoyed by sisters. Not that 'Semolina', as I teasingly called her, was a pushover; she would let me know from time to time just how angry she felt when I had taken her for granted, or expected her to cover for me when I had committed some misdemeanour of which she and I knew my parents would disapprove. It was all very innocent, of course. At least in the early days. And she did teach me French, which I thought a huge bore. I did not realise then – how could I – that it would come to be of so much value in my life, and the cause of so much heartache and joy in equal measure.

I hoped that I would get to know my father a little better as I reached my teenage years, but I suspect that he found me impossible to understand. To my mother, I was clearly a complete enigma. We were such different characters, you see; Mother was born during the reign of Queen Victoria and continued to harbour those mores – both social and domestic – all her life. She never really 'let go', and my father, being a good deal older than she, was similarly at sea when it came to understanding what made me 'tick'. I doubt for one moment that he ever knew what I got up to during the day.

When I was small I was woken, washed and dressed by Semolina (I really must stop calling her that now . . .) and we would then have lessons in the attic room next to my nursery before escaping mid-afternoon to play on the beach or walk in the woods. Celine had the room next door to mine – a tiny room in the eaves with a bed, a chest of drawers, a curtained-off cubby-hole for her always immaculately laundered aprons and dresses, and floral chintz curtains the same as my own. Most of the day she spent with me in my room, which was rather bigger than hers; it had a desk and two chairs as well as a bed and a dressing table where she would brush my hair each morning – thirty strokes a side (she said twenty was not suffi-cient and fifty was an indulgence). I was required to make my

own bed each morning and to tidy away my toys each afternoon
before we went down to tea. I was bathed once a week in front
of the fire in the parlour in a copper hip bath that makes me
smile just to think of it – soapsuds threatening to engulf me,
and Celine's hair showering me with hairgrips as she sponged
my back and let me do my own nooks and crannies, or 'coins
et recoins' as she called them. It's funny what one remembers.
And how safe I felt in front of that fire each Friday night.

'Where are we going?' asked Rosamund of her governess one
Saturday in May, shortly after her eighth birthday.

'To Dartmouth.'

'Is it far?'

'Not too far.'

'How will we get there?'

'By train.'

Rosamund had never been on a train before. She had seen
pictures of them in magazines and books, and had stood at the
local station when they had pulled in or thundered through,
but her travelling of any great distance – which was rare – had
been undertaken either in her father's car or the estate pony
and trap which was still in use, despite its venerable age.

At first she was frightened by the noise and the size of the
great iron beast that clanked and wheezed its way into the
station. The compartment into which they climbed had a pecu-
liar smell and she examined the pictures of such exotic-sounding
resorts as Skegness and Ullapool, which were framed in glass
below the criss-cross stringing of the luggage rack into which
Celine deposited the wicker hamper containing their picnic.

This trip would be the first of many to Dartmouth and
Salcombe – a feeling of escape and delight at exploring new
places that would never leave her. To Celine's chagrin, Rosamund

learned how to lower the window on its leather strap so that she could lean out and inhale the smoke-filled air. If she did this quietly when Celine had dozed off, she could feel the wind in her hair for at least thirty seconds before the noise of the wind would wake her governess, who would then admonish her for her folly and heave on the leather strap to close the window with a resounding thud.

'If another train goes by, you will lose your head!' – almost always delivered at breakneck speed in French – which would reduce Rosamund to giggles and eventually cause Celine to sigh and murmur *'Sacré bleu'* in melodramatic tones.

The day would be spent looking in shops – pointing out hats that Celine especially took a shine to – and examining the boats in the harbour, with Celine conjuring up stories of where they had been and where they were bound for. The picnic – jam sandwiches (Celine's favourite made with plums from the orchard at Daneway) and lemonade, with a slice of ginger cake to finish off – were almost always taken on the harbour wall. Then, late in the afternoon, the two would board the train for the return journey, frequently falling asleep with Rosamund's head in Celine's lap. They would be met at the station by the pony and trap, and on returning to Daneway as a copper sun set over the sea, Celine would then have the job of scrubbing her charge to remove the smuts and smell of smoke, which were invariably detected by her father as she was presented to her parents each evening before their supper.

'What have we done today?' her father would ask absently from behind his local newspaper as his daughter stood in front of him, shepherded into the room by Celine.

'We saw a pirate ship and a very scary-looking captain in Dartmouth harbour,' said Rosamund.

Her father lowered his paper. 'Really? How do you know he was a pirate?'

'Because he had an eye patch.'

Her father nodded thoughtfully. 'Did he have a parrot on his shoulder?'

'Not that I could see.'

'Ah. Probably not a pirate then.'

Celine joined in. 'We did think that he looked as if he *could* be a pirate.'

'The child's imagination is running away with her,' admonished Rosamund's mother, looking up from the circle of embroidery now resting in her lap. 'Celine, you really must try to keep it under control. I'm sure it can only lead to problems.'

Celine suppressed the smile that was never far from her lips on these occasions.

'Do you think he had any treasure?' asked Valentine Hanbury.

'I think it quite likely, sir,' answered Celine.

'Yes,' confirmed Rosamund. 'Doubloons and gold moidores.'

Mrs Hanbury tutted loudly and returned to her embroidery.

'I'm sure you're right,' said her father. 'Good for you. Well, goodnight. Sleep well.' He smiled, nodded at Celine, his fatherly duty completed for another evening.

Rosamund's parents would never get over the loss of her brother, Robert, and as she grew up she became wary of reopening old wounds. Like most children, she was adept at recognising atmospheres, much as her parents tried to cover them up by putting on brave faces and pretending that all was well. There is something in the air in families who have undergone personal tragedy, and no amount of cajoling and pretence will ever expunge it entirely.

When Rosamund was ten, a local schoolmaster was engaged

to enlarge her education rather more than Celine's modest capabilities would allow. He was astonished at the child's grasp of the French language – if rather irritated by the useful short-hand it facilitated between Celine and herself – but he soon realised that in other areas of academic achievement, Rosamund was somewhat lacking. Charles Langstone was young and hand-some and valued the extra income this tutelage would provide, for he had four small children and a wife to look after. Rosamund suspected that this state of affairs must have disappointed Celine, for on more than one occasion she caught her regarding him with a dreamy look in her eyes. The family lived in a tiny cottage in the village and Mr Langstone came three evenings a week, on two of which he tried – in vain – to teach Rosamund mathematics. She hated it.

'What is the hypotenuse?' he would ask.

'An animal a bit like a rhinoceros?' Rosamund would respond, to his endless exasperation.

But Mr Langstone also opened her eyes – and ears – to English literature, when he read aloud to her at the end of each lesson – everything from *Treasure Island* and *The Wind in the Willows* to *Cranford* and *David Copperfield*. Celine would sneak into the schoolroom for these stories, since Charles Langstone was blessed with a mellifluous speaking voice – lyrical and beauti-fully modulated. He could make Rosamund shiver with excitement and cower in fear with just a slight inflection or a difference in tone or accent.

In order to make sure that Rosamund had company of her own age, her parents arranged for the daughter of the neigh-bouring estate to accompany her during some of these lessons. Diana Molyneux had been headstrong since she could crawl, and after the usual tricky start – when two competitive spirits find themselves quite frequently at loggerheads – she and

Rosamund had forged a firm friendship based on a common love for the countryside and a willingness to take risks, whether that involved riding horses or taunting the local boys. As the two of them grew up together, the good-natured rivalry manifested itself in attempts to shock one another with tales of derring-do; few of them based on fact, and most of them ending in peals of laughter. The occasions when these rivalries were set aside were invariably when Mr Langstone was transporting them to tropical islands on a pirate ship, to Jane Austen's Hampshire, to Charles Dickens's London or Jonathan Swift's Lilliput. Then they would sit close together in rapt delight, their eyes wide open and their imaginations taking flight.

Those early encounters with English literature would have a lasting effect on both of them, but as they entered their teens, Diana's occasional trips to London and her parents' willingness to let their daughter visit relations in Dorchester and Barnstaple would ensure that her wider experiences of life would give her a more sophisticated air than that of her friend whose own adventures were confined to the more rural parts of Devonshire. But by the time they reached the age of fifteen, both had one topic of conversation which eclipsed all others: they loved nothing better than talking about boys.

Chapter 2

DEVONSHIRE

1936-38

'The wise girl will remember that boys are at best a
distraction and at worst a disaster.
But wise girls have no fun.'

Margot Lethbridge, *Encounters*, 1922

Diana Molyneux had long, dark, lustrous hair – the very opposite of Rosamund's fly-away blonde locks. She also had about
her an air of worldliness; a confidence that was foreign to
Rosamund and which consequently entranced her. Thanks to
her travels further afield than even Salcombe and Dartmouth,
Diana seemed to know everything – about boys, and people,
and London – and even maths; she could never understand how
Rosamund found numbers so puzzling.

But above all, Diana Molyneux had learned how to enjoy
herself. It was she who introduced Rosamund to the delights
of riding bareback along the beach, clinging on to the mane of
her highly strung pony for dear life. It was something Rosamund
chose to hide from her mother, lest the pursuit be banned on

the grounds that it was foolhardy, which it undoubtedly was. Riding like a lady was one thing; riding like a circus performer was quite another.

During the summer holidays, when Mr Langstone was given a few weeks off, Rosamund and Diana would spend almost all their time outdoors – on the beach or going for long walks in the woods between the two family estates of Daneway and Falconleigh, where Diana's family had lived for even longer than the Hanburys next door.

On these daily sorties – when Diana would often smuggle out a bottle of beer to accompany their sandwiches – the conversation invariably turned to boys, and the relative merits of those examples of early manhood the girls came into contact with in their relatively restricted world.

'Edward. What about Edward?' asked Diana, seeking Rosamund's verdict on her latest fancy.

'The groom at Falconleigh?'

'Yes.'

'He's ancient.'

'He's twenty-two.'

'As I said, he's ancient.'

'But he's good-looking. He's got amazing muscles.'

Rosamund turned to face her friend. They were lying on the sand dunes above the beach, their horses tethered to large stones, while their riders watched the incoming tide between bites of their sandwiches and gulps of the shared bottle of illicit beer. Both were dressed in cotton shorts, their floral blouses knotted at the waist, their feet bare and their hair billowing around their faces in the warm breeze. 'How do you know he's got amazing muscles?' she asked, wide-eyed.

'How do you think?' asked Diana conspiratorially.

'You haven't!'

'Haven't what?' asked her friend, smiling.

'You know . . . done it.' Innocent of such intimate personal experiences though she was, Rosamund had seen enough bulls and cows and horses mating to make any kind of instruction on that sort of thing superfluous.

'God no!'

'But how do you know . . . ?'

'Because he likes to take his shirt off when he's mucking out.'

'That's shocking! Does your father know?'

'Heavens no! He wouldn't do it when Daddy is around; he only does it when he knows there's no one looking but me.' Diana threw her head back. 'Last week he let me feel his biceps.'

'That's disgusting.'

'No, it's not. I bet you don't even know where his biceps are.'

'Yes, I do. Mr Langstone has charts – for biology.'

'Anyway, I think Edward is a bit dishy.'

'But you wouldn't . . . ?'

'Certainly not. I'm saving myself,' said Diana archly. 'But it doesn't stop me admiring someone's physique.'

'No, I suppose not,' said Rosamund. 'But you ought to be careful all the same. I mean, you don't want to lead him on, do you?'

'Oh, just a little . . . there's no harm in it . . . provided it doesn't go too far.'

'Or *he* doesn't go too far,' added Rosamund with a hint of admonishment in her voice.

'Don't tell me you've never been kissed!' teased Diana.

Rosamund blushed. 'Alright, I won't tell you.'

Diana propped herself up on her elbows, her eyes wide and her expression expectant. 'You have, haven't you?'

'Yes, I have, as it happens.'

'Who by?' There was genuine excitement in Diana's voice now.

'I think you're meant to say "by whom",' admonished Rosamund.

'Oh, don't be such a tease! Who was it? And was it just the once or did you go back for more?'

'That sounds dreadful.' Rosamund paused and turned away, but not far enough to hide the dreamy look in her eye from Diana.

'I know who it was. Davy Jennings! The boy who helps Wilding in your stables. That's who it was, wasn't it? I've seen you look at him.' Then, in a moment of realisation, 'But he's only sixteen. He's a boy!'

'At least he's not an old man of twenty-two! And he's a very good kisser.'

'Rosamund Hanbury, you dark horse! And there you were, telling me to be careful with our groom. You're nothing but a hypocrite!'

Rosamund smiled guiltily. 'Well, I didn't want to be left behind. You're so sophisticated and everything. Why should you have all the fun?'

'I will soon.'

'What do you mean?'

Diana grinned. 'Next year I'm moving to London. Daddy has made arrangements for me to stay there with my uncle and aunt. I shall be "coming out".'

'What's "coming out"?' asked Rosamund, her brow furrowed at such a strange expression.

'Being presented at court. To the King. You have to wear three feathers in your hair and curtsey to him alongside your mother.'

Rosamund giggled. 'You're not serious? Wearing three feathers and curtseying to the King? You're making it up!'

'I'm not. It's what all young ladies like us have to do when we enter society.'

'Well, I'm not going to. There's no need to do all that in Devonshire. I mean, people would laugh.'

'I suppose they would, down here. But that's London. I can't wait.'

'To wear three feathers in your hair?' Rosamund began to laugh and leaned over to tickle Diana on the waist. 'This is what feathers are for; for tickling, not for wearing in your hair in front of the King.'

Diana began to giggle, and in a few moments the two of them were rolling round among the sand dunes, incapable with laughter.

When Diana eventually departed for London, the two girls promised lifelong devotion and regular communication. Rosamund kept to her part of the bargain, but when Diana's letters became fewer and more sporadic, she realised with regret, but without any trace of rancour, that Diana was growing up in the city with all its attractions and distractions and now had more exciting things to do with her life than to write to an old friend marooned in the depths of Devonshire. She accepted the situation for what it was and hoped that one day she would be in a position to rekindle a friendship that had taught her more than she would otherwise have known of the ways of the world. Like other letters and souvenirs of events, they were tied with ribbon and kept safe in a box of treasures at the bottom of her wardrobe.

Rosamund never really talked much to Celine about men. Oh, she tried on occasion to elicit more information about her 'beau', but little was forthcoming and enquiries were usually batted off with a 'That's for me to know and you to wonder' sort of comment; swiftly followed by an instruction to clear away the supper plates or go and wash her hair.

What Rosamund also discovered was that Celine seemed to have a sixth sense about her own dalliances – brief and relatively innocent though they might have been. Brushing Rosamund's hair after a day's riding, she would hold up a strand of hay found tangled in her charge's locks and enquire how it came to be there.

'Horses eat hay,' Rosamund would explain.

'Yes, but that hay tends to be in their manger. Funny how it often ends up in your hair . . .'

Rosamund would glance at Celine in the mirror and see her suppressing a smile as she busied herself with the brush, applying a little more pressure by way of making her point.

'Just be careful, *ma cherie*; that's all.'

'Oh Semolina! Be careful, be careful . . . ! It's only a bit of fun.'

'Mmm. It's funny what a bit of fun can turn into if you are not careful.'

The words that came from Celine had so often been translated and passed on to Diana. Now she would have no one except Celine in whom to confide.

Celine's 'beau' seemed to be around for quite some time, although Rosamund never saw him. And then Celine suddenly stopped talking about him and for a few weeks her mood was darker and her aspect more stern.

It was some time before Rosamund plucked up the courage to ask after him, fully expecting the usual rebuff. It was bedtime, as it most often was when conversations of any import occurred. A time for reflection on the day or, in this case, on the last year. Celine's reply was matter-of-fact. 'He has gone,' she said.

'Gone where?'

'Back to his mother.'

Rosamund was confused. Celine read her expression and said,

'It's what happens sometimes. Things do not work out as expected. His mother had become ill and she asked him to go and look after her – in Northumberland. I understood that he must look after her, as any good son should, but when I offered to move up north with him – although it filled me with horror, leaving you and your family – he said that his mother would not approve. In the end he had to choose between his love for me and his love of his mother. Well, he chose his mother and I . . .' Here the words stopped and Celine turned away as the tears began to flow.

'But you still have me!' said Rosamund.

Celine dried her eyes and managed a brave smile. 'Yes, *cherie*, I still have you. Now come on . . . into bed.' And that was the last time Celine ever mentioned the gentleman she had always called her 'beau'.

Rosamund would have been happy to have remained in Devonshire – with perhaps the occasional trip to the 'bright lights' of Dartmouth and Salcombe – had not a change in her circumstances occurred quite suddenly.

She came back from riding alone one Friday afternoon, as she did regularly after Diana's departure for London, to discover Celine sitting on a stout wooden chair in the front hall, weeping uncontrollably.

Rosamund had never seen Celine give way to such emotion: Celine, the one person so in control of her feelings, so unwilling to express herself except when exasperated by her charge's unreasonable behaviour or annoyed at the inconsiderate or insolent attitude of tradesmen. Her chest was heaving and her words – a mixture of English and French, as often happened when she was overwrought – made little sense. Rosamund crouched by her and asked, 'What on earth is the matter?'

Celine looked up, and as she did so, the door of Valentine Hanbury's study opened and Dr Armstrong – the family physician – came out and walked towards her. His expression was grave. Rosamund felt her heart leap.

'I have spoken to the cottage hospital,' he said, directing his words to Celine. 'It is as I thought.' He shook his head and asked, 'Are you sure you would not prefer it if I . . . ?'

At this, Celine gathered herself together, rose from her chair and blew her nose. 'No. It is my responsibility,' she said, drying her eyes. 'Thank you, Dr Armstrong.'

Rosamund stood rooted to the spot, staring at the doctor in his long black coat and pinstripe trousers. He wore a wing collar and his eyebrows were long and upturned, giving him the look of a rather frightening owl. He bowed curtly to the two women and quietly took his leave; the front door closed behind him with an ominous thud.

'It is bad news I am afraid, *cherie*. Come with me.' Celine led the way into the deserted drawing room where the slanting rays of the sun caught the motes of dust that danced like gnats in the still, stale air. A heavy silence enveloped them. Celine dabbed at her eyes with her handkerchief and motioned Rosamund to sit in a large armchair, then, kneeling at her feet and holding both her hands, she said softly, 'Your mother and father were driving into Dartmouth.'

Rosamund nodded. 'I know. They are going to lunch with those friends who have a house above the harbour. What is it, Semolina? What's the matter?'

'Their car was involved in a collision.'

Rosamund found herself unable to speak. Her head spun; her chest tightened and she found it hard to breathe.

'I am afraid they are both . . . gone. I am so sorry, *ma cherie*. So very sorry . . .'

The words echoed around Rosamund's head and seemed to hang in the still air along with the millions of flecks of dust as Celine tried with all her might to stifle her uncontrollable sobs. Rosamund put a hand on her shoulder, to comfort her but also to steady herself. Her head pounded and a feeling of nausea overwhelmed her.

She had left the house two hours earlier a happy, carefree teenager, off for a gallop along the beach with her favourite pony. On her return she became an orphan, and thanks to the strange processes of English law, an orphan with nowhere to live.

Chapter 3

LONDON

SEPTEMBER 1938

'Oh, London is a fine town,
A very famous city,
Where all the streets are paved with gold,
And all the maidens pretty.'

George Colman, the Younger, *The Heir at Law*, 1797

'But why can't I stay there? There's plenty for me to do. I like working on the farm with the men, and riding my horse in the afternoons.'

'Now don't be ridiculous, dear. You couldn't possibly live there alone and you're most certainly not old enough to manage a farm.'

'I've got Semo – Celine, I mean. She can help.'

'You are seventeen. Even with Celine at your elbow you cannot run a farm. And, the entailment means it is no longer yours anyway. It passes to your cousin James.'

'Second cousin. I don't even know him. I've never met him . . .'
Rosamund's lip began to tremble.

Her aunt Venetia, sitting up in bed in her house in Eaton Square, patted the counterpane beside her. 'Come here. Come along. Dry your eyes and let's talk things through.'

The sudden and unexpected death of both her parents had precipitated a dramatic change in Rosamund's circumstances. She had never thought of living anywhere other than Devonshire; she had never needed to. The life of long summer days and brisk winter walks inspired by a raging sea contributed to a scenario she expected to go on forever. But all that had changed almost overnight.

She remembered her father talking about her 'going up to London, to your aunt Venetia's' on several occasions, but that had always seemed far ahead in the future, and when she had asked why she must do so, he had murmured something about being 'finished off' and 'prepared' – but prepared for what he never seemed to have got round to explaining. Now here she was, bundled off to London within the week and given shelter by her aunt. Heaven knows what her mother would have thought, for her mother and Venetia had never got along – the one a dyed-in-the-wool puritan, the other a hedonistic pleasure seeker.

Venetia, Lady Reeves, was Valentine Hanbury's sister. Unlike her brother, she had married young and had married well – an ageing baronet who had conveniently died within a few years of their union, leaving her with a house in Eaton Square and a generous income for life. It was just as well, for Venetia had expensive tastes; tastes which she indulged on a regular basis – boxes at the opera, dinners at The Ritz and frequent jaunts to Venice, Florence and Paris, her watering holes of choice. She breakfasted in bed and seldom rose before eleven, filling her afternoons with shopping trips and tea parties, as befitted the widow of an admittedly obscure and relatively minor member of the British aristocracy. She was a snob, but a fair one, and she would have no truck with those who were mean-spirited or who treated their servants poorly. Good manners were, to her, the stuff of life, and although she appeared to do very little of a practical and purposeful nature, she was a minor player in a game whose prime exponents were society hostesses of the calibre of Edith, Lady Londonderry, Sybil Colefax and Emerald Cunard, and she enjoyed to the full her subtle role as a facilitator of such productive encounters, albeit on a slightly lowlier plane than that of her more notorious counterparts.

Propped up against her lace-edged pillows in her second-floor bedroom, and framed by an elaborately tasselled half-tester whose passementerie alone must have taken up half the life of several dexterous needlewomen, Venetia patted her silver grey hair into place, drew her silk wrap over her shoulders and took the small and poorly manicured hand of her niece in hers. She stroked it gently, endeavouring to pacify this slip of a country girl, and at the same time wondering if she would ever be able to turn her into a lady. For that had been her brother's intention. He had spoken to Venetia only a few weeks before his tragic death, explaining that he was worried that his daughter's sights were set on unsuitable goals. It was his own fault, he'd admitted: allowing her to roam at will through the Devonshire countryside, to make her own amusement, to go her own way, to spend her days in the company of cowmen and stable lads. She had had one suitable companion in another local landowner's daughter, but Diana Molyneux had been shipped off to London and perhaps that was the moment when he, too, should have taken matters in hand. Valentine had explained that he had done his best with Rosamund's education – thanks to Celine she had become fluent in French, and a tutor he had engaged had filled in other academic gaps. She was surprisingly literate, spending her evenings making up fanciful stories which she copied down in notebook after notebook in her neat italic script, but when it came to wider society, he knew that his daughter was poorly prepared. What did Venetia think he should do?

Venetia had been quite clear about what he should do. He should send the girl to live with her in London. She had no shortage of accommodation, she had a butler, a cook and a maid, and if Celine came with her, the child would have a companion and Venetia would be able to make use of the girl's governess around the house, where another pair of hands would certainly come in useful.

The fact that events had caused all this to come to pass so quickly was unfortunate – tragic – but at least there had been some sort of plan in place and the fact that it was being executed sooner rather than later would, in the long term, probably prove beneficial to the girl's ultimate development.

'I'm so sorry, my dear.' Venetia stroked the rough skin at the back of Rosamund's hand. 'None of us saw this coming, but come it has and I fear we will have to make the best of it.'

Venetia watched as Rosamund gazed transfixed at the pattern on the counterpane – an elaborate mixture of intertwined leaves and rosebuds. Only a few days ago, the poor thing had been looking at real ones on the sun-drenched walls of Daneway; now, here she was in the heart of London, so far from sea and field, from woodland and stream; the prospect must seem worse than death itself.

'I know how much you loved Devonshire. And I know why. I was a country girl once myself, remember. I was brought up there with your father. It is a special place; a place for dreaming and for feeling at one with nature. Looking at me lying here in my bed, you are probably wondering how I can possibly know how you are feeling, but I, too, rode horses along the beach and had picnics on the sand.'

Rosamund looked up. 'Really?'

'Oh yes.' Venetia's eyes took on a dreamy quality as she reminisced. 'I thought I should stay there forever. But then I began to feel some kind of unease; a feeling that I was missing something. That there was a life outside my own that could offer me untold riches.'

Rosamund pulled back a little and glanced about the room – at the fine furniture, the paintings and sumptuous fabrics that seemed to envelope her aunt in a kind of luxurious cocoon.

Venetia saw what was going through Rosamund's mind. 'No, not these sorts of riches, lovely as they are. But the riches of society in its true sense. Meeting people, finding out their likes and dislikes, observing their sensibilities and being conscious and considerate of them.' Then, seeing her niece's wide-eyed expression, 'I know it makes no sense to you whatsoever at the moment, but it will. You will meet new people . . .'

'But I'm not sure I want to . . .'

'Oh, you will. It will be hard at first. You will feel like a fish out of water. I know I did. There were times when I wanted to bolt back to Devonshire and leave the city – and the people – behind. But you must remember one thing: Devonshire will always be there. No one is going to take it away . . .'

'But they *have* taken it away,' interrupted Rosamund. 'Taken it away completely—'

Her aunt cut in: 'Your father has left you an annual income which will make sure you want for very little – for the foreseeable future, anyway. And the sea will still be yours, and the sand, and the combe, and the stream. No one really "owns" them, you know. You can still keep them in your heart, no one can stop that – not an entailment, not an Act of Parliament, not anything.'

Venetia lifted Rosamund's chin and fixed her with a knowing

gaze. 'When you look around this room, you will probably think that I am a materialistic sort of aunt. One who revels in possessions. I enjoy them, it's true, and I am lucky enough to live a life of comparative luxury. But I do not regard it as an entitlement, and I know that one day, when I pass out of this world, I can take none of it with me. I am a custodian; I look after these things while I am here, and when I am gone, it will be someone else's pleasure to take care of them for the generations that follow.'

Venetia saw the tears welling in Rosamund's eyes. She curved her arm around the girl's neck and drew the small, blonde head on to her shoulder. 'You've had a great shock, my child. A very great shock. Your entire world has fallen apart and you have been expelled from the one place you knew and loved more than any other. That cannot be helped. But what can be helped is where we go from here. I can't bring Daneway back to you, but I can show you the alternatives. I can open your eyes to what else is out there.'

Rosamund sat up and made to protest, but Venetia interrupted her. 'Your father made me promise that I would help, and help I shall. Celine has come with you, so you will not be entirely alone, and the things you find you cannot say to me, you will be able to confide in her when you are alone together.'

Taking both of Rosamund's hands in her own, she fixed her with a penetrating gaze and asked, 'So. Are you prepared to give it a go, or are you going to sulk and pine for Devonshire for the rest of your life?'

Before Rosamund could speak, Venetia added: 'It would be such a waste, you know. There is a whole world out there for you to explore, and it is a world that is – at the moment I am afraid – full of unrest. But no one is going to improve matters except us. The politicians may do what they will, but it really is down to you and me to make the best of our own lot. If we really do "come this way only once", then we need to make the best of it, don't you think?'

It was Celine more than anyone who guided Rosamund through the darkness. It was she who knew her charge inside out – her strengths, her weaknesses, her abilities and her failings. Seventeen years of companionship had taught her when to intervene and when to leave well alone. For the most part she listened, and in the first few weeks there was little to listen to, for Rosamund went into herself more than Celine had ever known. But just by being there, by occasionally simply putting her arm around Rosamund and holding her as she sobbed silently, Celine took on the role of mender.

It was Celine who brought the meals that remained uneaten, the cups of tea that remained un-drunk, and who laid out the clothes that were not worn. It was she who dared to enter the room and open the curtains and explain that the sun was shining, until eventually the cloud of sorrow, while not disappearing, did begin to lift a little.

I remember feeling as though life as I knew it had ended. Well, it had, of course. But my aunt Venetia, in spite of her apparent love of the finer and more frivolous things in life, was a wise old bird. She knew that if she did not chivvy me along then I would go back into myself and become a sullen, sulky girl who was unlikely to make anything of herself at all. I wanted to

protest, but it did occur to me that my aunt's summary of the situation was probably an accurate one. I went back to my room and pulled from the drawer a small wooden box filled with some of the seashells I had collected as a child. They were my one tangible connection with Devonshire; a touchstone, if you like. But I knew that I must move on; I would keep them forever and remember my roots, but I had to look forwards and, as my aunt said, make something of myself. I suppose I did in a way . . .

Not that it happened all at once. Night after night I would sit on the wide window seat of my bedroom that overlooked Eaton Square, watching people coming and going from the opera or from supper and dinner parties. It seemed that I spent much of my childhood and youth sitting in window seats watching the world go by. But the view from this one was quite different from the one in Devonshire.

I would hear voices below me in the house, and the sound of laughter. I wanted nothing to do with it at first and my aunt, very sensibly, did not force me to be present at her gatherings and tea parties. At least, not for a while. I suppose she knew that it would take time, and she was prepared to give me a chance to come round. After all, any child who has lost both parents at once – and I was really still a child at seventeen, not at all what we would now call 'streetwise' – needs to be given space to come to terms with their loss. Without Celine I would have taken so much longer to come round to the belief that life was still worth living, for it was she more than anyone who gave me the impetus to pull myself together. I have no doubt that she and my aunt had many discussions on how best to sort me out. Eventually, between the two of them, they worked their magic.

It all began rather gently. About a month after we had arrived,

Aunt Venetia would invite me to take tea with her in the after-
noons in her drawing room. She was alone at first, then perhaps
one of her friends would come to join us. I was paralysed with
fear to begin with. Yes, I had been taught good table manners
and suchlike – what my aunt would call 'the social graces' – but
I had very little in the way of conversation about current affairs
or . . . well . . . almost anything of any interest to men and
women of the world. Naïve as I was, nevertheless I knew they
would not be interested in the finer points of mackerel fishing
or the harvesting of wheat.

'So do you think we should be a peaceable nation, child, or are
you all for going to war?'

It was the first time in her life that anyone had asked
Rosamund for an opinion on a matter of national importance.
The questioner was Lady Felicity Campion, one of Venetia's
friends who was a regular at her afternoon tea parties. She was
a silver-haired woman with a ramrod-straight back who would
always sit on the very edge of the sofa with her cup in one hand
and her saucer in the other. She wore a high toque and a fox
fur around her neck over her favourite lavender-blue two-piece
suit which clearly owed its cut to a Bruton Street salon. The
fox fur would be pulled apart to reveal an impressive three-
stranded pearl necklace, which, along with the toque, gave its
owner more than a passing resemblance to Queen Mary. Lady
Felicity's voice was equally querulous and intimidating.

Rosamund felt herself colouring up, but as the room fell silent
and her Aunt Venetia glanced at her with a worried look, she
was aware that she must respond and not let her down. The
three other ladies present all turned towards her with a mixture
of expressions that varied from the kindly to the disdainful.

'It rather depends on the outcome of the talks, doesn't it?'

'Which talks are they, dear?' asked Lady Felicity.

'The talks between the Prime Minister and Herr Hitler, and whether or not we can trust him.'

'And do you think we can?'

'I'm not certain, but I think it unlikely.'

'Really? So what then? Will you side with Mr Churchill?'

'We have to defend ourselves if we are threatened. I don't see how we cannot.' Rosamund was warming to her subject now and saw a gentle smile creeping over her aunt Venetia's face. 'And we cannot stand by and see other countries invaded. Surely we have to stand together and help each other in such circumstances. We can't just turn a blind eye, can we?'

Just as she was about to launch into an impassioned speech about the responsibilities of a civilised society, Venetia cut in. 'Yes, well, we all clearly have different feelings but I do think fairness is common to us all. Now then, who's for a little more seed cake?'

I learned early on the pitfalls of expressing myself too frequently and too passionately, and so I listened a lot, and handed round the finger sandwiches and iced fancies. I learned about Mr Chamberlain and Mr Churchill and discovered how Aunt Venetia's friends were divided in their opinions – some supporting Chamberlain, 'the appeaser', and others supporting Churchill, whom my aunt referred to as 'the warmonger'. They talked about Germany having annexed Austria, and then invading

Sudetenland – part of Czechoslovakia – which, even to my young ears, seemed quite wrong. It surprised me that Aunt Venetia was not more exercised by it, but I realise now that her acquaintanceship with Lord Halifax – an appeaser and ally of Chamberlain's – probably coloured her judgement. It was one of those occasions – and there were several – where, much as I came to love her, my aunt and I did not see eye to eye.

Cities and countries that hitherto I had never heard of came under discussion. I spent time looking at an atlas to work out where all these strange-sounding places were. It was not long before I grasped that even small, sheltered worlds like the one I had inhabited in the West Country would be affected by what went on in these seemingly far distant lands. It was, I suppose, my first realisation that the world could be an unkind place; that not everyone was willing to rub along with the next man. Just as there were school bullies, so there were bullies on the national stage as well, and putting one's head in the sand and ignoring them was unlikely to make them go away.

Did I side with Mr Chamberlain or Mr Churchill? In the beginning I was not sure. I most certainly did not want a war that might damage the country I loved so much – which was clearly my aunt Venetia's point of view – but at the same time I felt so sorry for those people in Austria and Sudetenland whose own country had been taken from them. How would I feel if Hitler had annexed Devonshire? It seems rather simple when put in those terms, but from that moment on I knew I would most certainly fight to protect the land and the people I loved, for if I did not, what was I worth?

Chapter 4

LONDON

SEPTEMBER 1939 – JUNE 1940

'There never was a good war, or a bad peace.'

Benjamin Franklin, 1783

'Well, I suppose it was inevitable. But I can't help feeling sorry for dear old Neville Chamberlain. He meant well, but that's possibly the worst thing to have written on one's tombstone. I can't see him lasting long as Prime Minister . . .'

It was a Monday morning. Venetia Reeves was in her usual antemeridian position, propped up on her lace-edged pillows, thumbing through the *Daily Sketch*, while Rosamund was sitting on the window seat in her aunt's bedroom, looking out over the square below. Celine was busying herself folding newly washed clothing. It was something Rosamund tried to dissuade her from doing, now that she was of an age where she felt she should undertake the task herself, but Celine had insisted that it was something she had always done and she would be happiest if it could continue that way. At least Rosamund could insist that Celine do the job in the company of her and her aunt, rather than in the laundry room as though she were some kind of skivvy. On this particular morning it had taken longer than usual to discuss the previous day's news. Mr Chamberlain had addressed the nation via the wireless the day before – Sunday 3rd September. The Germans had invaded Poland. It was a state of affairs, he had explained in a voice of gloomy resignation, which meant that 'this country is now at war with Germany'.

That particular Sunday, a warm and sunny end-of-summer's day, had hardly seemed a suitable day to declare war. In Rosamund's mind, war meant winter – grey skies, rain, snow, sleet and slithering rivers of mud – not blue skies and birds singing.

Air raid sirens had sounded that night and Celine was convinced that they would be 'bombed to bits' if they did not immediately take to the air raid shelter. Rosamund was torn; her aunt refused to budge from Eaton Square – 'I would rather die alone in my house than in some ghastly underground shelter with the heaving masses of humanity,' she explained, momentarily forgetting her usual dictum that all men were equal under the Lord. Rosamund stayed with her. There were no planes growling overhead that night, and no explosions. It would be the best part of a year before 'the phoney war' came to an end and the first bomb fell on London.

There were compensations, though at first Rosamund found it hard to regard them as such.

'Today we visit Mr Hartnell,' her aunt informed her.

'Who is Mr Hartnell?'

Celine giggled, eavesdropping on the conversation between Venetia and her niece as she tidied away the newspapers and magazines in the drawing room.

'Celine knows, but then Celine keeps a weather eye on those

magazines she is sorting out,' said Aunt Venetia with mock asperity. 'Mr Hartnell is a dressmaker – a couturier,' she added with a nod to Celine. 'And rather a good one.'

'He makes dresses for the Queen,' added Celine, clearly impressed.

'And you need a new dress?' asked Rosamund of her aunt.

'No, my dear. You need several.' She noticed her niece's surprised expression. 'There is no need to look like that. He won't hurt you. It is quite a painless process; you might even come to enjoy it. It is time you had your first ballgown.'

'Ballgown!'

'Goodness me, the girl has ears. Yes; ballgown. You'll need more than one but we can start slowly. And you'll need some daywear as well.'

'But what's wrong with the clothes I have? They are perfectly serviceable – and comfortable.'

Venetia looked heavenwards and then threw a glance at Celine. 'You have been too good at your job, Celine. My niece has a sense of rural frugality that does her credit. Alas, it will not wash in London society.' She turned again to Rosamund. 'Celine can come with us; she has an eye for these things.' Venetia winked at Celine, who looked as though such excitement might actually cause her to burst. 'Ooh-la-la!' she murmured, and Rosamund laughed at her pantomime expression, at the same time nervous of the implications. Ballgowns and daywear. She really would have to behave like a grown-up now.

I suppose I had begun to be seduced by 'the bright lights of London', which, it seemed, were about to be extinguished just as I had come to enjoy them. And I did enjoy them – even though I never expected to. At first, when Aunt Venetia would take me to some couturier to have a fitting for a smart two-piece suit, or a ballgown – a ballgown! I had never dreamt of such a thing – I would be embarrassed and annoyed at such a point-less waste of money. But, rather to my surprise, I began to enjoy myself in the brief twelve months of peace that remained before the outbreak of war. I was, after all, an eighteen-year-old girl, and eighteen-year-old-girls – most of them at least – are rather captivated by fashion.

I determined before very long that as this was the life I had been plunged into as a result of circumstances beyond my control, I had better make the most of it. The events of 1938 had convinced me that nothing would or could last forever. If ever anyone had been made aware of the wisdom of that Latin phrase Carpe diem it was yours truly, Rosamund Hanbury, at the age of seventeen.

Aunt Venetia must have been secretly delighted. She was clever enough to offer tantalising glimpses of a way of life that only an ungrateful wretch would have turned his or her back on. I might not have approved of all its excesses, but I convinced myself that I deserved a little light relief after the loss of both my parents – and the house and the land that I so loved – and for the time being, I would throw caution to the wind and enter into the spirit of things.

At first I was relatively circumspect. I insisted that my clothing – although fashionable – should also be practical. I could see the barely-suppressed smile on my aunt's face when she took me for fittings, and when Mr Hartnell in his smart pinstripe suit and exquisitely furnished salon in Bruton Street would look me up and down and scratch his chin before saying to my aunt, 'I think we have just the fabric, Lady Reeves.' He was a charming, polite gentleman, but I found those early fittings to be enormously intimidating. Here, after all, was the man responsible for dressing our new queen. Elegant, slender young women would sweep up and down in front of us in the most glorious gowns that I felt I could never carry off. But I did grow a little, and eventually managed to look quite passable, I think.

I was taken to a Mayfair salon to have my hair properly styled – my long, fly-away blonde locks cut shorter and curled at the ends. I remember coming back and staring at myself in the looking-glass, realising that as well as cutting off my hair, I had somehow cut off my previous life. The person who gazed back at me had a seeming degree of sophistication that I found hard to reconcile with what I knew to be inside. I wore silk stockings – a strange sensation after bare feet or thick woollen socks. Thanks to Celine's encouragement, I also took to poring over fashion magazines – Vogue, McCalls and Harper's Bazaar – even the society pages of my aunt's newspapers. I might not have approved of all such goings-on, but it captured my imagination, this hitherto unknown tableau of life, which in Devonshire, I barely knew existed.

Celine watched as I tried on my new clothes in front of the looking glass. That was the one thing that convinced me to make the most of this new life – the thrill and the pure joy that Celine evinced not only in watching me wear the creations of Mr Hartnell and Victor Stiebel, but her own pleasure in handling them. It was as if she, too, had been allowed to spread her wings and fly – no longer confined to caring for the workaday attire of country folk whose idea of dressing up was a floral dress kept for the weekend. My guilt at such extravagances was tempered by Celine's pure delight and the sparkle in her eyes when she asked me to walk up and down in front of her wearing a new day or evening dress. She would clasp her hands to her mouth and murmur, 'Mon dieu! C'est parfait!'

It was all part of a transformation of a kind, but one that I was determined would not erase 'the real me', for I remained loyal to what I like to think was an innate sense of justice and down-to-earth common sense.

Once I had got over my initial lack of confidence, I would go with Aunt Venetia to visit her friends – other fashionable women who would chew over the latest topics of conversation – some unspeakably frivolous, others of national importance – and bit by bit I began to know my own mind, courtesy of a wide range of opinions that came my way, as disparate as they were colourful.

I had little time for gossip – not least because I knew so few of the individuals in question – but gradually, as the principal players in my aunt's circle became more familiar, I began to differentiate between idle, unfounded chit-chat and well-informed opinion. I soon learned whose thoughts and judgements I valued and whose I could ignore as ill-founded speculation. Occasionally I would be asked for my own view on a particular person or situation, and took care to think before giving an answer. I was not at all sure if my own opinions were really of any interest or importance to my aunt's friends, or if they were simply being polite in including me in their conversation. To this day I am uncertain.

In the evening we would most often dine in. There were

supper parties, usually for six or eight, for Aunt Venetia maintained that larger numbers would split the table into factions which precluded her from understanding all that was going on. It is something I have come to believe in and practise myself. More frequently – and certainly once the bombs began to fall – we would dine alone; my aunt and I discussing the events of the day in much the same way as Celine and I did each morning.

Dear Celine; what would I have done without her? Like me, she took some time to recover from the shock of my parents' sudden death, but eventually she formed her own circle of friends in London – most of them connected to the social circle of my aunt – dressers and lady's maids, of which there were still a few around before the outbreak of war. And in the grander households, a skeleton staff would hold the fort even when conscription came in and many of the men joined up.

Celine's duties were not arduous. I think Aunt Venetia considered that she had done quite enough work bringing me up; now she was acting as my confidante and companion. Her duties around the house at Eaton Square were quite light – arranging flowers and helping lay the table for dinner – so she had a degree of freedom which allowed her to act as a French teacher to several of Aunt Venetia's friends' daughters. She would go round to their houses of an afternoon and come back to regale me with stories of how slow to learn her new charges were, and how their accents were simply execrable. 'Do you know, one of them said to me, "Daddy says it is important that my accent is not too good because that way it helps to keep the Froggies in their place"? I ask you. The very nerve of it. I had to bite my lip. Zut!'

In our private conversations we invariably spoke in French, not least because in some way that seemed to make them more private, more intimate. But, for all our closeness, I could sense *that Celine was beginning to keep a respectful distance between us. I had a feeling that although we had grown up together, and could say almost anything to one another, she knew that we were becoming different. We inhabited the same universe, but were in different orbits. In Devonshire we seemed to be cut from the same cloth; now there was a kind of divergence between us which, although unspoken, was mutually acknowledged. But along with this grew a determination on my part that we would not become too distanced from one another. Celine, I knew, was concerned that she should not hold me back; her reticence was one based on affection for me and a desire to avoid standing in my way. I feel a certain wistfulness about this, for it seems that Celine looked upon me as though I were like Wendy growing up and leaving Peter Pan and his childish exploits behind. Not that there was anything childish about Celine, apart from a lifelong love of jam sandwiches, which she never lost . . .*

On those evenings before war was declared, when Aunt Venetia and I dined out, she would whisk me off with her to The Ritz, or Quaglino's, where we would enjoy supper with a couple of her friends – most usually a husband and wife, such as the royal courtier Sir Basil Flynn and his wife, or Lord and Lady Belgate who had a large estate in Somerset and an imposing house in Belgrave Square.

The 'country mouse' began to turn into a young lady who could 'hold her own at the dinner table' as Aunt Venetia would say, so much so that on occasion she would look in my direction and clear her throat gently, implying in her own subtle way that I had said quite enough for the time being. But those occasions were rare, and I think that for the most part she was quite proud of the way that her charge was opening up – rather after the fashion of a rose in the sunshine. Sometimes, when I was declaiming rather too passionately, I would catch her out of the corner of my eye, smiling and checking the reaction of her friends as they listened to me expressing my feelings on subjects upon which 'nice young ladies' were not really expected to have opinions.

The most dramatic event of those early years of the war was the evacuation of Dunkirk. It created in us a mixture of pride and despair, if you can understand that contradiction. In late May and early June of 1940, the Germans advanced on the Allied forces and pushed them across northern France towards the English Channel, forcing the British Expeditionary Force into the sea. Day after day we listened to the news on the wireless, our hearts in our mouths for fear of what might happen to 'our boys'.

What could have been a complete disaster was averted by the arrival, not only of naval vessels to pick up the evacuees, but also around 700 'little ships' – all kinds of craft, from steam packets and fishing smacks to tiny pleasure boats – that set out from England to rescue our soldiers. There were many fatalities, of course, but over the space of eight days more than 300,000 Allied troops were saved. It made us feel that even those of us who had not enlisted were able to do something for the war effort. Celine found the whole operation heartbreaking, for the land she thought of as home was now totally in the hands of the German army. It made her, if anything, even more patriotic.

Once I had turned eighteen, and when I had quite clearly proved that I was capable of standing on my own two feet, my aunt announced that it was time I enjoyed the company of people my own age. There were places I could go with 'the young' – the sons and daughters of her society friends. These were respectable young men and women who would 'know the ropes', as she put it, and who would be more likely than some of her own intimates to introduce me to the intricacies of the life that I was now expected to lead. The Café de Paris was a favourite watering hole for the sons and daughters of society. The champagne was good – if pricey – the food delicious, and the music of the very best.

Until that point I had never fallen in love. How quickly that was to change.

Chapter 5

LONDON

JULY 1940

'London is a modern Babylon.'

Benjamin Disraeli, *Tancred*, 1847

'Shall we?'

Rosamund looked up to see Harry Napier smiling and holding out his hand. The band at the Café de Paris had struck up a popular Cole Porter number – 'Begin the Beguine' – and Harry was a good dancer. Rosamund smiled back, took Harry's hand and followed him to the dance floor. His arm was round her waist and his cheek thrillingly close to hers. She had known him (from afar at least) for just a few months – quite long enough to fall madly in love. She hadn't thought he'd even noticed her properly. She felt herself blushing as he steered her gently round the dance floor.

'Do you like Cole Porter?' he asked.

Rosamund nodded.

'Me too.'

Rosamund felt her throat tightening. This was the first time that Harry had ever asked her to dance. Normally it would be the rather eager Billy Belgate who asked her. Billy was a sweet, stocky lad who was good fun in a brotherly kind of way with his blond curls and smiley eyes – 'Come along, Ros, old girl,' he would say, 'let's trip the light fantastic' – and he would whisk her around the floor, his patent leather shoes glinting in the spotlights. But Harry was something else – tall, dark and brooding, he could melt a girl's heart with the raise of his eyebrow.

Billy, the son of Lord and Lady Belgate – Aunt Venetia's friends – had been charged with looking after Rosamund and introducing her to a group of people her own age – mainly the sons and daughters of the nobility. He was a nice young man, given to bursts of enthusiasm about jazz and the latest fashions, but he was not Rosamund's idea of the perfect match. Not that her aunt was in any way matchmaking; simply making sure that her niece was well integrated into London society. Harry Napier was a part of that set but seemed always to be standing on the edge of it, rather bemused by the often raucous excesses of his friends. She had hardly spoken to him, let alone danced with him, and he always seemed to be coupled with a girl called Henrietta who barely gave Rosamund a second glance.

'So how are you enjoying it? London, I mean.' Harry's voice had a velvety quality, but there was a naturalness about him which Rosamund found captivating. There were other men in 'the set' who were bristling with self-confidence: ladykillers of the first order. But Harry was different. He might have been tall (six feet three inches), dark (a full head of rich, lustrous hair) and handsome (a long face with a firm mouth and a square jaw; his eyes green and his smile . . . melting) but it was his total lack of self-awareness that Rosamund found so engaging. Of course, the fact that he was good-looking and that every girl in the room seemed to glance at him or go out of her way to brush past him, did help to give him a certain magnetic quality.

'I think I've got used to it,' Rosamund replied. She noticed the envious glances from other girls around the floor and blushed slightly.

'Not your scene really then?'

'It wasn't. But . . . well . . . here I am and I might as well get used to it.'

'That sounds a bit resigned. Does it bore you?'

Rosamund was suddenly aware that she might have sounded rude, ungrateful even. She stammered out, 'No! No, not at all. It's just that it is so different from Devonshire. From life on a farm. But I think I'm beginning to enjoy it.'

'Good.'

The music's lilt set her heart beating faster, and the gentle pressure of Harry's hand in the small of her back left her feeling sure that he must feel it through the fabric of her dress.

'Well,' he said, 'we'd better make the most of it. I fear it won't last.'

'It's been awfully quiet so far,' responded Rosamund.

'It may have been quiet here, but it's hotting up in Europe. I fear we'll be next.'

'You think so?'

'I know so. The Germans are flexing their muscles. Getting ready for the fray. I can't see that we'll be dancing like this for much longer.'

'No.' Rosamund felt a stab of sadness and regret. For the first time in her life, she was being swept around a dance floor by a dashing 'beau', as Celine would say, and circumstances would seem to be conspiring against her. It just wasn't fair. She tried to put it out of her mind. To live the moment – a moment which might never come again. The sound of the clarinet and the lyrical tones of the slick young vocalist at the microphone filled the glittering room. Faces of other dancers swirled by as the words of 'Begin the Beguine' seeped into her head. But the dream was broken suddenly as she brushed past a figure she knew.

'Diana!'

'Rosamund! What are you doing here?'

It was three years since Diana Molyneux had left Devonshire for London. Now, here she was on the same dance floor and looking . . . well . . . just as pretty as she always had, her once long, dark locks cut into a smart bob, her now shapely body encased in a sheath of emerald green slubbed silk.

Without thinking, Rosamund let go of her dance partner and threw her arms around her old friend; then, aware of her apparent lack of manners, she turned back to Harry, only to find him laughing at her.

'Shall I go?' he said.

'No! No! Please! I'm so sorry. It's just that Diana and I . . . well . . . we used to live near one another . . .'

'In Devonshire?' he offered teasingly.

'Yes.'

'And you haven't seen each other for . . . ?

'Three years,' said Diana, helping to explain her friend's unintentional rudeness.

'Well then . . . why don't I leave you to catch up?' And then, seeing the look of dismay on Rosamund's face, he offered, 'Unless we all three sit down and have a drink?'

'Oh, yes, please!' blurted Rosamund, suddenly aware that she was probably sounding far too eager.

'There's a spare table there,' said Harry, indicating a small booth at the far end of the dance floor. 'You go and sit down;

I'll order a bottle of champagne and have it sent over.' He nodded at Diana, turned on his heel and went off to find a waiter.

'Well!' said Diana, looping her arm through Rosamund's and walking with her across to the table. 'How did you manage that? Harry Napier, the most eligible man in the room! And the dishiest!'

'Really?'

'Oh, come on, Ros! Don't tell me you haven't noticed the looks of all the other girls! If they could kill you and walk all over you they would.'

'Well, I know he's dishy but . . . eligible?'

'My dear girl, he has just dumped – well, not dumped exactly, Harry would never be that rude – but he has just . . . said farewell, shall we say, to Henrietta Westmorland. He's available.'

'I've seen her but I'm afraid I don't know . . .'

'She's landed. Stinking rich, but a bit of a shit. He's well rid of her.'

'Oh.' Rosamund looked bewildered.

'Oh, it's good to see you. I've missed you so much. And I was so sorry to hear about your ma and pa. I wanted to write but I didn't know where to find you. So what are you doing here?'

Rosamund began to explain to Diana the events of the intervening years, Harry arriving as the conversation got under way. Rosamund made to change the subject, but Harry begged her to carry on and listened intently as the story unfolded. At first Rosamund was self-conscious, but the attentiveness of her two companions soon relaxed her and, between restorative sips of champagne, she told the story of her parents' deaths, how she and Celine had been whisked off to Aunt Venetia's house, and about how life had changed – and how she herself had changed – in the years since they had parted.

'And Celine?' asked Diana. 'Do you still speak French together?'

'All the time.'

Harry looked quizzical.

Diana explained: 'Ros was brought up by a governess – a sort of minder – Celine.'

'French?' enquired Harry.

'Her father was,' qualified Rosamund.

Diana continued, 'It used to make me so cross. When they wanted to exclude me they would just chatter away, and French not being my strong point, I was left out in the cold – completely.'

'Oh, that's not very fair!' protested Rosamund.

'No. Not really. It didn't happen very often. Only when I'd ridden faster than her on the beach, or caught the eye of a groom that she quite fancied.'

'I don't recall ever fancying a groom! Certainly not one old enough to be my . . . !' retorted Rosamund.

'No. They weren't much of a catch, were they? And some of them were far too young . . .' interrupted Diana with a knowing glint in her eye.

'Anyway,' said Rosamund, 'you were much better at maths so you could always get one over on me when it came to numbers.'

'Not your thing?' asked Harry.

'No.'

'Shame.'

'Why do you say that?' asked Rosamund.

'Oh . . . no reason.' He took another sip of champagne and asked, 'So, now that you've met up again, what will you do?'

'Well, we've a lot of catching up to do,' said Diana. 'We must swap telephone numbers. Where are you living?'

'Eaton Square,' replied Rosamund.

'No! I'm just round the corner in Draycott Place. There is absolutely no excuse for us not to see each other. Belgravia ten-sixty-six. Easy to remember. Call me as soon as you can.'

'I will!' said Rosamund brightly.

Diana made to get up. 'But in the meantime, I have a man I need to dance with . . .' She nodded to a small group on the other side of the dance floor, among them the rather crestfallen youth she had summarily dismissed when she had bumped into Rosamund. 'Don't think me rude, Mr Napier.' She reached out and shook his hand.

'Not at all,' replied Harry. 'It's been a pleasure to meet you, Miss Molyneux.'

'Oh! You know my name?'

Harry nodded. 'Yes.'

Diana did not, as a rule, blush. But at that moment she came as near to doing so as ever she had. She kissed Rosamund on the cheek. 'Soon!' she said. Then, casting a smile at Harry, she left to rejoin her group.

'Fancy you knowing Diana Molyneux,' said Harry.

'I think she was rather surprised that *you* knew *her*,' responded Rosamund.

'Ah. Yes.'

'So how *do* you know her?'

'Through a friend of a friend.'

'That sounds rather sinister,' said Rosamund, finally regaining her composure and relaxing into the encounter.

'No. Not sinister. Just . . .' he shrugged as if to make light of the matter.

'So what do *you* do?' asked Rosamund. 'You now know my life story. What about yours?'

'Oh, rather dull in comparison. Minor public school, Oxford University . . .'

'Impressive!'

'Not really – only managed a second . . . and then a spell at that big house at the end of The Mall.'

'Buckingham Palace?'

Harry nodded.

'Gosh!'

'Oh, don't get too excited. Nothing very regal. I'm a phil-atelist.'

Rosamund looked surprised. 'Stamps?'

'Yes. Boring, isn't it?'

'Not necessarily. Surprising though. How does a philatelist come to be working at Buckingham Palace?'

'Because the King has probably the finest stamp collection in the world. Thanks to his father. Volumes and volumes of them. Albums of red, and now blue. Hugely valuable.'

'And you look after them?'

'I *helped* to look after them. The man who's really in charge of them is Sir John Wilson. But I'm now having to do something else. The albums are being transferred to the vaults of a bank in Pall Mall for the duration of the war. For safety.'

'Goodness.' Rosamund looked thoughtful. 'So what will you do now?'

'Oh, my future will be pretty much like every other twenty-something for the next few years. Part of the war effort.'

'Of course. Army, navy or air force?'

'Yes.'

Rosamund felt slightly uncomfortable. 'Oh. I see.'

'Do you?'

'Yes. I think so. Something . . . secret.'

'Sort of. Dunkirk was a bit of a watershed. Life changed then. For all of us.' Harry drained his glass, then stood up and asked, 'Shall I see you home?'

'Oh!' Rosamund glanced at her wristwatch. 'Goodness! Yes. I mean, thank you. If you're sure . . .' Rosamund nodded in the direction of the party that Harry had left to dance with her.

'I'm sure. They can get along quite well without me.'

'You didn't come with anybody then?'

'No. But I think you'd worked that out, hadn't you?' Harry smiled at her, and she blushed. Unlike her friend Diana, the blood would rush to Rosamund's cheeks far too frequently for her liking.

He walked her from the Café de Paris to his car – a shiny black Talbot Sports Tourer.

Rosamund gazed at it wide-eyed.

'I know. She's rather lovely, isn't she? I don't know how long I'll be able to keep her. Bought her three or four years ago in a fit of madness. There she sat in the Rootes showroom in Piccadilly, all 3½ litres of her. Fell in love.' Then, clearing his throat, he said, 'Eaton Square, wasn't it?'

'Yes.' Rosamund slipped into the passenger seat and Harry closed the door behind her, then walked around the front of the car, slid into the driver's seat and started up the powerful engine.

She sat quietly as they turned right into Panton Street, then into Haymarket and down The Mall through a dark and unilluminated London towards Buckingham Palace.

'Are you all right?' asked Harry, noticing that Rosamund looked a little pale.

'Yes. I'm fine. Sorry. It's just that – weirdly – I'm still a little nervous of fast cars. Since the accident. It's almost two years ago now. You'd think I'd be over it . . .'

Harry slowed down. 'Not at all. I don't think one can ever get over something like that. The suddenness of it, especially.'

Rosamund felt comforted that he understood. 'Will you go back to the palace?' she asked. 'After the war I mean?'

'Who knows? Who knows when it will all end? Or what sort of state we'll be in.' Harry drove on through Belgravia, seeming to know his way about in spite of the diluted beam of the headlights and the lack of street lighting in the wartime blackout. 'Or when I'll be able to drive this beauty again. She's going into storage. I've been able to use her for . . .' he hesitated, then continued, 'work . . . but petrol rationing will mean she'll have to have a holiday for a while.'

'What a shame.'

Harry glanced at Rosamund. 'You like her?'

'I think she's wonderful.' Rosamund pulled her fur wrap high up round her neck, feeling unspeakably decadent as she nestled into the deep leather seat.

He grinned, and they drove on through Belgravia in comfortable silence, finally reaching Eaton Square and pulling up outside the house that Rosamund indicated.

Harry switched off the engine and turned to her. 'Can I take you out to dinner next week?'

The question was unexpected. Rosamund had been steeling herself for the moment when Harry would say, 'Well, it's been a lot of fun. I hope we meet again one day. Thank you so much.' Instead, he was asking to see her again. She did her best to seem relaxed about it. 'Yes, of course. That would be lovely.'

She smiled at him and he leaned over and kissed her tenderly. It was the first time she had ever been kissed on the lips by anyone other than a stable lad. The difference was astonishing. She understood now all those seemingly trite songs about the earth moving beneath your feet, the sound of bells, and birds singing. Harry's kiss was like something she had never encountered before and, truth be told, like something she'd never believed really existed. She felt sure he must now feel – or even hear – her heart beating within her chest. As he leaned back from her and smiled, she smiled back and tried hard to stop the tears from welling up in her eyes.

As if he knew that this was not the time for further conversation, Harry opened his door, got out of the car and walked around to help Rosamund out of the passenger seat. As he took her arm and raised her to her feet, his cheek brushed hers, and he held her in his arms briefly before pulling back a little and smiling. 'Welcome to London, Miss Hanbury,' he said softly. 'I'll be in touch.'

She waved briefly from the open doorway as he drove off with a smile and a nod, then she locked the door behind her and climbed the stairs to her room. The house was silent. Aunt Venetia had retired, but as she turned the handle of her bedroom door, Celine's head popped out from her own room further along the landing.

'You are back safely?' she whispered.

'Yes,' Rosamund whispered back. 'But you shouldn't have waited up.'

Celine shrugged. 'I like to know you are safe.' Then, smiling, 'Have you had a good time?'

Rosamund beckoned her to join her in her room, and after quietly closing the door, she turned to Celine and said, 'Can you keep a secret?'

Celine shook her head and smiled. 'You have to ask? After all this time?'

Then she saw the look in Rosamund's eyes – the dreamy, faraway look that she recognised. 'You have met somebody?' She began to undo the hooks down the back of Rosamund's dress, preparing her for bed as she had done thousands of times for going on twenty years.

'Yes.'

'And is he special?'

'Gosh, yes. I had no idea he even noticed me. I mean, he never showed that he did.'

'But you noticed him?'

'Yes. But I tried to put him out of my mind. I mean, why would a handsome man-about-town notice a little country mouse among all those elegant women?'

Celine smiled indulgently. 'But you are no longer a little country mouse, are you?'

'Aren't I?'

Celine shook her head. 'Not any more, *cherie*. You are beautiful and sophisticated now.'

'Oh, Semolina, stop it! I'm not at all sophisticated. I feel such a fraud.'

'Still?'

Rosamund was thoughtful. 'Not as much as I did, I suppose.'

Celine helped Rosamund into a silk dressing gown and sat beside her at the dressing table as she applied Pond's cold cream to remove her make-up. 'Look at me! Make-up and all. What has happened to me, Semolina? What has happened?'

'You have grown up. That is all. You cannot stay a girl forever.'

'I know. But I am still me, aren't I?' She took a small box from the drawer of the dressing table, opened it and showed Celine the contents. 'I am still the Rosamund who collected these shells from the beach in Devonshire. Tell me I am still the real me, not some shallow London socialite.'

'You are as real as those shells, and as long as you remember that, and as long as you value all those things – the shells, the memories and the events that made you what you are – you will be fine. Don't reproach yourself for growing up. Hang on to the important things – the values and the happy memories – but have the freedom to make new ones. And new friends.'

'And lovers?'

'Yes. And lovers.'

'Even if they break your heart?' she asked, remembering Celine's beau.

'They may break your heart, but who wants a heart that does not feel; that does not take risks?'

'Is it worth it? The heartache, I mean?'

Celine shrugged. 'Who can say? All I know is that you have to follow your heart wherever it leads – whether that be to heaven or to hell. There is no way of knowing which until you take the risk.' She smiled. 'Is he very handsome?'

'Ridiculously!'

'And kind? Tell me he is kind.'

'Very kind.'

'And you are . . . head over heels?'

'I'm afraid so.'

'Then there is nothing more to be said. We are at war. Live each day as it comes and do not be afraid to love. It is all that matters in the end.' She bent and kissed Rosamund on top of her head and walked to the door.

'And you?' asked Rosamund. 'Will you love again?'

Celine paused, holding on to the door handle. She looked away and said quietly, 'Maybe. There is someone; but it is too early to say.'

For a moment Rosamund was a child again; she rushed at Celine and said, 'Oh Semolina, do tell me! Who is he? Where did you meet him? What is he like?'

Celine smiled wearily. 'I told you; it is too early. But he has been kind to me, as your man has to you. He is an older cousin of one of the families whose children I teach French. I am not rushing things. I have given my heart before and paid the price. This time I want to be sure . . .'

'Oh, but do tell me . . .' Rosamund said no more, for Celine laid her finger gently upon her charge's lips and murmured, 'One day; when I am more certain. For now I am happy to . . . gentle it along. Perhaps one day I shall have the life of my dreams.'

'And where will that be?' asked Rosamund excitedly.

'In a house on the coast.'

'In Devonshire.'

Celine shook her head. 'In the south of France. Near Cap Ferrat, where there are beautiful villas and the sea is the colour of sapphires. Where the scent of lavender fills the air and the sun makes the wavelets glisten like diamonds.' She came out of her reveries and added, 'Now go to bed! Sweet dreams, *ma cherie*, sweet dreams.' Then she quietly closed the door.

Before she got into bed, Rosamund took out the journal she kept in her dressing table drawer. It was a small school exercise book that Mr Langstone had given her and she would jot down things that had amused or interested her or which might – who knows – come in useful later in life. In red ink she wrote the date and then, in her usual italic script, just twelve words: 'I think I am in love. And I think Celine is, too.'

Chapter 6

LONDON

AUGUST 1940

'One need not write in a diary what one is to remember for ever.'

Sylvia Townsend Warner, 1930

True to his word, Harry took Rosamund out for supper the following week; not to The Ritz or The Savoy Grill, where high society met in all its defiant wartime glory – conflict permitting – but to a small restaurant in St James's where the staff seemed to know him and the two of them were closeted in a small and intimate booth where their conversation could not be overheard. It was here that Harry talked about his childhood in Yorkshire, schooling at Ampleforth and holidays with the family at Whitby.

'Whitby? I've never been. Isn't there a ruined abbey?'

'Yes. With the most amazing view out across the North Sea.'

'Do you like the sea?' she asked.

'"Like" is a bit of an understatement. I love the sea – its moods, its majesty, its . . . vastness. I love the fact that we have no control over it.'

'Some people find that scary,' said Rosamund, taking a sip of wine.

'Yes. But perhaps they feel unnerved by its power. I think it keeps us in our place; reminds us that we are not as omnipotent as we sometimes think we are. It proves that there are forces in life far greater and more significant than we are. What about you?'

'I was born and brought up by the sea. I can't imagine living anywhere other than on the coast.'

'And yet here you are in London.'

'Circumstances. But I plan to live by the sea again one day.'

'That's funny. I've always felt the same.'

'You're just saying that to be kind.'

'No, I'm not. It's perfectly true.'

'So why did you come to London?' asked Rosamund, taking a mouthful of the modest sliver of fried plaice that constituted the highlight of their five-shilling meal.

'The job. I can't think where else I would have found a way of earning a living from my childhood hobby. When it comes to employment, philately is a bit specialised and I didn't fancy selling stamps in Stanley Gibbons. I'm not very good at bargaining with people, and a lot of stamp collectors are hard bargainers.' He grinned. 'I'd have had to do something else altogether – perhaps worked in a garage. Now that would have been a thing; I could have tinkered with cars to my heart's content. Then the job at the palace cropped up.'

'And now?'

'Yes. All that's over and I must "do my bit" for the war effort.'

'Do you mind?'

Harry looked directly at her. 'That doesn't really come into it. We are at war and I want to serve my country.'

'How?'

'Oh, you know. This and that . . .'

She took a sip of her wine. 'I see . . .' Then she looked away, feeling that she had pried too much.

Harry reached across the table for her hand. 'It won't be long, you know. Before the bombs start to fall and we tumble headlong into heaven-knows-what. I'm just involved in trying to make sure that we're on the winning side.'

Rosamund smiled. 'Yes.'

'And you?' asked Harry. 'What are you going to do?'

Rosamund shrugged. 'Look after Aunt Venetia, I suppose – while she looks after me.'

'Is that all?'

'Isn't that enough?'

'That's for you to say.'

Rosamund was taken aback by the remark. She hesitated. 'I mean, what can I do? I suppose I could go and work in a munitions factory, but I think that would send Aunt Venetia apoplectic. I could join the ATS, or the Air Transport Auxiliary and deliver Spitfires, but I'd have to learn to fly first and by that time the war would be over . . .'

'God willing!' added Harry.

'There's not much else left . . . apart from going back to Devonshire as a Land Girl; I'd do that like a shot . . .'

'Would you? That would be rather a waste.'

Rosamund nodded at her plate. 'Well, we need food, and with so many men joining up and leaving the land there are plenty of opportunities for women.'

'Planting potatoes? Cutting hay? A bit of a waste of your talents, I'd say.'

Rosamund laughed. 'What talents? I haven't got any, apart from a vivid imagination, so my aunt tells me.'

'You speak French, don't you? Fluently?'

'As well as I speak English, but that's not much use here except to order a meal in a French restaurant . . . if I could get one.'

'How wedded are you to a life in London?'

'I'm sorry?' She looked puzzled.

'Supposing you were able to do your bit . . . in France.'

'But it's occupied. The Germans invaded in May.'

'Exactly.'

Rosamund hesitated. 'I'm not sure what you're suggesting . . .'

Harry took a sip of wine and replaced the glass on the table. Then he leaned forward, took both her hands in his and said, 'You could be really useful in occupied France.'

Rosamund was shocked and hurt. She drew her hands from his and sat back in her chair. 'Is that what this is all about? Is this why you have invited me out to dinner?'

Harry shook his head emphatically. 'No. I've asked you out to dinner because I enjoy your company and because . . . I want to get to know you better.'

'So you can work out if I'd be suitable material to send over to France as . . . what? A spy?'

'Keep your voice down. And please . . . I was only suggesting that if you did want to "do your bit", there are better ways of utilising your talents than . . . planting potatoes.'

'Utilising my talents. Very romantic . . .'

'Look, just forget it. I didn't mean to upset you, and I certainly didn't ask you out to dinner so that I could . . .'

'Recruit me?'

'No. Not at all. Please. Let's not talk about it any more. It was just that . . . well . . . I didn't know if you wanted to spend the rest of the war in London with your aunt or . . .'

'Doing something useful?'

Harry shrugged.

Rosamund considered for a moment, then said, 'You don't really like that set you go around with, do you?'

'I don't *dislike* them.'

'But you don't feel their behaviour is . . . appropriate.'

'Not now. Not really. But some of them are already doing their bit, and most of them will be called up soon to join those that have already enlisted, so I suppose they're just enjoying their freedom while they can. Who can blame them?'

'I see.'

Harry leaned forward again. 'Look, I know we've only just met, and that I'm probably being a bit forward, a bit premature, but it's just that I saw something in you that I don't very often see in a society girl. I mean, a woman. You're bright, you're intelligent – far more intelligent than most of them in "the set", as you call it.'

'Even Diana? She's much better at maths.'

'Yes. And her talents are being used already.'

'Diana's?'

'Yes.'

'Is that how you knew her . . . and she doesn't know you?'

'She knew my name.'

'Only by reputation and because you're . . .' her words faded away.

'Because I'm what?'

Rosamund took a deep breath. 'Because you are a good catch.'

Harry laughed.

'You are!'

'Well, I'm very grateful for the compliment. Not that it's strictly true. I've very little money to speak of – no country estate . . .'

'Neither have I . . . now . . .' Then she asked the question again: 'So how do you know Diana?'

'There's a place where we can use people with a flair for numbers. It's a part of the intelligence network. It's based at Moor Park in Hertfordshire.' He hesitated. 'I shouldn't have told you that. But . . .' he shrugged, 'you seem like a nice girl . . .'

Rosamund smiled and shook her head. 'What am I to make of you, Mr Napier?'

'That's entirely up to you. Shall I get the bill?'

'Thank you. And do I get a lift home in your lovely motor car?'

'Only if you'll think about what I've said.'

'Mmm,' said Rosamund. Nothing more.

My mind was in a whirl after that first evening. It took me an age to get off to sleep. I could not help wondering if Harry really did like me or if taking me out to supper was simply a ploy to get me to be a part of . . . what? It all seemed so unlikely, so cloak and dagger. And, after all, he hardly knew me. Why did he risk telling me such things?

What Aunt Venetia would have made of it I could not imagine. I would not tell her, of course; she would have had a fit. I felt sure that as far as she was concerned, she and I would be living together for the duration of the war and I would be steered in the direction of a suitable man with whom I could make my future – she had intimated as much. But we were at war now; all 'suitable men' were being called up – either as officers (clearly my aunt's only consideration) or as private soldiers. Men that my aunt would have thought 'eligible' were not exactly thick on the ground unless they were in reserved occupations, which meant they were doctors, farmers or teachers. There were coal-miners, dockers and railway workers as well but they were hardly likely to come into my aunt's sphere. I laughed at the thought of coming back to Eaton Square and saying that I had met a wonderful man down at the docks!

I realise that I am talking as though I were living in Jane Austen's England, with my guardian deciding on a suitable match. It was not quite as bad as that, but as I now moved in this circle of upper class men and women, they were the ones I met on a daily basis. It simply did not occur to me to look outside that circle. I was not then – and am not now – remotely snobbish, but one is only likely to fall in love with the people one meets socially, and these were they. Oh, and I did love Harry. In spite of my suspicions that he saw the relationship as a way of getting me to be a part of some wartime operation in which he was involved.

I will never forget that first supper together. Not only because of being with him, alone, and looking into those wonderful green smiling eyes, and being worried that he did not love me as much as I loved him, but also because later that night the first bomb fell on London. The evacuation of Dunkirk in May and June had made us all defiant and determined, and the 'Battle of Britain', as we came to call it, had strengthened our resolve, but when Hitler started to bomb London, we knew then that it really was a fight to the death. For all of us, not just 'the few'.

I became more and more uneasy at the thought of doing nothing during the war; of simply living with Aunt Venetia and marking time until the hostilities were over. It seemed morally wrong that I should not do my bit, even if that meant leaving *what we would nowadays call 'my comfort zone'. But what to do? I had not the brains to do what Diana was doing – our aptitudes were so different – and the prospect of flying terrified me, so joining the Air Transport Auxiliary and delivering planes was out of the question. Perhaps I really would have to become a Land Girl. Unless, of course, I followed Harry's advice.*

Chapter 7

LONDON

SEPTEMBER 1940

'O herald skylark, stay thy flight
One moment for a nightingale
Floods us with sorrow and delight.
Tomorrow thou shalt hoist the sail;
Leave us tonight the nightingale.'

Christina Rossetti, 'Bird Raptures', 1876

True to her word, Aunt Venetia refused to totter along to the nearest air raid shelter swathed in furs when the bombs began falling that September. Instead she made sure that she and Rosamund and Celine and Mrs Heffer – the amply proportioned cook and sole remaining member of the original household staff, whose 'Mrs' was bestowed as a courtesy title by Venetia, for she had never married – were safely ensconced in the cellar at 29, Eaton Square, its walls and ceiling reinforced with stout wooden planks thanks to 'an obliging little builder from Fulham'.

Each night they would play draughts and gin rummy and whist as the bombs fell around them, keeping up their own spirits with a little help from the liquid variety. Aunt Venetia's cellar was never to be found wanting during the war, thanks, Rosamund assumed, to the precautions taken to keep it filled up during the 1920s and 30s. It was odd, though, how extra bottles seemed to keep appearing.

Instead of hosting dinner parties – altogether too risky during the Blitz – Aunt Venetia would have her friends round to lunch, when Mrs Heffer would use her imagination to cobble together what appeared to be some gastronomic delicacy from the meagre rations available at the local butcher and grocer, along with a generous supply of vegetables from her brother's allotment in Putney. The produce of 'Dig For Victory' was much appreciated in Lady Reeves' household, and Mrs Heffer was not known for her parsimony. Wartime privations or not, Aunt Venetia saw no reason to revise her dictum: 'Never trust a thin cook.' Mrs Heffer was clearly a magician of sorts, for her meals always seemed to be greater than the sum of their parts.

It was at one of Aunt Venetia's lunches that Rosamund found herself in a compromising situation. Seated around the table were Lord and Lady Belgate (their son Billy had recently joined the RAF), and Sir Patrick and Lady Felpham. Sir Patrick had been a friend of Venetia's late husband, Sir Oscar Reeves; his wife was a birdlike woman with glasses, looking as though even the slightest breeze would blow her over. So small was she that two cushions had to be placed on her chair in order that she could reach her knife and fork. Sir Patrick, on the other hand, was a large, florid man (probably on account of eating his wife's ration as well as his own, suggested Aunt Venetia to Rosamund before their guests arrived).

Rosamund liked the Belgates. He, an archetypal patrician gentleman, tall and besuited with a neatly trimmed grey moustache; she, slender, elegant and well preserved for her years, always gracious and enquiring after Rosamunds' well-being.

But it was another enquiry which almost wrong-footed Rosamund on this occasion. Hardly surprisingly, the conversation revolved around the war – especially the Blitz and how long it was likely to continue. The Belgates' house had narrowly escaped a direct hit a few nights before – the two of them, like the Eaton Square household, had been holed up in the cellar and showered in plaster. Rosamund tried to imagine the pair of them covered in dust and found the task beyond even her imagination, so beautifully turned out were they at all times.

Then, from the other side of the table, Sir Patrick, between mouthfuls, began to explain that as well as fighting on the front line, there was also fighting behind the enemy lines, or so he had heard. 'There's some place in Hertfordshire,' he said, 'where they are working on intelligence. Cracking codes and suchlike. Very important work apparently. They're recruiting bright young things to help with the job.' He turned to Rosamund. 'You must have heard of it. It's just the place for a sharp girl like you.'

Rosamund smiled at him. Without hesitation, she replied, 'No, I'm afraid not.'

'Oh. Shame. I'd like to have known more.' Sir Patrick harrumphed and helped himself to more potatoes, while his wife made figure-of-eight movements with her fork around a lonely carrot in the centre of her plate.

Aunt Venetia looked across at Rosamund and frowned, while the bulky Sir Patrick continued to work at maintaining his commendable girth.

Lord Belgate, laying down his own knife and fork, having disposed of a more modest portion, chipped in. 'Where did you get that information from, Felpham?'

'Oh, some fellah at my club. Says its vital work apparently. Very hush-hush.'

Lord Belgate winked at Rosamund. 'Oh, just the sort of thing that Rosamund would tell you then, if she knew?'

Sir Patrick huffed and puffed and finally said, 'Well, I suppose not. Just thought it was interesting, that's all.'

'Very interesting, I should think,' said Lord Belgate. 'And yes, vital, too. We need all the help we can get to win this damned war. There are those who said it would all be over by now. How wrong they were. I suspect we're in for another couple of years at least.'

'Two years! Heaven forbid!' exclaimed Aunt Venetia.

'I'm afraid so, my dear. You'd better tell Mrs Heffer to get her brother to order more seeds for next year's crops. How else are we to eat so well?' He ended his advice with a knowing wink.

Aunt Venetia smiled wanly. 'Yes. Well, I'm afraid that pudding is blancmange, and a rather watery one at that.'

Sir Patrick put down his own knife and fork and harrumphed once more. 'Churchill might have told us that it's going to be "blood, toil, tears and sweat", but he didn't tell us that it was going to be blancmange instead of jam roly-poly.'

His wife sniffed. The rest of the company smiled wistfully.

People ask if we were frightened during the Blitz. I suppose we were. But what I remember most is laughter. Laughter and determination. Every night, as the bombs fell around us, rather than clutching each other and shaking with fear, we gritted our

teeth and carried on talking down in the cellar, telling silly stories and learning childish French songs from Celine like 'Sur le pont d'Avignon'. But then there is a limit to how long you can sit like a rabbit in the headlights, waiting to be hit, and the Blitz just seemed to go on and on.

Poor Celine. She worried so much about France, which, in spite of never having lived there, she always thought of as her homeland. At the very mention of 'pâté de fois gras' or 'croque monsieur', her eyes would become misty and take on a faraway look. Not that during the war we had much contact with either.

The rest of us shared her sorrow for France, but we were annoyed more than anything; annoyed that we couldn't get on with our lives. Except that we did. As best we could. We became so used to finding a different landscape each morning when we emerged, and to steeling ourselves in case anyone we knew had been killed, as was all too frequently the case. Filth was every-where. As fast as Celine and I cleared away the dust, so it settled yet again. You could write your name on polished furniture within an hour of it being cleaned. Mrs Heffer's brother's house was destroyed, but he kept on with his allotment in a sort of bloody-minded defiance. Without a good gardener, I don't know how we would have kept body and soul together.

Much to my surprise, Harry asked me out again a few days later. We went boating on the Thames at Henley. I remember the date exactly – it was one of those wonderfully warm, late summer days. It was hard to believe we were at war. I felt like a princess, sitting in the back of the rowing boat with a parasol to shade my eyes from the sun, and Harry with his sleeves rolled up, rowing us under the bridge with its masks of Isis and Thamesis looking up and downstream. It was as though we were in a dream that neither of us wanted to break. Well, I knew I didn't, and I hoped that Harry felt the same.

We picnicked on the riverbank at Hambleden. There was a wistfulness about Harry now, as though some of the time his mind was elsewhere. I did not want to push him too hard in case I broke the spell. What I did want him to understand was that I was determined to play my part in the war and not just sit at home waiting. He smiled at me – that smile which always melted my heart – and I knew that he would not push me into anything I felt I could not undertake willingly.

There were ducks quacking in the shallows, and Harry, lying back on a plaid rug spread out on the grass, was idly throwing them crumbs of bread.

'Are we allowed to do that? Don't you know there's a war on?' asked Rosamund teasingly.

'Stale. Or, it would have been by the time we got it home.'

'Mmm. I'm not sure I believe you.'

'It's true. And I never lie.'

'Never?'

'Well, hardly ever. Only when it is for the greater good.'

'Oh, that sounds to me like a very convenient excuse.'

'*Ich sage die Wahrheit.* I'm telling the truth!'

Rosamund sat up. 'I didn't know you spoke German.'

'*Es gibt Dinge über mich, selbst du weist es nicht.*'

'Meaning?'

Harry grinned. 'There are things about me even you don't know.'

Rosamund frowned. 'I think there's quite a lot about you I don't know.'

'Oh, nothing sinister, I assure you.'

'And the German?'

'I studied it at University. As a hobby.'

'A strange thing to study . . . as a hobby.'

'Not really.' Harry became more serious. 'I saw the way the

wind was blowing. I thought it might be useful. And it is, as things have turned out.'

Rosamund flopped back on the rug. 'I don't think I want to talk about things like that. Not on a day like today, when the sun is shining and the ripples on the water are shimmering like diamonds, and the wands of the willow trees are gently swaying in the breeze . . .'

'You're such a romantic,' murmured Harry.

'Incurable, I know. I can't help it.'

'Don't you ever get depressed?'

'Oh, goodness. If you knew how long it has taken me to get out of that dreadful state, and how scared I am that I could go back there, you wouldn't ask that . . .'

'I'm sorry.'

'No. Don't be. It's just that I've realised it's better to look for the good in people, rather than the bad. As Celine says, "*Si vous cherchez le bien, vous le trouverez*".'

'If you look for the good, you will find it.'

'Exactly.'

'And have you?' he asked pointedly.

Rosamund paused and then said, 'I'm not sure. I think so. I hope so.'

There was silence between them for a few moments, then Harry flopped back on the rug, put his hands behind his head and closed his eyes before asking, 'So when this lousy war is over, Miss Hanbury, what will you do?'

Rosamund drew her knees up under her chin and wrapped her arms around them; then she gazed across the water to where two swans were swimming, occasionally tapping their beaks together in some kind of mute conversation. 'Oh, I shall get married and have children, and when they are grown up, I shall earn my living by writing romantic stories.'

Harry laughed. 'Well, that's you sorted then.'

'Yes. That's me sorted.'

Harry sat up. 'We'd better be off. We need to get the boat back by six, and then I must drive you home.'

Rosamund smiled, unsure as to how he had taken her revelations. She half wished she had not been so frank; wondered if it would have been better to have been more vague. But she did know, in her heart of hearts, that what she had said was absolutely true.

She need not have worried. Harry did call again, and seemed not at all perturbed by the fact that she had been so open with him. Quite the reverse, in fact.

He took her to Brighton. It seemed to Rosamund quite an adventurous trip. They went in his car, travelling over the downs with the roof of the Talbot folded back and the wind in her hair. They walked along the promenade – which seemed to be putting on a brave face in spite of wartime privations – and had a lunch of fish and chips. Harry had offered to take her for lunch at The Grand Hotel, but Rosamund had said it would be more fun to eat fish and chips out of newspaper.

'That's what I like about you,' he said as they sat side by side on a bench on the promenade. The sun shone and the gentle breeze was beginning to strengthen.

'What?'

'You've got no class,' he said.

She laughed. 'I thought you were going to say something nice!' she teased.

'Sorry to let you down.'

'Will you?'

'What?'

'Let me down?' She popped another chip into her mouth.

'Goodness, I hope not. What a thing to say.'

'Well, as long as your intentions are honourable.'

'Goodness! Do you know *Pygmalion*? By George Bernard Shaw?'

'No. Should I?'

Harry gazed out to sea, collecting his thoughts. 'Henry Higgins asks his friend Colonel Pickering if he has ever met a man of good character where women are concerned.'

'What's the answer?'

'Higgins says that there is no such thing.'

'Do you believe him?'

'I'll make it my mission to prove him wrong.'

Rosamund looked at him quizzically. 'And how will you do that?'

'You'll have to wait and see, won't you?' He screwed up the newspaper that had held his meal and threw his last chip at a seagull prospecting on the promenade. Within seconds others had come to investigate the arrival of free food, and both Harry and Rosamund found themselves running away from the flock of scavengers and laughing at the folly of Harry's ill-timed generosity.

As they walked along the promenade towards the car, the sky began to darken and a distant rumble of thunder indicated that the weather was about to take a turn for the worse. They reached the car as large droplets of rain began to fall.

'Quickly, help me put the hood up!' instructed Harry.

Rosamund looked puzzled at the collection of struts and folds of canvas. 'Where do I start?'

'That rod there,' said Harry, pointing. 'Pull it forwards and then push the one behind it backwards. Hurry! It's getting harder!'

It took a full two minutes to get the hood in place and for the two of them to scramble into the car, soaked to the skin, panting for breath.

'You smell like a wet sheep,' muttered Rosamund.

'You don't smell so good yourself,' retorted Harry. Then the two of them began to laugh as the rain drummed on the canvas roof of the car. The laughter only stopped when Harry put his arms around her and kissed her.

When, several minutes later, they eased apart, she rested her head on his shoulder and said, 'What a lovely day.'

'Really? In this weather?'

'Who cares about the weather. Here we are, together, by the sea.'

'Yes,' he agreed. 'By the sea and with a girl in my arms. My idea of heaven.'

'Just any girl?' she asked.

'No. Not just any girl. *The* girl.'

Rosamund smiled and kissed him gently on the cheek. She could not remember ever being so happy.

I remember quite vividly my last meeting with Harry. We had been out together several times in the intervening weeks, and it had taken all my resolve not to appear too keen, or to throw myself at him, though, goodness knows, I wanted to. He was the only man I had ever met in whose presence I felt completely comfortable, completely safe.

When he called and asked if we could have lunch at the Savoy Grill, I suspected it was to say goodbye. I was not wrong.

*

There was a look on Harry's face that gave Rosamund cause for concern. He seemed distracted. His eyes darted up and down the menu, then he closed it and said, 'I think I'll just have a Bloody Mary.'

'Not hungry?'

'Not really. I had a big breakfast,' he offered by way of an excuse.

'What?'

'Toast and coffee.'

'That's hardly big!'

'No, well, things on my mind. Things to do, I'm afraid . . .'

Rosamund closed her own menu. 'I see.' She thought for a moment and then said, 'Is this it? Is this goodbye?'

'Sort of. For a while.'

She looked down, unwilling and unable to meet his gaze.

'It's not out of choice. I've been posted. Can't tell you where.'

'Of course you can't.'

The waiter came and Harry ordered his Bloody Mary. Rosamund settled for coffee and toast.

'Are you copying me?' asked Harry, forcing a smile.

'Something like that.' There was a profound sadness in her voice. She had found a man in whose company she felt secure and alive. Yes; that was it – alive. And now he was going away and she would . . . wither probably. She breathed deeply, telling herself that this was the case with all young women in this damned war. It wasn't just her; everyone her age was in the same boat. Unfair it might be, but it was the way of the world right now in 1940. What a year to fall in love!

The coffee came, along with Harry's Bloody Mary, from which he took a generous gulp. 'There's something I want to say.'

'Oh dear,' said Rosamund, almost involuntarily. She feared the worst was yet to come.

'You remember that first night when I took you out?'

'How could I forget?' she murmured, not meeting his eye.

'Well, you might have thought that the only reason I did so was to persuade you to play your part in the war. But that wasn't the case. I asked you out because . . .'

Rosamund looked up.

'Because I love you. I have done from the moment I first laid my eyes on you.'

It came like a bolt from the blue. They had been out together several times now, and she knew her own feelings quite clearly – had done since the very first time she had spotted him across the dance floor, had watched him from afar – the way he moved, the way he smiled – and had strained to hear his voice. But until he'd asked her to dance, she hadn't thought he had been aware of her existence.

'But . . . how could you . . . I mean, I didn't think you had even noticed me. '

'Oh, I noticed you. For the best part of a year I watched you, at a distance, too afraid to come over and say hello. I've seen you with others. I've watched you laugh, watched you engage in conversation, and compared your life with mine. I realised how little I had in common with Henrietta, and how the only person in the world whose company I really wanted was always on the other side of the dance floor with her arm round somebody else. I wanted to be that somebody. Why couldn't it be me and not . . . Billy Belgate? And because I now have to go away, for heaven knows how long, I don't want you to think that the only reason I asked you out was because I saw in you the sort of person who could help with the war effort. I asked you out because . . . well . . . I've told you now.'

Rosamund was aware that her mouth was wide open. She closed it and felt tears springing to her eyes. She reached across the table and squeezed his hand with all her might. 'I am so sorry.'

He shook his head.

'Sorry that I thought what I thought. It was only that I couldn't possibly believe my luck. Believe my good fortune. Men like you don't fall for girls like me.'

'This one did.'

Rosamund smiled through the tears and rummaged in her handbag for a handkerchief. 'At least these aren't rationed,' she murmured, blowing her nose.

And then, pointing to Harry's Bloody Mary, 'Do you think I might have one of those?'

Their meeting lasted for three hours, both of them aware that they might not meet again for some time, and not daring for a moment to think that they might never meet again.

'You'll be in danger, won't you?' she asked matter-of-factly as they got up from the table.

'Yes.'

'And . . . in another country?'

'Yes.'

She put her arm through his as they walked to the door. 'It's all right. I won't ask any more questions. You can trust me.'

'I know I can.'

'Really?'

'Yes.'

As they walked along the Embankment, he said, 'You remember that lunch party you had with your aunt?'

'Which one?'

'The one with Lord and Lady Belgate and Sir Patrick and Lady Felpham.'

'Yes. But how did you know about that?'

'Sir Patrick asked if you knew where this secret place was where they worked on code-breaking?'

'Yes, he did.' She stopped walking and turned to look at Harry; her face the picture of concern.

'And you told him you had no idea?'

'Yes.'

'But I had told you just a few days before that it was at Moor Park in Hertfordshire.'

'Yes.'

'You must forgive me. Because as well as being madly in love with you, I had to find out if I could trust you.'

'You mean . . . ?'

'Sir Patrick, old fossil that he appears to be – all bluster and expanding waistline – is a bright old bird and part of the code-breaking set up, which is not at Moor Park but at a place in Buckinghamshire called Bletchley Park. I can tell you that now because I know that I can trust you with my life.'

Rosamund made to speak, but Harry interrupted her: 'And if you now want to hit me, and tell me that you never want to see me again – which, in the balance of probability in this wretched war, there is a chance that might well be the case – I shall completely understand.'

Rosamund stopped walking and turned to face him. 'So you deliberately gave me false information to see if I would pass it on to anybody else?'

'Yes. And before you say anything else, it was unworthy of me and I deserve everything you throw at me.'

'But . . .'

'But please understand that I just wanted to be sure that you were the sort of woman I thought you were and I wasn't just being blinded by love.' He stopped and raised his arms in supplication. 'So there you have it.'

Rosamund looked at him, then slowly shook her head. 'I suppose I should be angry.'

'Yes.'

'And tell you to . . . bugger off.'

'Yes.'

'But you're going to do that anyway.'

'Yes.'

'Oh, Harry. Why did we have to fall in love?'

'You mean you . . . ?'

'Oh yes. Absolutely, totally and completely . . . you rotten bastard.'

She threw her arms around him and kissed him passionately, as the air raid siren sounded and the distant growl of aircraft began to rend the air.

Chapter 8

LONDON

SPRING 1941

'This is no war of chieftains or of princes, of dynasties
or national ambition; it is a war of peoples and of
causes. There are vast numbers, not only in this island
but in every land, who will render faithful service in this
war, but whose names will never be known, whose deeds
will never be recorded.'

Winston Churchill, 14 July 1940

It was after Harry left that Rosamund began regularly to keep
a journal. It replaced, in some way, the notebooks she filled
with stories in her youth and childhood. It was not so much a
diary or even a daily recording of events, more jottings of this
and that – key moments of her life, amusing or momentous
events that she wanted to record in the otherwise dark days of
war. She wrote her notes in red ink for the simple reason that
she found a pot of it in the desk in Aunt Venetia's drawing
room, and it seemed much less portentous in these times of
conflict than funereal black or gloomy blue.

'Red ink,' muttered Aunt Venetia, 'is usually an indication of debt – but I suppose we are in debt as a country, not least to those who are fighting for us.'

Tough old bird that she was, there were moments when Rosamund could see something of her father's broodiness in his sister. For all her *joie de vivre* and waspish asides, Aunt Venetia remained silent on her deepest inner feelings – for the most part, at least – just occasionally giving vent to her spleen and shouting at the enemy planes that roared and growled overhead: 'Oh, bugger off!' The exhortation seemed to take on a humorous side when it came from a well-spoken dowager in furs and diamonds, which Aunt Venetia would occasionally appear in of an evening, in defiance of the woes of the world around her.

Once or twice a month she would persuade a few friends to come to dinner, rather than lunch, insisting that the men don black tie (she had reluctantly accepted the demise of white tie and tails) and the ladies wear long dresses, gloves and jewels. Those who objected – whether on the grounds that they would like as not be robbed on their way to Eaton Square, or simply that such outward demonstrations of wealth did not seem fitting during the war – were told to get a grip; this was defiance, not ostentation. Most did. Those who did not were not invited again.

As the weeks since Harry left turned into months, Rosamund clung on to the hope that she would hear from him; that he was at least alive, if nothing more. It was a long time before any message came. When it did, in the spring of 1941, it was on a single sheet of paper sealed in a small, plain envelope. It bore no indication of its exact point of origin and it was delivered by a uniformed messenger on a motorbike:

Somewhere far away . . . Spring . . .

My darling Rosamund,

This is to let you know that I am safe and carrying on as best I can, though it is not easy. I miss you so very much. I have to say, in reference to the matter of which we spoke before I left, that I was misguided. Not in matters of the heart – that still stands resolute – but in terms of your future employment. Please do not think of doing anything or going anywhere. It is too risky. Stay where you are, look after your aunt and be safe. I will need you there when I return, though I am as yet unsure when that will be. I cannot say more in this letter for obvious reasons, but be absolutely certain that this comes with all my love,

Always,

Harry xxx

I kept that letter inside the cover of my commonplace book, reading the message every morning of every day, and then folding it away neatly and murmuring as I did so an earnest plea to the Almighty to keep Harry safe.

Although I knew I could not send it – for I had no idea how to reach him at this point – I wrote Harry a reply. It seemed only right that if he was prepared to express his feelings for me, that I should do the same for him, if only to satisfy myself. I hoped one day at least he might read it:

My Dearest Harry,

Please, please, PLEASE take care of yourself. I know you are concerned about me, which is sweet and kind of you and no less than I would have expected, but you must remember how precious you are to me. I do not think I have ever met anyone in my life – apart from Celine, and that is different! – who means so much to me in so many ways. We seem so in tune, so absolutely a part of one another that I cannot bear to imagine being without you. Your love for the things I love, your kindnesses and your . . . well, I run out of words to express my feelings. Perhaps I should guard them more closely, but this wretched war makes me want to tell you how I feel, and to explain that without you, my life would be empty.

Be safe, my darling, be careful and come back soon to
Your loving Rosamund

I had little appetite for frivolity, in spite of the fact that Diana Molyneux, on her occasional evenings off from Bletchley Park, would beg me to come out dancing, or to join her and 'the set' for supper 'in a darling little restaurant we have found in Maiden Lane where they do the most amazing five-shilling meal. You simply wouldn't believe . . . !'

The Café de Paris continued to defy Hitler and play the tuneful music of Cole Porter and George Gershwin, Jimmy Dorsey and Irving Berlin, for all those who needed a break from the daily grind of wartime work, for airmen between missions, and for those who were intent on one last fling before joining up.

It was on the evening of 8 March 1941 that Diana begged

Rosamund to meet her there, along with Billy Belgate who was on leave and had to return to his squadron at Biggin Hill the following day. 'Billy says he knows you have "someone else" now, but he'd like one more dance for old times' sake.'

Rosamund was torn. She did not want to let her friends down – they must think of her as a real stick-in-the-mud already – but somehow it did not seem right to celebrate while all around families were losing their homes and their loved ones in the nightly raids.

She spoke to Celine about it. 'I really need to find a way to contribute, Semolina, but every time I think I have a solution, my plans seem to go awry. I mean, I can't just say "I want to go to France and help the war effort. Please can I become a secret agent?", can I?'

Celine looked at her incredulously. Rosamund had been thinking out loud. The one thing she had not shared with Celine was her conversation with Harry about her war work, and the prospect of her own involvement in an undercover role. She knew that such an idea would horrify Celine.

'Secret agent?'

'Oh, just me being silly. Think nothing of it. But I do need to do something. I feel so shallow going to all these parties.'

'And it is dangerous to be out at night,' added Celine. 'I worry every time I go, but I will not let Hitler keep me a prisoner in my own room.' She put on her beret and her coat and said, 'I will not be long' before blowing Rosamund a kiss and leaving the house.

The risk of losing her own life in the Blitz, Rosamund had come to terms with – most Londoners had learned to live with that risk for the last six months or more. It seemed cowardly to exhibit any hint of fear. What was needed was a brave and determined front. And, anyway, the Café de Paris was regarded as a relatively safe haven, the dance floor being in the basement.

Diana pleaded with her that night: 'Do come, Ros. You could do with a break from all those old fogies.'

Rosamund had finally made up her mind to go – had even changed to go 'out on the toot' as Aunt Venetia called it – when fate took a hand and she was deterred. She dialled Belgravia 1066 and explained to Diana that she was all dressed up and ready to go, but that her aunt had retired with the most pounding of heads and Rosamund did not want to leave her alone. Celine was out seeing friends herself and Mrs Heffer had gone to help her brother who had been re-housed in Putney.

'I really do want to come,' she explained, though probably a trifle unconvincingly, 'but I just don't feel I can leave her alone.'

'Oh, alright,' said Diana resignedly. 'But next time I won't take no for an answer, even if your wretched aunt breaks a leg, OK?'

That night at 9.45 p.m. the Café de Paris received two direct hits. 'Oh, Johnny, Oh, Johnny, Oh Johnny, oh . . .' sang Ken 'Snakehips' Johnson before his head was severed from his body by the blast. He was twenty-six years old. Altogether thirty-four people – from the saxophonist Dave 'Baba' Williams to waiters and diners – were killed.

'At least I won't have to pay for my dinner,' explained one diner, as he was stretchered out of the wreckage. The courageous spirit remained resolute among the carnage and the tragedy, and the bombs continued to fall on London.

I felt numb the following morning when I heard the news from one of our neighbours. It was not just that I could have been there, but fear and dread that I should discover my friends were among the casualties. I could not help thinking about Diana and Billy Belgate and wonderful 'Snakehips' Johnson. He had such an easy way with him – and he was so young, so full of life and music. His was a voice that had charmed us, had taken us out of ourselves when we most needed it, and it would never be heard again. I sat by the telephone and looked out of the window, hardly daring to lift the receiver and make the call to Diana's number. And when I did the line was dead. How could I have expected otherwise? It had been lucky to survive for so long, while all around us telephone wires hung across the streets like washing lines.

Aunt Venetia had recovered from her migraine and sat up in bed looking pale and drawn. I sat beside her on the rose-patterned counterpane. 'I am so glad you stayed with me,' she said, her voice weak and dispirited.

'Yes,' was all I could offer in reply. I stroked her hand for some time, saying nothing, and then explained that I simply must go round to Diana's house in Draycott Place. Whatever the news, I could not go on being kept in the dark.

I picked my way through the devastation – mountains of rubble that were once houses, now collapsed across the streets; everything littered with the signs of everyday domestic life – a tea towel, a dressing gown, pairs of knickers, a single shoe hanging by its laces from a spike of wood that had once been a floorboard or a rafter holding up the third floor of a tenement block. Brightly patterned wallpaper decorated bare walls, where flying ducks still took wing over fireplaces suspended in mid-air. The head of a child's doll poked through shattered plaster. Burst water mains spewed fountains high into the air. All of this chaotic drama was accompanied by the sound of men shouting and the shrill clarion of fire engines' bells. At the sight of an ambulance I would look the other way, rather than gawping, as many did, at the disfigured bodies that were being wrested from the wreckage of what had once been happy homes. Everywhere one walked, broken glass crunched underfoot. The air was thick with brick dust and filth; the smell of smoke and charred yet sodden wood I can smell to this day. Hoses played on flames that continued to lick the ruins where the previous night's incendiary bombs had done their worst, until finally I arrived at Diana's door.

There have been several times in my life when my mouth has been dry with fear and my heart has pounded as though it would explode. This was one of them. I feared the very worst. Then the door opened and there stood Diana. I fell into her arms and the two of us wept uncontrollably for what seemed like an age.

When we did speak it was in fits and starts. 'Are you alright?'

'Yes, yes, I'm fine.'

'And Billy?'

'He's been patched up. He'll be fine too. We were so lucky. I'd just nipped out to powder my nose, and Billy had gone to buy cigarettes from the counter. Otherwise . . . if we'd been dancing . . .' Diana stopped talking and the tears came again. Then she pulled herself upright and sniffed. 'Anyway, we bloody well carry on, don't we?'

And we bloody well did. For quite some time, as it turned out.

Chapter 9

LONDON

11 MAY 1941

'505 bombers flew to London on the night of 10 May, the full moon lighting their snaking path along the Thames. The German pilots had fifteen minutes to locate and bomb their targets once they reached London, but still the bombing lasted nearly seven hours . . .'

Alex Nunn, *West End at War*, 2011

The very worst nights of the Blitz were endured by Londoners that spring, just as they were endured in other cities that had become prime targets for the German Luftwaffe – Portsmouth, Bristol, Coventry, Hull, Liverpool, Plymouth, Southampton and Glasgow among them. Families and property alike were devastated by night after night of bombing. On the night of the 10th May, London took the hardest pounding it had so far experienced, from both high explosives and incendiary devices. It

seemed that what was not destroyed by blast was burned to ashes. Our mood changed from the sombre to the dauntless almost on a daily basis.

Aunt Venetia and Rosamund, alone in the dimly lit cellar at Eaton Place, realised that this was a night like no other.

Aunt Venetia was untypically edgy. 'Why is Celine not here?' she asked, her eyes alight with alarm. 'Where is she?'

'I told you; she was invited to one of her pupil's houses for some kind of celebration. She did not say exactly. I think it might be to celebrate her passing her French exam.'

'French exams! The very idea! Ridiculous. Don't they know there's a war on?' Aunt Venetia drew the tall collar of her sable coat high around her neck as she huddled on the cushioned bench in the gloom of the cellar. 'I mean, there's little point in learning French now, is there? It's not as if one can go to Cannes or Deauville on holiday any more.' Thus she tut-tutted her way through the night, sipping champagne from a coupe, with Rosamund singing *'Sur le pont d'Avignon'*. It was only when her vocalisations had deteriorated to the level of *'La plume de ma tante, et sur le bureau de mon oncle'* that she managed to get her aged relative to raise a reluctant smile. 'We should have Celine here,' complained Aunt Venetia, 'she has a much better voice than either of us.'

Come the next morning, the scene that greeted their eyes was one of utter devastation. Eaton Terrace had been badly hit; water and gas mains were ruptured and the handsome frontages of the stucco houses in the Square had been damaged. Worse news was to come. The trench shelter in the centre of Eaton Square had been struck by a high explosive bomb. Twenty-two people had been gathered there, but by some great good fortune the bomb had not fallen on the main part of the shelter. There had been a handful of casualties who had been treated in hospital, but only two fatalities – the Mayor of Westminster, who had been doing the round of the air raid shelters that night, and one other, unknown, explained the next-door neighbour, who appeared to have some kind of direct line to the news gatherers of the day, if not to the Almighty Himself.

'I sometimes wonder if that woman doesn't have a direct line to Adolf Hitler,' complained Aunt Venetia, 'except that her telephone wire must be down as well.'

When Celine had not arrived by 10 a.m. that morning, both Aunt Venetia and Rosamund began to worry. Perhaps she had stayed with the people she had been visiting the night before; the raid was intense and she – and they – may have felt it was safer for her not to return home.

'I'll go and see them. We must make sure she is safe,' explained Rosamund to her aunt.

'Don't be long!' pleaded Aunt Venetia from the porticoed porch, now peppered with scars from flying debris, as Rosamund picked her way carefully through the rubble and wreckage.

'I'll be as quick as I can,' Rosamund replied, hardly able to look up for fear of missing her footing. 'You go in. And keep warm.'

It is only with the benefit of hindsight that one realises how lucky one has been in life to have been surrounded by people one loves, and who love one back, seemingly unconditionally.

I had never really thought about life without Celine, quite simply because she had always been there, and I had paid her the supreme compliment (or so it seemed to me) of assuming that she always would be there. She was, after all, not so much older than me, and we were often taken for sisters by those who did not know us, simply because we had grown so alike in the way we behaved, and the way we joked and spoke in French to one another.

The family in Cadogan Square explained that Celine had not stayed with them, but had left that evening just before the air raid started, assuring them that she would get back home safely or – if the worst came to the worst – she could take to the shelter in Eaton Square. It was, after all, only a short walk away. The bombs had started falling within minutes of her departure, but they had no way of contacting anyone to check that Celine had reached safety. Like me, they were worried on discovering that she had not made it back home. They suggested I should enquire at the hospital where many of the casualties had been taken. The master of the house – a Mr Vansittart – offered to come with me, but I declined. At such a time I did not want to have to make pleasant conversation with a complete stranger, exacerbated by the fact that I was unsure what we were going to discover. It took me a while to walk to the hospital – the bombing had made access to some streets completely impossible.

On arrival the scenes that met Rosamund's eyes upset her deeply. Among the weeping mothers and children, the ashen-faced fathers and sons, it took her some time to find anyone to whom she could make herself or her mission understood. She was asked to wait in a corridor that was already overcrowded with casualties and their loved ones waiting for news. Eventually she was seen by a rather harassed young doctor in a white coat that was smeared with blood. He seemed rather embarrassed by his appearance and began to apologise, but Rosamund made it clear she did not care a jot for what he looked like when all around them was chaos. She explained where she lived, and about Celine being missing. Carefully the doctor took down details then asked her to wait while he made enquiries. She stood in a corner, trying desperately to keep out of the way of stretcher cases that were still being brought in – one or two of them completely covered in sheets, so that it became obvious they were fatalities, even though the stretcher-bearers tried to hurry past without anyone noticing.

It seemed to take an age for the doctor to return – but before he did, Rosamund had her answer. A stretcher was carried past, and protruding from the sheet that covered the body was a foot wearing a shoe that she had come to know so well. Rosamund could not speak, but stood, rooted to the spot as the stretcher passed by.

Time stood still, and Rosamund had little concept of how long it was before the doctor returned, shaking his head at having failed to ascertain the whereabouts of her missing person. He could tell from her expression that something had happened in the interim. She stammered out that she had seen what she thought might have been her friend on a stretcher that had just been brought in. 'Was your friend in Eaton Square?' he asked.

'I don't know. She could have been. I'm not sure. She was on her way home.'

'Are you . . . I mean . . . would you . . . do you feel up to identifying her?'

Rosamund could no longer find any words, but nodded her head.

The doctor motioned her to follow him down the crowded corridor that now seemed eerily quiet, except for the occasional moans of those who were injured or the disconsolate weeping of those bereft. They turned eventually into a side room that contained rows of stretchers, and Rosamund saw again the shoe she knew so well, still sticking out from beneath the sheet. With one hand to her mouth in an attempt to hold back the tears, she pointed toward it.

'Are you sure you feel able to?' asked the doctor gently.

Scarcely daring to breathe, Rosamund nodded; the doctor carefully drew back the sheet. There lay her own darling Semolina without a mark on her body, her face calm and untroubled, seemingly in a deep sleep, but totally devoid of any spark of life. Rosamund reached down to touch her friend's hand. It was Celine's left hand, and on the third finger was a ring set with a small but shining stone the colour of her beloved Mediterranean sea. An engagement ring. It had not been there when Celine had left the house, she knew that. And surely if Celine had expected a proposal, she would have told Rosamund. Wouldn't she? It must have come as a surprise to her. And now . . . Rosamund felt her eyes brimming with tears.

'This is your friend?' asked the doctor.

Rosamund nodded as the tears began to course down her cheeks and her body was wracked with sobs.

The doctor replaced the sheet with the utmost care, then put his arm around her shoulder and said, 'Blast, I'm afraid. So often the case. Do you think you could give us a few details? This lady had no bag with her, and nothing to offer identification.'

Rosamund nodded again and found herself, within just a few minutes, sitting in a room bristling with doctors and nurses bustling in and out, many with cardboard folders in which they were jotting down the details of casualties.

A cup of hot, sweet tea was put into her hand and she was

urged to drink it. The saucer held a rich tea biscuit, and it struck her how odd and normal and polite that seemed in the face of such carnage. She had never taken sugar, but she sipped the hot liquid and tried to find sufficient breath to explain who her friend was and where she lived.

'We live in Eaton Square,' she confirmed. 'Number 29. My friend's name is . . . was . . . Celine de Rossignol. We have grown up together.' She found herself bursting to explain how close they were; how important Celine was. The kindly doctor, no doubt rushed off his feet with other casualties and emergencies, listened attentively as Rosamund told him of moving from Devonshire to London, and how much Celine had meant to her. She was, in all but name, a sister.

'Celine de Rossignol,' he repeated, checking his notes.

'Yes.'

'The nightingale.'

Rosamund managed a smile. 'That's right. And she could sing so beautifully, too.'

Chapter 10

LONDON

JULY 1941

'The night of 10-11 May 1941 marked the last major
raid of the Blitz. It inflicted the highest number of
casualties of any single night of the London Blitz:
1,436 Londoners killed and over 2,000 others seriously
injured.'

Alex Nunn, *West End at War*, 2011

Celine's death changed Rosamund. She felt a degree of anger
that was, for much of the time, hard to suppress. For weeks
afterwards she became, by turns, moody, taciturn, terse and
tearful. Aunt Venetia, by contrast, found hidden reserves of
strength, which she knew she would need to get her niece
through the days and months ahead. Rosamund had already
lost both parents; now she had also been deprived of her dearest
friend and lifelong companion; it was a burden of unspeakable
weight.

There were many days when she stayed closeted in her room;
others when she had to be forced from her bed to eat, to drink,

and even to exist. Having lived under clouds so dark that gloomier skies seemed impossible to conceive, she now found herself in the very depths of despair.

Sometimes she sat trance-like in the window seat of her room, gazing out across the square with unseeing eyes. In her mind played out scenes of a young girl and her governess on a Devonshire beach – the former dodging the waves, and the latter scolding her good-naturedly as she brushed sand from her charge's hair in an effort to make her presentable for her parents. The singing of songs, the secret conversations in French, the sharing of a furtive glance at some perceived absurdity of a particular person or situation. It was a world now long gone; a world which, since that fateful May night, had ceased to exist.

Aunt Venetia knew that it would take time for Rosamund to recover from the shock, the anger and the seismic change that Celine's death had wrought in her life. She herself had lived through the Great War, experienced at first hand the loss of friends, and seen in her brother and sister-in-law the effect of losing a son. She had been fond of Robert, and had not only mourned his death but also the breakdown of his parents' marriage during that deep, dark time of their bereavement.

And now history was repeating itself. Would this human tragedy never end? Would mankind never learn from past mistakes; mistakes that were made within living memory and which should surely have diverted nations from sliding into conflict with one another in the vain hope of making the world a better place for some at the expense of others? Had Hitler learned nothing from Napoleon of the folly and ultimate futility of empire building?

But she must not let her lack of faith in humanity show, and she could also not risk trying to bounce her niece out of her grief. It would take time for Rosamund to work through those serried ranks of emotions that always accompanied personal loss: profound sorrow, anger, frustration and – most destructive of all – despair.

Bit by little bit, as the weeks wore on and both aunt and niece endeavoured to make some kind of sense of the life that remained, there gradually came about a change in Rosamund. It was a kind of hardness – a resilience that she knew would be needed if she were not only to get through the war itself, but if she were to make any kind of a life for herself in its aftermath.

Aunt Venetia watched as the change was wrought in her niece; watched knowing that such a transformation had to happen if Rosamund was to find a way forward, but also with sadness at the diminution of the vital spark of youth that war could so effectively extinguish. It was all such a waste . . .

It was the fact of realising that Celine had died in vain which galvanised me. Her life snuffed out at its most vibrant, as though her very existence had been pointless. I did not want that to be the case. I wanted her to have lived for a reason, to have achieved something, and the only accomplishment I could think of was that of my own upbringing. I was Celine's achievement. If I failed to do my bit in life or to make a mark, then her life – as well as my own – really would have been for naught. It was an uncomfortable admission, but one that I knew I could not escape. But how to make my life worthwhile? That was not an easy question to answer. At least not at first. And then I remembered

there was a way; that I was – thanks to Celine's instruction and encouragement – amply fitted to do something to help us survive this war. And it really was survival. 'Winning' the war seemed to me an unfortunate phrase. A war was not there to be won; it was there to be survived. I knew that in order to survive, an enemy had to be defeated; that wickedness and cruelty had to be vanquished, but that did not mean triumphalism. All these strange and sometimes childish contradictions whirled around in my head until I finally saw with crystal clarity the path that lay ahead. It had already been suggested to me by Harry; albeit countermanded when he realised what it would entail. Aunt Venetia would, in all probability, not be happy with my decision, but I hoped that she would respect my wishes and my determination. It was the only way that I could make sense of the past and cherish any hope of a meaningful life in the future.

Diana Molyneux was delighted that Rosamund had emerged from her self-imposed exile. It was two months since Celine's death, and Diana had almost given up hope of ever seeing her childhood friend again.

They were out to lunch when Rosamund posed the question directly: 'What do you actually do at Bletchley Park?'

Diana was taken aback. 'Well, I can't really say . . .'

Rosamund realised the indelicacy of the situation; knew that she had phrased her enquiry clumsily. 'I know. Sorry. What I mean is . . . without going into detail . . . is it something that I could help with?'

Bletchley Park had been mentioned before in one of their conversations, so Diana knew that Rosamund was aware of her place of work, if not the precise ins and outs of what that work entailed. She also knew – not least from their childhood, as well as later from a conversation she had had with Harry Napier

– that Rosamund was totally trustworthy and the least likely of her friends to entertain idle gossip. Quite the reverse; there had been times in their Devonshire youth and childhood when Rosamund's secretive nature had driven Diana mad with irritation and curiosity.

'Are you good with numbers?' she asked.

'Hopeless. Absolute Greek to me. Words are my thing.'

'Oh. That's a shame. Bletchley is all about numbers, you see. But then I think you've probably worked that out already . . .'

Rosamund nodded. 'Yes.' Then, lowering her voice, 'I'm absolutely hopeless at cracking codes. Can't work up any interest at all over digits; they make my mind spin . . .'

'But you speak French.'

'Yes.'

'Fluently.'

'*Absolument.*'

'So . . .'

'So what?'

Stirring her cup of tea and doing her best to look as though this was nothing more than two young women sharing secrets about boyfriends, Diana lowered her voice and asked softly, 'Have you heard of "The Firm"?'

'I'm sorry?' Rosamund looked at her blankly.

'That's what they call it. Or "The Outfit", or, when they are being rude, "The Racket".'

'No. Oh dear; that sounds a bit too high powered for me.'

A man taking tea with a well-dressed woman a few tables away cast his eye in their direction.

Diana raised her voice in reply to Rosamund's exclamation: 'There's nothing high powered about driving a jeep!'

The man smiled indulgently and turned back to talk to his companion.

'Keep your voice down,' murmured Diana. 'Think about it. Look at what you *can* do, rather than highlighting what you can't. You're bright, you speak French so well that you could pass as a native, and you want to do your bit.'

'That's true.'

'The only thing is, the work is not without danger.' Diana regarded her friend with a serious expression. 'This is important work, Ros, and not to be undertaken lightly.'

Rosamund met Diana's gaze but said nothing.

'It involves working behind enemy lines and it also involves a serious amount of risk.'

'I can see that.'

'I'm not sure you can. While I'm comfortably ensconced in Buckinghamshire, you'd be over in France. The place is swarming with Germans whose intelligence network is strong and sophisticated.'

Rosamund put down her cup and said in soft, measured tones, 'I'm not stupid, Diana. I might be a bit dopey with numbers but I do have a brain and I am not afraid to use it. Neither am I afraid to risk my life. There are thousands of soldiers, sailors and airmen out there doing as much already, and I'm not going to sit idly by enjoying dinner parties in Mayfair and going to bring-and-buy sales or knitting mufflers for the troops. While I have breath in my body, I want to use my talents to do something serious and positive to help bring this bloody war to an end. The last one took my brother. This one has taken my dearest and closest friend. There is no way that I am going to sit back and hope that through the efforts of others and great good fortune we might come through it. I'm not made like that.' She paused and took another sip of tea. Then she said, in a louder voice, 'Do I get to drive lorries as well?'

The man at the other table looked over again and smiled.

Diana's eyes gleamed. 'Right. Well, good for you.'

Rosamund shrugged. 'It's taken me a while to realise it, and to admit as much to myself, but I think I probably do have a few talents that might in some way be useful to my country. I could never forgive myself if I did not use them. It would make Celine's death absolutely pointless and futile.'

Diana countered in a voice no more than a whisper, 'Yes, but again, this is dangerous work . . .'

Rosamund murmured softly, 'French speakers are needed. And I am a French speaker . . .'

'Better than any I know.'

'Well then, what do I do? How do I let them know I am willing to sign up?'

Diana shook her head. 'You don't. You'll have to wait for what they rather delicately call "the tap on the shoulder".'

'I see. I can wait. But not for too long, I hope.'

The two friends paid the modest bill and left the small café in Greek Street to a merry wave from their friend at the other table.

'Are you really sure about this?' Diana said, as they walked along the pavement in the direction of Piccadilly.

'Quite sure,' responded Rosamund.

Diana stopped and turned to face her. 'There is one thing you ought to know. Before you make up your mind.'

'Only one?'

'The most important one.'

'Which is?' asked Rosamund, half-smiling.

'At least half of those who join The Firm never come home.'

'You mean they stay in France? Live there?'

'No, Ros. I mean they never come home. To any home.'

Chapter 11

LONDON

LATE SUMMER 1941

'To combat may be glorious, and success perhaps may
crown us; but to fly is safe.'

William Cowper, 'The Task', 1785

*It was a little while before the 'tap on the shoulder' came. I
had half-expected Sir Patrick Felpham – whom Harry had
indicated was involved with the intelligence service – to take
me to the side at one of Aunt Venetia's lunch or dinner
parties. Whenever he was in attendance, I would glance in
his direction for a knowing look. Or when he sat next to
me, as he occasionally did, I waited for him – between
harrumphings – to whisper furtively in my ear. It was not a
pleasant prospect, but then neither of these imaginings translated into reality. Sir Patrick barely looked at anyone during
these gatherings, reserving his searing gaze for the contents*

of the plate or bowl immediately in front of him, and offering his pronouncements on this and that without ever looking up.

It was a Thursday morning. Rosamund was shopping for a new blouse in the eastern wing of Bourne & Hollingsworth in Oxford Street – the only part of the store which had survived the bombings and continued to trade daringly. She felt it showed solidarity to patronise those shops that had not capitulated to Hitler, but which had remained open in some capacity in spite of the difficulties imposed by crumbling façades and a lack of much in the way of lighting and heating.

She was making her way out through the side door with her purchase when a tall gentleman in a dark coat almost knocked her over. The neatly tied brown-paper parcel slipped from her hands and on to the newly swept pavement.

'I am so sorry! How clumsy of me. I must look where I am going.' The man raised his bowler hat in apology and then stopped: 'Bless my soul. Rosamund! How are you?'

He bent down to retrieve her package as she exclaimed, 'Lord Belgate!'

'I really am sorry. I was so busy looking to see if they were open that I didn't notice you coming out. Are you alright? Is your parcel intact?' He turned it over and examined the brown-paper package for damage. 'I see that it is. That's something at least.' He handed it back to her with a respectful nod.

'Yes. It's such a relief that they are still in business,' confirmed Rosamund. 'You never know from day to day who will be open and who will be closed, but at least they've swept up most of the glass.'

'Thank the Lord. One got so used to crunching everywhere one went.' He smiled at her and replaced his hat. 'Just nipping in for some new socks; it's so hard to find anything nowadays, but I can't believe they will have had a run on those. Your aunt is well?'

'Yes, thank you.'

'And you? You seem to be weathering the storm . . . and that terrible business . . .' His voice trailed off.

'Yes.' Rosamund looked down, but managed a faint smile. 'Weathering is a good word. I'm trying to.' Then she raised her head and looked him in the eye.

'I'm going to do my bit, Lord Belgate. I'm not sure how just yet, but I can't sit by and watch everyone else fighting this war without playing my own part.'

'Good for you! But then you are already playing your part. You're looking after your aunt, and I should think that is pretty much a full-time job.' There was a knowing twinkle in his eye as he looked down at her kindly. His neatly trimmed moustache, which seemed somewhat whiter than it used to be, bristled as he spoke.

'Oh, I think she'll manage. Mrs Heffer won't let her get into mischief,' Rosamund assured him.

'Mmm. From my experience, it will take more than Mrs Heffer to keep Venetia Reeves in order. She's a force of nature . . .'

'Yes. That's true. How's Billy?'

'He's fine, from what we hear – which isn't much, as you can imagine. He's been away for a couple of months now. It's a worry, of course, so many of them fail to return from their . . . sorties, you know. His mother frets about him. As do I. But then that's war, isn't it? The sons and daughters do the fighting and the mothers and fathers do the worrying.' Then he murmured, almost to himself, 'I'm not sure which is the harder task really . . .'

'No. I do see that.'

Her words jolted him out of his reverie. 'Well, good luck, my dear. Whatever you decide to do.'

'Thank you.'

'And remember me to your aunt. It must be about time for another of her lunch parties, I should think. Haven't been to see you for a few weeks. Must make up for that soon.' Lord Belgate raised his hat again as he bade Rosamund farewell, then walked briskly away down Oxford Street.

'What about your socks . . . ?' Rosamund's words echoed after him. But he did not turn round.

An hour later she laid the parcel on her bed and picked at the knot in the string which held it together. As she peeled back the brown paper, she saw not only the cotton blouse, but also a neatly folded square of paper lying on top of it. She assumed it was the receipt, and put it to one side before shaking out the blouse, holding it up to the light to admire it, and then transferring it to a coat hanger inside the wardrobe. Then she wound up the string and folded the brown paper, placing both in a drawer of her dressing table – this was a time of 'make do and mend', when nothing that could be used again was disposed of until it fell into such a state of disrepair and decrepitude that its demise was inevitable.

She checked in the mirror before brushing her hair and making ready to go down to lunch. As she crossed the room, she noticed the discarded square of paper lying on the silken counterpane. She picked it up and unfolded it to check that the transaction had been properly recorded. But the slip of paper made no reference to pounds, shillings and pence. Instead, it bore a brief message:

Please call PAD 1739.

C.B.

How had it got there? And what did it mean? It did not take her long to answer both questions. Lord Belgate must have slipped it inside the parcel when he bent to pick it up. And it meant that her life was about to change.

I suppose I should have realised that Lord Belgate would be involved in the war effort in some way, despite his age. (He and Lady Belgate had Billy relatively late in life – Billy always used to say he was an afterthought – so Charles was past retirement age when war broke out.) The fact that Lord Belgate mostly sat quietly at Aunt Venetia's luncheons, and that when he did 'chip in', as he put it, his remarks were always thoughtfully considered rather than impetuous, made it quite clear that if he were not an active part of wartime proceedings, then at least his grasp of them was comprehensive and well-reasoned. It made perfect sense that such an intellect should not be wasted.

After discovering the note, I went down to lunch with Aunt Venetia. When we had no visitors, Aunt Venetia still insisted on having our modest meal at the round table in the upstairs first-floor window on what she still referred to as the 'piano nobile' – a phrase which caused the more worldly of her guests to raise an eyebrow or disguise a smile. There would be a neatly ironed white damask cloth ('cleanliness and standards are not rationed', she would regularly inform Mrs Heffer, who would occasionally try to cut corners by turning yesterday's cloth upside down to get two meals out of it instead of just the one) and the best silver and crystal would be laid for just the two of us.

This, I came to realise, was my aunt's way of showing Hitler that he was not going to change her habits of a lifetime – or at least that part of her life which she had enjoyed since her marriage and her move to 29, Eaton Square. I can see, now, with the benefit of old age, why it meant so much to her.

There were few in the Second World War who felt quite so impotent as the elderly. If they had fought in the Great War, the apparent futility of such conflict – when 700,000 British soldiers were killed – came home to roost. That was meant to be 'the war to end all wars' and yet here we were, sending our young men – and in some cases, women – off to fight on our behalf once more. The 'Homes Fit For Heroes' had, in most cases, not materialised; the few that did were enjoyed for just twenty years before war was declared once more.

'Why can't they send the old?' my aunt would ask from time to time, her voice ringing with anger and frustration at yet more reports of loss of life in her morning perusal of the Daily Sketch. 'At least we've had a life.'

I soon discovered that the only way to jolt her out of her depressing reverie was to tease her. 'Because I doubt you could even lift a Bren gun, Auntie, let alone stay upright when you fire it.'

'I could try,' she would reply defiantly.

'Just the once?'

'A Lewis gun, then. You operate those lying down.'

'That's alright then. You can join the Home Guard. They have a few Lewis guns at their disposal. We can position you in your nightie and nightcap on the top of the white cliffs of Dover and you can have a pop at anything coming over.'

At this point Aunt Venetia would realise that I was unlikely *ever to take seriously her offer of volunteering for close combat. Then she would say, resignedly, 'Well, I suppose I'd better just stick to my dinner parties.'*

'What do you know about Lord Belgate?' I asked her over our lunch – a rather watery soup that Mrs Heffer was pleased to call 'cock-a-leekie', though it owed more to boiled greens than either chicken or leeks.

'What makes you ask?' my aunt replied without looking up.

'It's just that of all your lunch and dinner guests, he seems to be the one who says least and knows most.'

Aunt Venetia laid down her spoon. 'Very observant. Patrick Felpham makes the most noise but Charles Belgate is the better informed. Is that what you are suggesting?'

I didn't answer her immediately, simply because I didn't know what I was suggesting, really; I just wanted to find out why he would have put a piece of paper in my parcel which carried a phone number and his two initials and nothing else. Maybe he just wanted me to call him . . . socially. No! Lord Belgate could not be that sort of man, surely? And so, for my own peace of mind as much as anything, I asked my aunt if he was anything to do with the war, rather than the retired old gentleman he appeared to be. I have not forgotten her answer: 'Never judge a book by its cover, Rosamund. And when it comes to men, the quiet ones are always the deepest.'

Later that evening, when my aunt had retired to bed having heard that the Germans were laying siege to Leningrad, I picked up the telephone to dial the number. I knew it would be futile. The line had been down for weeks. I listened. There was a dial tone. The line had been repaired. It did occur to me at that point that perhaps one of 'the quiet ones' had been responsible.

I dialled PAD 1739. There were barely two rings at the other

*end of the line before my call was answered: 'Who's speaking?'
It was a woman's voice – young, brisk, efficient.*

*I said that I was Rosamund Hanbury and half expected to
be told by my interlocutor that I had the wrong number. But
instead she said, 'Just a moment, please.'*

*I waited, and after a few moments and various clicks another
woman's voice came on the line. She asked me to confirm that
I was Miss Hanbury and when I said I was, she said that it was
good of me to call, and that she wondered if we might meet.
I muttered something to the effect that we could, and she asked
if it was convenient to meet at eleven o'clock the following
morning in St James's Park. She explained that there was a
bench by a weeping willow tree near the water and that I would
recognise it because there was a slat missing on the back. It's
funny what you remember . . .*

*It all sounded terribly cloak-and-dagger, and I felt my heart
pounding. It was all I could do to answer in the affirmative. I
asked for her name, but she did not give me one. Instead, she
said that she would be easy to recognise because she would be
wearing a blue two-piece and a black hat, and carrying a brown-
paper parcel. (Brown-paper parcels were obviously going to be
some kind of leitmotif from now on.)*

*I don't think I slept at all that night. And the following day
at eleven o'clock in St James's Park I met the woman who would
be instrumental in changing the course of my life. Her name
was Doris Kilgarth.*

Chapter 12

LONDON

AUGUST 1941

'Courage is the price that Life exacts for granting peace.
The soul that knows it not, knows no release
From little things.'

Amelia Earhart, 'Courage', 1927

Doris Kilgarth was not the sort of woman to mince words; neither was she fond of overdramatising. The term 'matter-of-fact' could have been invented for her. Not that she was without humanity, or good humour; it was just that neither of these sensibilities evidenced themselves with any frequency, and certainly not on first meeting. Rosamund would eventually come to like her, and from the very beginning felt that she could trust her, though she was never quite sure just how much she ever really knew this small, stocky woman with the bob of white hair, which framed her face like the wimple of a nun.

Their first meeting in St James's Park was conducted cautiously by both parties: Doris Kilgarth scrutinised Rosamund through her round, horn-rimmed glasses rather as an entomologist might examine a hitherto-unknown species of beetle, and Rosamund was wary of committing herself to anything until she was sure she could trust her.

At first the conversation involved little more than pleasantries. Doris Kilgarth was the first person Rosamund had ever met who used small talk as a weapon. Not given to such time-wasting habits as a rule, Miss Kilgarth appreciated its usefulness not just at warming people up but also at catching the unwary off guard. She enquired about Rosamund's childhood, her affinity with the countryside and her current daily activities. Then, having satisfied herself that her prey was completely relaxed, she asked, 'And you speak French?'

'Yes.'

'Fluently?'

'Yes.'

'Celine de Rossignol was a good teacher?'

'The best.' The reply came out before Rosamund realised that at no point in their conversation had she made any mention of Celine. 'Oh, but I never . . .'

'No, you didn't. But you don't think you would have got even this far without us making a few enquiries, do you?'

'No. Of course not.' Rosamund was crestfallen.

Miss Kilgarth obviously realised that as far as the loss of Celine de Rossignol was concerned, the wound was still raw. 'We all have reasons for doing what we do, Miss Hanbury. Those reasons are often based on tragedy. Or on wanting some kind of revenge.' She spoke evenly, with unemotional and measured tones. 'It's as well to put these motivations on one side. They can make us irrational, and irrationality clouds judgement. You'll need all your wits about you if you are to succeed in this job.'

'But I . . .'

'You don't even know what that job is yet? Yes, I know.'

Rosamund began to feel discomfited by Doris Kilgarth's unfailing ability to predict her every thought; to anticipate her every question.

'You'll find my manner irritating, infuriating even, but years of experience and more than a few interviews have taught me a lot – not least, what goes through the minds of new recruits.'

Rosamund was rattled. 'But I've not agreed to anything yet.'

'No. You haven't. But I hope that you will. Everything I know about you, everything I've found out about you – and that's quite a lot – leads me to believe that you could be very useful.'

'To whom?' she asked, a touch more belligerently than she intended.

'To your country. To the people you care about; though, as I say, it is as well to leave them out of your reckoning. The more dispassionate you can become, the less you'll be hurt in the long run.'

'It all sounds rather soulless. Rather cold-blooded.' Rosamund turned her head away and looked across the park, her mind reeling under a mixture of confusing and conflicting emotions.

'It's not easy, that's for sure. But from what I know of your abilities, you can do it. And you'll find it rather more challenging than holding bring-and-buy sales and knitting mufflers.'

Now Rosamund was really unnerved. It was as if Doris Kilgarth had been an invisible presence at conversations she had had over the past few weeks – not just with the likes of Lord Belgate and Sir Patrick Felpham, but even with Diana Molyneux and her aunt Venetia. She was reminded of the fact that she had so far said nothing to her aunt about her intention of being part of the war effort; that it would come as a great shock to her.

'Of course, I shall have to talk to my aunt.' Then, realising that her remark might be misconstrued, 'To tell her that I plan to . . . enlist . . . join up or whatever. I won't give any details, obviously, but I can't just disappear. She'd worry . . .'

Doris Kilgarth shook her head. 'I think you'll discover that she knows more than you think.'

'She can't. I've not said anything – to anyone – and certainly not to her. The only person who knows is . . .' she chose her words carefully, 'someone who works in another department.'

Miss Kilgarth smiled, almost pityingly, it seemed. 'Diana Molyneux is not the only person who knows of your talents, and neither is she the only person who is apprised of what I hope are your intentions.'

Rosamund stared at the older woman in disbelief, laced with more than a hint of wariness.

'But . . .'

'Your aunt is worldly wise, take my word for it. She might look fragile, and appear to be intent on nothing more than a life of pleasure, but she knows that pleasure comes at a price. It's a price she pays through all manner of machinations.'

Before Rosamund could ask what she meant by that remark, Doris Kilgarth stood up. 'Is that the time? I must be off.' Fixing Rosamund with her gimlet eye, she added, 'Don't be long making up your mind. I think you know what this job entails – to some degree, at any rate. You will be far from home, you will be in considerable danger and you will find it hard to know who to trust. But I think you have what it takes, and if you can keep your wits about you, I think you can make a great contribution to the war effort. And that's what you want to do, I suspect? I'll give you till the end of the week, Miss Hanbury. You have my number. Goodbye.'

Rosamund watched as the sturdy being that was Doris Kilgarth set off at a brisk pace in the direction from whence she came, with a sinking feeling in the pit of her stomach and a battery of unanswered questions in her head– more than a handful of them concerning her aunt Venetia.

'I don't know whether to be angry or relieved!' confessed Rosamund to her aunt. They were taking tea in the first-floor drawing room; Rosamund was perched as usual on the edge of the padded window seat, while her aunt, in a floral Hartnell creation, half reclined on a sofa so generously furnished with brocade-covered cushions that she seemed in serious danger of suffocation. It was an elegant room, as befitted an elegant woman – the furniture a mixture of Regency and Louis Quinze, the carpet Aubusson and the pale yellow walls decorated with portraits of minor aristocrats painted by Romney and Ramsay. The overall feeling was of studied elegance, but there was clearly much about her aunt Venetia that was studied – not least her knowledge of what was going on around her. She might give the impression of being unworldly and ethereal, but the razor-sharp mind was clearly in no need of a whetstone.

'Never underestimate the elderly,' murmured her aunt, as she poured more hot water from the kettle into the silver teapot beside it.

Rosamund became reflective. 'I did wonder how we were always able to get food . . .'

'Now don't go thinking that I get special treatment. Not on that sort of scale anyway. There are enough people in this country trying to beat the system – petrol, meat and suchlike – and I refuse to be a party to it, however much I might feel the pinch at times. The black market: I won't have any truck with that. The powers that be are kind enough to help us out – a little – but I most certainly do not use their supplies for my own – *our* own – needs. It is strictly for my lunch and dinner parties. A means to an end. A little entertaining to oil the wheels.

The rest of the time we really do have to rely on Mrs Heffer's brother and what he can produce on that little patch of earth in Putney. You would hardly call her cock-a-leekie soup a gastronomic triumph, now would you?'

The recollection struck Rosamund forcibly. 'No.'

'Well then . . .'

Rosamund turned the conversation back to her own circumstances. 'But you really don't mind me . . . doing my bit?'

'Of course I mind. The prospect terrifies me. You could have a quiet time here – well, as quiet a time as the bombs and the devastation will permit. But how would you feel later in life, and how would I feel, having selfishly clung on to you?' The old woman put down her cup and saucer and sat back among the cushions. 'Certain circumstances demand certain actions. There is nothing I would like more than the freedom to visit Venice and Rome and Florence again, to dine regularly at The Ritz and The Dorchester. But to be able to do that, we have to fight for it – each and every one of us. And since you won't allow me to use a Bren gun, whatever that might be, I shall have to fight by other means, and so will you.'

'I thought you'd be horrified,' explained Rosamund, with a note of surprise in her voice.

'I am horrified. Horrified at what your mother and father would think of me encouraging you. And don't imagine that I am totally convinced that I am doing the right thing. I already wake up at nights shivering sometimes, wondering why on earth I do what I do, and why I should expect you to be a part of it when you haven't even begun your own life. Please don't imagine for a second that I rest easy at the prospect.'

Rosamund got up from the window seat and walked across to her aunt, kneeling at her feet and taking both her hands in her own. 'Don't worry . . .'

'Fatuous thing to say! Of course I shall worry – day and night until you return. And I shall think it all my own fault if anything should happen to you.'

'You mustn't. Really you mustn't. It's my decision and mine alone.'

Aunt Venetia shook her head. 'Why don't you just drive buses? Or act as a chauffeur for some government bigwig? I have plenty of contacts; I know I could fix it for you.'

'Too late to back down now. And, anyway, you know it would be a waste of what little talent I have. I learned to drive on the farm in Devonshire, but it's my French – thanks to darling Celine – that makes me useful. I should use it. I must use it. Somehow it's the only way to make sense of Celine's death, don't you see?'

Aunt Venetia flopped back amid her nest of cushions. 'Oh, I do see; that's the trouble. But I'm not at all sure that I should encourage you.'

'Well, don't. Just resign yourself to the fact that I'm a young girl from the country who is headstrong and wilful and so determined that you will never deflect me from my intentions.'

'Mmm.' Her aunt pushed herself into an upright position and picked up her cup once more. 'And how much of these "intentions" are at the behest of Mr Napier?'

Rosamund sat back on her heels, at first surprised, but then reminded herself that she must get used to the fact that her aunt knew far more about her circumstances than she had been given credit for. 'I don't know.' She hesitated.

'I mean, it was Harry who set me off on the trail . . . but then the letter I had from him tried to discourage me from following it up.'

'You mean, once he realised the danger in which he would be putting you?'

'Yes. He told me on no account to go. Said that I should stay at home. Stay safe.'

'So you would be flying in the face of that advice? Good advice probably.'

'Yes.' Rosamund seemed lost in thought.

'Do you love him?'

For the second time in as many minutes, Rosamund was taken aback by her aunt's directness. 'Yes, I do,' she answered. 'Very much.'

'After such a short acquaintance?'

'Long enough. Especially in the current circumstances.'

'And yet you want to go against his wishes and put yourself in danger in spite of the fact that he warned you not to?'

'That was before Celine died. Before I knew I couldn't just sit back and do nothing. It took me ages to make sense of it all, but then I realised that I'd been given a chance to make a difference – perhaps just a very small one, but a difference all the same – and that if I didn't accept the challenge, I would always feel that Celine's life had been wasted. This is my chance to prove that was not the case. Does that make sense?'

Aunt Venetia smiled. 'Perfectly. You must do what you feel you have to do, and I must learn to live with it.' She sighed heavily. 'You're a brave girl, Rosamund. And I am very proud of you. But please take care. Do not put yourself at more risk than you have to. Promise?'

'I promise.'

Her aunt rose unsteadily to her feet. 'Now then, we must get on. We have people coming to dinner.'

'Again?'

'I'm afraid so. You're going to do your bit and I must do mine, though I have to say that I'm not much looking forward to this evening.'

'Why?'

'Tricky company.'

Rosamund looked at her questioningly.

'The Belgates,' said her aunt.

'Well, they're not tricky; you like them.'

'Yes, but they're bringing with them someone who is notoriously hard work.'

Rosamund laughed. 'Oh dear, who's that?'

'General de Gaulle.'

Rosamund's eyes widened.

Her aunt made to leave the room. 'He'll enjoy your company, I shouldn't wonder – and he'll be grateful to speak French, being stuck here in London away from his homeland. But if I were you, I wouldn't mention your plans to him. He's a suspicious sort and he might think we have an ulterior motive in inviting him. As it is, we just want to keep him on side.'

Aunt Venetia left the room, and Rosamund was left alone with her thoughts. Not for the first time that day, she wondered what on earth she had let herself in for.

I suppose it was a baptism by fire really. I reasoned that if I could keep my head that evening then I could at least prove to Aunt Venetia – and to Lord Belgate – that I had what it took. But throwing General de Gaulle into the mix was a cruel twist, not least because Aunt Venetia seated me next to him. She sat across the table to the right of Lord Belgate, whom I had not

encountered since our meeting outside Bourne & Hollingsworth.
I was sorely tempted to ask if he had managed to find any
socks, but I resisted. Nor did I say anything about the note. He
didn't refer to it either, but I was aware of both him and Aunt
Venetia frequently casting an eye in my direction to see how I
was faring. There was also a French attaché – more personable
than de Gaulle – Gaston Palewski his name was. Aunt Venetia
told me he was a friend of Nancy Mitford – rather more than
a friend as it turned out – and Patience Westmacott, a shrill-
voiced, widowed friend of Aunt Venetia who was clearly there
to make up the numbers.

De Gaulle was quite chilly at first – wondering, I expect, why
he had been seated next to a young girl rather than someone
of greater importance (though Lady Belgate was on his right).
He said little over the first course of egg mayonnaise and I
wondered if he would bother with me at all. When he turned
to me as the main course arrived, he said just one word – 'Poulet!'
– and I wondered if that would be the sum total of our conversation. I remembered the story of an American woman being
seated next to the American President Calvin Coolidge in the
late 1920s. He was famously monosyllabic, and the American
lady said, 'Mr President, I've made a large bet that I can get
you to say more than two words over dinner', to which the
President replied: 'You lose.'

I was quite convinced that I would find myself in the same
situation, until I found the courage to reply 'Oui. Nourriture
des dieux.' He sat back in his chair and smiled, and then the
conversation took a different turn. We spoke in French for the
entire meal, and he hardly turned to Lady Belgate. I noticed
Aunt Venetia and Lord Belgate smile knowingly at one another
and, to be honest, I felt rather proud of myself. Of course, I
was careful not to talk about my plans, but we did talk about

France, and how he missed being there, and how he was convinced that eventually he would return. He was clearly a great reader and asked what I thought of Victor Hugo. When I said that I enjoyed reading Zola, he raised an eyebrow. I think I must have shocked him. I suppose because of the fact that I made an effort, and because – without being boastful – my French was so good, he began to unbend a little. I remember how tall he was, and how imposing, and how haughty he looked when his face was in repose. But like many people who do not smile a lot, when he did, his face lit up and it completely transformed his appearance. He had little to smile about at that time, of course, and although he knew the British were supporting the French Resistance movement – at the behest of Winston Churchill – he could never accept that there was not some ulterior and subversive motive in our actions.

After the meal we moved to the drawing room for coffee (another example of Aunt Venetia's good fortune, since it betrayed not a hint of chicory). Here the general held a lengthy conversation with Lord Belgate, which seemed to involve a lot of Gallic shrugs. Aunt Venetia came across to me as I was sitting on the sofa next to Lady Belgate and smiled, nodding in the direction of Monsieur Palewski; he had something of a reputation as a ladies' man but looked faintly uneasy, having been backed into a corner of the room where he was being grilled in appalling French by Patience Westmacott. Eventually Palewski pointed to his watch and gestured in the direction of the general, who grasped the situation and explained that they must leave, for he had a meeting the following morning with the Prime Minister. For one brief moment, I suddenly felt at the very centre of things, and that the decision I had made was the right one. I knew I was only a very tiny little cog, but surely that was better than being a spectator?

The general bowed smartly to the assembled company then came over to thank Aunt Venetia for her hospitality. I wondered if he might kiss her. He did not, but took her hand and shook it quite formally, thanking her, in English, for the best meal he had enjoyed in quite some time. I eased back, hoping to slip into the shadows, but he looked up and leaned forward towards me. 'Au revoir, mam'selle,' he said. Then, with the faintest of smiles: 'Jusqu'à la prochaine fois. En France.'

I know that I blushed as I smiled back. But it seemed to my way of thinking that my plans now had some kind of seal of approval. Not for the first time in my life I felt – without meaning to sound melodramatic – that this was my destiny. The wheels had been set in motion and now there was no way of stopping them.

A week later I found myself on the threshold of the next phase of my life. It filled me with apprehension and with fear, but I would be lying if I did not also admit that I found the prospect more than a little exciting. Oh, how little I knew of what was to come.

Chapter 13

SURREY

SEPTEMBER 1941

'Upon the whole it was an excellent journey & very
thoroughly enjoyed by me; the weather was delightful
the greatest part of the day . . . I never saw the country
from the Hogsback so advantageously.'

Jane Austen, in a letter to her sister Cassandra, 1813

The journey from Guildford station was a short one. Sitting in
the back of a staff car with her suitcase beside her, Rosamund
looked for clues as to their destination. The car travelled along
the Hog's Back – that ridge in the North Downs that separates
the sprawl of robust Aldershot from the more delicate consti-
tution of Godalming – and then turned off the ridge and
descended northwards to the tiny village of Wanborough. After
many twists and turns along a narrow country lane, the car
finally drew up at its destination.

Doris Kilgarth had been pleased that Rosamund had agreed
to sign up, and at a subsequent meeting where very little had
been given away as to the nature of her future task, she had

explained that before anything else could happen, Rosamund would have to be assessed for her suitability for the job in hand. Speaking fluent French was clearly very useful, but there were many other attributes she would need in order to be of any use to 'The Outfit', as she called it.

The Outfit, or The Firm, had several training schools, divided up according to which part of Europe those who successfully completed the two- or three-week training course would be posted. The French school was situated at Wanborough Manor, a rambling half-timbered house dating from the late seventeenth century. As Rosamund walked up the steps to the heavy front door, accompanied by her army driver, a sense of foreboding flooded over her. She looked up at the uneven agglomeration of chimneys and pointed roofs, stacked almost like playing cards, their dull orange tiles encrusted with moss and lichen, and felt that she was about to enter some hinterland of the underworld. In a way, she was.

Wanborough Manor was staffed by a small number of Army Non-Commissioned Officers who would put the new recruits through their paces – a dozen or so at any one time. A smattering of general service soldiers were responsible for the day-to-day running of the establishment, and members of the sinister-sounding Field Security branch of the Intelligence Corps had the job of fending off nosey locals, explaining to them that the inmates of Wanborough were undergoing commando training. That was as much as they needed to know.

The students themselves were told only a little more, the powers that be realising that many of them would fail to come up to the mark. They knew that their job would be undercover, that it would encompass deception, subterfuge, intelligence gathering and even, when occasion demanded, combat. That much was clear. But the less detail they knew when they were returned to wider society, the better for all concerned.

The door of Wanborough Manor was opened by a soldier in battledress, and at that moment Rosamund realised there was no turning back.

Up to that point, this undertaking had seemed, in prospect, like 'an awfully big adventure'. Having weathered the profound sadness of losing my parents, and of Celine's death, and of being parted from Harry and knowing that he was most likely in mortal danger, the prospect of doing something to redress the balance did, I admit, light some kind of fire in me. There were frightening moments in London during the Blitz, but this was something altogether different. I was handing over my life not only to fate, and to an ageing aunt, but also to outside agencies which would not be as well disposed towards me as my family and friends. If the deaths of those nearest and dearest to me had caused me to grow from being a girl into a young woman, then this was clearly the next step in my journey – that of facing something which would, in a completely different way, be supremely demanding. It would test my powers of physical and mental endurance to the limit. I knew that, and, to be honest, I questioned my ability to prove myself equal to the task. I was determined not to fail, but at the same time – deep in my heart – not at all sure that I really had the necessary steel to see it through.

I passed the first test at least. For much of the day – and always at mealtimes – nothing but French was spoken at Wanborough, and from the moment I was greeted inside the door by a smart and businesslike female in a tweed two-piece suit, I slipped into my former way of conversing with Celine as though it had been yesterday.

Every morning before breakfast, we underwent physical training – intensive exercise in the grounds of the Manor as well as cross-country runs, which I rather enjoyed. They gave us a chance to escape the confines of the building and breathe in the fresh air of the North Downs, which I loved. It was not Devonshire, but it was a refreshing change from the dust-filled wreckage of London.

I was not at all sure about the combat, but I learned to look after myself, much to the surprise of the NCO in charge of our physical training. Wagstaff was his name – a wiry little man with a big nose and a thin pencil moustache. The sight of him was rather comical, but there was nothing amusing about his way of putting us through our paces. It was punishing. Having had rather a 'soft' life in London, it was some time before I felt less than completely shattered at the end of the day. Our basic weapons training involved the use of an assortment of firearms and target practice; there were life-sized paper outlines of men fastened on frames attached to the high wall in the garden, and we learned where to aim and how to keep our weapons – light automatic guns and pistols – in good working order.

The breadth and intricacy of our learning over the two weeks had come as a surprise to all of us. We had expected to be schooled in the use of firearms and unarmed combat (we knew that we would need to be taught how to protect ourselves in extreme and often unexpected circumstances), and French classes were de rigueur for those whose grasp of the language

was slight. And yet it was the more mundane, domestic knowledge that was equally important, if we were not to stand out
as outsiders, interlopers and subversives. What did a French
ration card look like, and what did it entitle you to? Was coffee
available on this particular day in this particular café? Such
local intelligence – tailored to the part of France in which a
particular cell would operate – could turn out to be the difference between life and death.

In unarmed combat, I think I amused Sergeant Wagstaff. I
might have become a woman-about-town, but thanks to my
early days of wrestling with stable lads, I seldom came off too
badly. I noticed that after the first week, when I unfortunately
kneed him in the groin, he avoided demonstrating on me and
instead picked out a slender youth who departed the course
shortly after. I felt rather sorry for him. There were eleven of
us at the beginning of the course, and by the end of two weeks
we had been whittled down to three.

There were certain prevailing attitudes towards the women
who were recruited to The Outfit. Those like Doris Kilgarth
were treated with respect and caution, which usually manifested
itself in avoidance of contact. Most men were wary of her,
unsure of just how much power she possessed and knowing
that she might well be involved in their final selection – or
rejection. As for the female 'rank and file' recruits like myself,
we were made aware of the need to be every bit as tough as
the men (maybe not so much physically, but certainly mentally)
and it was possible, in time, to earn the respect of one's
colleagues – with just a few exceptions.

Some tasks suited men more than women, but all of us –
regardless of gender – had things we were good at and things
we found more difficult to grasp. That said, it was clear that a
variety of aptitudes was needed in those who joined what I

later realised was called the Special Operations Executive – the SOE. At the time, we never used the acronym; it was only after the war that we understood just how important it had been, and just how complex an 'outfit' it was. As far as I am concerned, I will forever be grateful that it taught me things I'd never known about myself – but it also highlighted weaknesses in my character of which I had been all too aware.

I gradually got to grips with wireless operating, and worked hard at mastering codes – never my strong point, as I had explained to Diana.

Then there were the lessons in demolition in a chalk quarry on the Hog's Back. I could see that most of the men on the course were looking forward to this – males do seem to have an inbuilt desire to destroy. It evinces itself in early childhood and is then mercifully overtaken by a desire to build rather than demolish. But it is surprising how that facility comes to the fore once more when a man is given an opportunity to knock something down.

Much to my embarrassment, I proved to be particularly adept at dealing with explosives and incendiaries. One or two of the recruits referred to me as 'Miss Dynamite', which had little to do with my sexual allure, and more to do with my ability to reduce buildings to rubble.

There were attractive men there, of course, and men who occasionally 'tried it on', including one particular Frenchman – Thierry – who had a twinkle in his eye, the most disarming smile and a fine line in small talk of the flattering kind, but the thought of Harry in Europe was never far from my mind. I had frequent pangs of guilt at going against his wishes and joining The Outfit, but it seemed to me that if I was doing nothing else, at least I was showing solidarity with him. I hoped that if he ever heard about it that he would – after the initial annoyance, or even anger, at my ignoring his plea – be proud of my intentions. I put out of my mind the thought that I might never see him again. That, more than anything, would be just too much to bear.

All the while, we were aware that we were being monitored. Our abilities in all branches of combat, intelligence gathering, wireless operating and coding were constantly assessed and, rather like an Agatha Christie murder mystery, it was not unusual for us to come down to breakfast and discover that one or more of our number had disappeared – either moved to other work, or else sent home as 'unsuitable material'. I remembered Mr Langstone reading me Treasure Island *as a child, and half expected one day to find a piece of paper with the 'Black Spot' slipped into my hand.*

The dangers of being in occupied France were brought home to us on a daily basis. The Gestapo were ever present. The term was used to cover both the Abwehr (the German military intelligence service) and Himmler's SS – of which the SD, the Sicherheitsdienst security service, had a reputation for brutality – especially the branch based in Lyon. Then there was the Milice, which operated against the SOE on behalf of the French administration in Vichy, plus the German military police (the Feldpolizei) and the Gendarmerie. The whole thing was a confusing minefield, but it made us all the more determined to keep ourselves to ourselves and to be very careful who we trusted, for it seemed that more were briefed to undermine us and expose our weaknesses than were there to encourage us.

Wherever we were from, whatever our background, we were aware that we must always be on our guard. We had a brief social life in the evenings, but even then we knew that we were being watched and often plied with rather more alcohol than was good for us to see if we let anything slip. We were sometimes woken up in the middle of the night – one of the station supervisors would shake us awake to see if we said 'Mon Dieu' or 'Good God'. If you blurted out the latter, you would probably find yourself on the next bus home. We needed to be French, not just act French.

Breakfast was another time for taking care, being sure not to mention things that those in charge would regard as better kept to one's self. The place was notorious for 'honeytraps', lulling each of us into a false sense of security in the hope that we might let ourselves down – and potentially those around us, too.

But I thank God I managed to survive them, and I met, during those two weeks at Wanborough, some of the most amazing people I have ever encountered.

Not least, the man in charge of The Outfit, Major Maurice Buckmaster.

'Your French is particularly good,' said the tall, thin man in the suit, speaking in English. He was clearly one of the 'bigwigs', for everyone was more than usually careful and courteous whenever he appeared. He had an upper-crust accent that betrayed his Eton education.

Rosamund thanked him, in French, without realising who he was. Major Maurice Buckmaster was a fluent French speaker himself, having been a tutor to various French families in the early 1930s. He had gone on to be put in charge of the Ford motor company in Paris, before being repatriated when the French decided that they wanted one of their own in charge. Then came the war.

Through various vicissitudes, and having survived the evacuation of Dunkirk, Buckmaster joined the Intelligence Corps and was eventually chosen to head up Special Training School No.

5 at Wanborough Manor. He spent much of his time in The Outfit's headquarters at Baker Street, but was a frequent visitor to Wanborough, where he liked to keep an eye on the quality of trainees coming through, some of whom were French nationals determined to fight the Nazis in the only way they could – by subversive activities.

This brief encounter with the head of STS 5, never to be repeated, was one that Rosamund would forever remember.

'You speak it fluently. Were you taught it at school?' he asked, now speaking in French.

Rosamund replied in the same language: 'No, I had a French governess as a child and we spoke French all the time.'

'Ah. The best way. I, too, learned that way. It makes a difference, don't you think?'

'I hope so,' replied Rosamund.

'Well, good luck!' Buckmaster nodded and moved on. It was only when he had gone that she realised he had probably been testing her to see if she were on her guard. 'Zut!' she muttered to herself.

Major Buckmaster was an impressive figure, and it was as much by good luck as good judgement that I did not let myself down when speaking to him. The thing about constantly speaking French is that you also start to think in French, which is why I answered in the tongue that I was now accustomed to using, though Sergeant Wagstaff and his men spoke English, the better

to ensure that we knew exactly what we were doing. They were tough but fair, and if I found Major Buckmaster a little intimidating, then it was probably the impression he liked to give.

The Commandant of the Manor, Major Roger de Wesselow, was rather more kindly and approachable, but he left us in no doubt as to what was expected of us – that the lives of our comrades depended on us entirely, and that we were entering an establishment which involved a high level of security: letters inward and outward would be censored, and we would be forbidden to use the telephone.

It surprised many on the course that I had never been to France, so fluent was my use of the language, but then I had travelled very little in my own country. I had never been to Scotland, for instance. I had always liked the sound of it: all those lochs and heather-covered mountains – just the sort of scenery to appeal to a girl with a romantic turn of mind.

When at last I made it there, it was not a disappointment – and neither was the company.

Chapter 14

SCOTLAND

SEPTEMBER 1941

'Still from the sire the son shall hear
Of the stern strife, and carnage drear,
Of Flodden's fatal field,
Where shivered was fair Scotland's spear,
And broken was her shield.'

Sir Walter Scott, 'Marmion', 1808

'Yer probably think y'erve come here for a holiday. Well, y'erve not. Y'erve come here to see if you can find yer way home in the dark.'

Sergeant Wagstaff was a small and slightly built Cockney with a glint in his eye. The sort of glint that demonstrates the confidence of one who has the upper hand and is assured of victory. Wagstaff enjoyed putting new recruits through their paces – some of them scions of the aristocracy who, in many cases, had not a hope of staying the course. He was glad to see the back of them. To those who did make the grade, he reluctantly offered his respect.

After two weeks at Wanborough, Rosamund and the other two surviving recruits were transferred by train to the Scottish Highlands; here they would be unceremoniously dumped in the wilderness, given a rudimentary map and a compass, and expected to find their way to a given rendezvous at dead of night – all without being seen. It was a simple exercise, a straightforward hurdle, but one at which many had fallen in the past. The trek across bog and mountain, heather and bracken, granite and icy stream could take several days, and if you were spotted, then worse was to follow. Interrogation and lack of sleep – both discomforts which they had undergone already, but not in tandem with mountain climbing and scrambling through waist-high heather – would follow if they broke cover and revealed themselves to the sentries who were posted at strategic and unmarked positions on their route. It was the final obstacle in their weeks of training.

Rosamund veered between exhaustion and elation – exhaustion as a result of the strenuous exercise, and elation at having got this far. There were just three of them left now: Rosamund, plus the auburn-headed Eric Ridley – an older recruit from Lancashire who had been spotted in the Royal Navy and singled out for his ability to repair radio transmitters that others would have confined to the scrapheap – and the French national, Thierry Foustier, who, from the very start, had taken a shine to Rosamund.

Foustier was, Rosamund had to admit to herself, the ultimate Gallic pin-up. A natural charmer, at whose feet women no doubt fell in battalions before the war; two years of conflict had done nothing to dent his allure. A little older than Rosamund, he was not particularly tall, but there was about him an attractive kind of insouciance. It was as if he had been born knowing what was expected of him, and confident that he had the necessary attributes to succeed. It was not a human trait that Rosamund usually found attractive, but Foustier's saving grace was his inability to take himself too seriously. He could discourse on the works of Marcel Proust and André Gide, start an argument as to their relative merits and then, with a shrug and a smile, admit that he had never read more than a few pages of either.

Rosamund would take him to task: 'You're such a fraud, Thierry Foustier!'

At which the Frenchman would grin, replying, 'Fraud? *Moi? Non! Je suis charmant!*' And then he would wink and whistle the 'Marseillaise' as he went on with the task in hand.

Rosamund had become used to his mischief-making, and reconciled herself to the fact that at least her comrade in arms was not dull. The same could not be said for Eric Ridley, whose own ability to converse was confined to a seemingly unfathomable litany of amps and ohms and watts and volts. Rosamund would find herself smiling at him indulgently as he explained with the patience of a saint why one particular radio valve was so much more effective and efficient than another. Ridley's saving grace was that in spite of his English being delivered with a strong Lancastrian accent, his spoken French was surprisingly good. Rosamund put it down to the fact that having a pair of earphones clamped to his head for so long, he must have developed a decent ear for accents. Most of his dispatches would be in Morse code – a system of communication mercifully devoid of accent and idiom – but it would be a great help that his French was up to par.

Rosamund would look at these two unlikely confederates from time to time, and wonder just what she had got herself into. One cheeky Frenchman and one apparently humourless Lancastrian – what a strange and unlikely pair of comrades in arms.

It had been months since I had heard from Harry. Not a day went by without my remembering our meetings and, most especially, the day he said goodbye. I tried to put out of my mind what Diana had said about only half of those who worked for The Outfit coming home. And, of course, I did not know whether Harry was indeed a part of The Outfit, or involved in something else altogether. I kept his letter with me at all times, carefully tucked away in the pocket of my jacket, though I knew that when I eventually was transferred to France I would have to leave it, and everything to do with Rosamund Hanbury, behind.

I realised at this point that the people who surrounded me now were the people I would have to live with and work with for the forseeable future – a future that would run into months, maybe even years. Who knew then just how long the war would last? My daily life involved building working relationships, and working relationships, if one is not careful, can so easily turn into something more personal, especially when placing one's very life in the hands of others.

There were times, on that long trek, when Rosamund felt she was bound to fail; to fall at the final fence. Eric Ridley – slender and gangly that he was – seemed to take it all in his awkward stride, even though he had to make the journey with a radio transmitter on his back. It was as if normal feelings did not encroach upon him, and he gave little away in terms of both fatigue and emotion. It seemed to Rosamund that he would be a shoo-in for the service, for he had probably given little away in civilian life, a facility that would stand him in good stead when faced with the enemy. He appeared to be one of those people who operated on a different wavelength to the rest of humanity, but then wavelengths, after all, were his own particular speciality.

'Are you alright?' he would ask, whenever Rosamund looked as if she was cracking under the physical strain of their operation.

'I'm fine, thanks,' she would invariably reply, grateful for his concern yet determined to prove her worth.

'I 'ave a sister, you know,' he confided as they butted their way up the side of one particularly steep and heather-filled gully.

'Yes?' Rosamund answered briefly, saving her breath for the climb.

'She'd not be able to do this.'

'Oh?'

'No. Too many fags. No breath to speak of.' He spoke in short, staccato sentences.

'Oh dear.'

'Pluck. That's what you've got. Pluck.'

'Thank you.' Rosamund would have laughed had she managed to summon up the energy.

Eric himself seemed to have no trouble breathing at all. His loping strides took him higher and higher with little apparent effort. He would stop every now and again and survey the scene, but Rosamund suspected this was to allow her to catch up a little rather than for any navigational reason.

As they reached the top of one particularly precipitous slope, Eric flopped on the ground and threw off his pack. 'Just checking me knobs,' he said as he unbuttoned the cover of the transmitter.

Now Rosamund did laugh, and Thierry allowed himself a knowing smile.

'How do you do that?' he asked mischievously.

'I give 'em a twiddle and listen for the atmospherics,' replied

Eric with no acknowledgement of having said anything humorous.

'Well, when you have "twiddled your knobs" to your satisfaction, can you tell us which way you think we should go?' asked Thierry. He glanced at Rosamund to observe her reaction, but she was grateful to Eric for his constant solicitude and said simply, 'I think we'll probably be grateful for Eric's knob twiddling before we've finished.' Then she rose to her feet and added, 'Shall we push on?'

Thierry gave a mock salute and rose to his feet. '*En avant!*' He, like Eric, could easily butt his way through the bracken and heather, leaping across streams like a gazelle in flight. Though, noting Eric's chivalry, he would occasionally suggest that they rest up, taking a moment to light a cigarette and talk of things other than the war – music, books that he *had* read, and his favourite foods. From his slender frame, no one would have guessed his liking of good food and fine wine, but then, as he pointed out to Rosamund (and Eric when he was not otherwise occupied tinkering with his radio) such things were a Frenchman's birthright.

'A bottle of Chateau Margaux and a plate of foie gras, that's what I would like now.'

'I'd settle for a bottle of brown ale and a fresh pork pie,' cut in Eric. 'One that you could drink the jelly from while it was still warm . . .' His eyes glazed over as he was transported in his mind back to some Lancashire pork butcher where the pies emerged hot and aromatic each morning. 'Two of them I could eat before nine o'clock, when I started work at the electrician's. Them were the days.' Then he took a screwdriver to his transmitter and continued with his endless tinkering.

'What about you, Fair Rosamund?' asked Thierry.

'I think I'd like a bath.'

'With bubbles?'

'Don't be cheeky! A hot bath followed by a cup of cocoa.'

'Ah, now you're talking,' chipped in Eric. 'Cocoa.'

'With your pork pie?' chided Thierry.

'Don't be daft. You don't drink cocoa with a pork pie.'

'What do you drink with it then?'

'Brown ale, as I said. Or tea, with three sugars, in a pint pot.'

'*Sacré bleu!*'

Rosamund laughed at the disparity between the two men and mused on the fact that only war could have brought them together.

They completed their first day's trek in the required time, helped by the round white face of a full moon, and arrived at a deserted croft on the edge of a reed-infested glen just as the amber sun rose up over the adjacent mountain. The warm September day – replete with midges that would force even the most resilient enemy agent to surrender – was the time to rest up, hidden from the view of the enemy. Rosamund sat with her back against the lumpy stone wall of the croft and began to rub Germolene (the only salve to be found in the small first-aid kit) into the bites on her calves that had clearly been administered by those midges that were content to operate nocturnally.

Eric, as ever, began to unscrew the panel on his radio transmitter – things were obviously getting serious as far as its internal workings were concerned – and Thierry, throwing his backpack to the ground, fished in his breast pocket for a packet of Gauloises, lit up and sat down next to her.

'How are you doing, *cherie*?'

Rosamund smiled wearily. 'Alright. Relieved to have made it this far.'

'Tougher than you thought?' He nodded to himself and murmured, 'Hard for a woman.'

'Hard for a man,' she batted back. Then, when they had settled themselves, she asked, 'So where did you learn to speak English so well?'

'I had an English governess until I was eleven years old.'

'And are you really a Count?'

'Of course. I am Count Thierry Foustier and my family have a chateau in the Garonne.'

'Impressive! Perhaps I should curtsey to you whenever we meet.'

Thierry gave a short laugh. 'Not really. Counts are ten-a-penny in France and the chateau is falling down. Well, not falling down, perhaps, but in a poor state of repair. Until I came to England to join STS 5, it was all I could do to stop the roof from leaking.'

'What will happen when the war ends?' she asked.

'If we succeed, I shall go back. If we fail, it will be somebody else's problem and I shall rely on my knowledge of German to get me by.'

'You speak German?'

'*Ja. Morgenstund hat Gold im Mund.*'

'I beg your pardon?'

'Morning hours have gold in mouth.'

'What's that supposed to mean?'

'It is the German equivalent of "It's the early bird that catches the worm". Speaking German might just help us to catch the worm and win this war.'

Rosamund looked thoughtful. 'I know someone else who surprised me by telling me they speak German,' she murmured.

'Sorry?'

'No, nothing.'

She rather admired Thierry's devil-may-care attitude, but suspected that beneath it lay a dogged determination to reclaim his birthright and his country.

And now, here they were, sheltering in a derelict crofter's cottage miles away from anywhere, in the hope that their success at finding their way home would allow them to do the same in another country where the stakes were rather higher. If they failed today, they would be sent home. If they failed in France, they might never see home again.

The sun disappeared from view behind lumbering grey clouds and a cold wind began to blow, rattling a sheet of corrugated iron on the roof of the crumbling building. Much of it had been dismantled to build drystone walls which were now themselves in a poor state of repair. The wind found its way in through the doorway and the long-broken window, and Rosamund felt its chill begin to gnaw at her bones. Even the midges would be sheltering now.

Eric Ridley had fallen asleep on his radio transmitter in the opposite corner of the building; perhaps, having been used, it was warm and acted like a heater, thought Rosamund, with just a hint of envy.

Thierry was sitting with his back to the wall alongside her, his knees tucked under his chin and the collar of his coarse woollen jacket pulled up in an attempt to intercept the wind.

She began to shiver.

'You are cold?' he asked.

Rosamund nodded.

'Have my coat.' He rose and began to unbutton it.

'No!' she protested. 'You're cold, too.'

'But not as cold as you. I have an inbuilt . . . how do you say . . . radiator.'

'No!' she insisted. 'We have to manage on our own. How would I feel if I stayed warm and then woke up to find you frozen to the marrow.' She pulled up her own collar, and Thierry shrugged and sat down again.

'Marrow? A vegetable, no?'

'Yes. But it's also what's inside your bones.'

'Frozen to the marrow . . .' he murmured. 'Frozen to the courgette . . .' He glanced sideways at Rosamund and smiled. 'That's what we say in French,' he said, adding, 'but then you know that . . .'

'I know no such thing. "Frozen to the courgette", indeed . . .' And then she began to laugh.

'Shhh!' exclaimed Thierry. 'You will wake our friend Eric.'

Rosamund glanced across to where Eric was now snoring gently. 'I don't think anything is going to wake Eric.'

'We could slip out and leave him to his dreams,' said Thierry mischievously.

'Tempting,' admitted Rosamund. 'But we'd better stick together.'

'Stick together, stick together,' murmured Thierry. 'Always stick together.'

He thought for a moment and then asked, 'Who do you stick together with, Rosamund? Is there a man? An *amour*?'

'Yes. There is.' She thought for a moment and then corrected herself. 'At least, there was.'

Thierry regarded her enquiringly.

'We met just a few weeks before he had to leave. That was a year ago.'

'Have you heard from him?'

'Just the once.'

'No more?'

'No. I don't think he can write. I mean, I don't think he's in a position to write. To communicate. His work is rather like ours will be.'

'Dangerous?'

'Yes. Very. At least, I think so.'

'But you will wait for him? Wait until he comes back?'

'Yes.'

'If he comes back?'

She turned to face him. 'Yes.'

Thierry nodded. 'Lucky man.'

'And you?' asked Rosamund.

'Me? Oh, I am . . . how shall I put it . . . a free agent.'

'Unattached?'

Thierry gave one of his habitual shrugs. 'I guess so.'

'You don't sound very sure . . .'

'It is as well during this war not to get too attached to anyone or anything, I fear. For both may be taken away. In war one must live from day to day and take love where one can find it.'

Rosamund shook her head. 'How very French.'

'But I *am* French.'

'Yes, you are. Very.'

'Is that so bad? You could be French yourself. You speak as though you were. You have no English accent, nor him, oddly . . .' he nodded in the direction of the slumbering radio operator. 'You, too, could be more . . . philosophical, more . . . relaxed. Perhaps you would find it more enjoyable.'

Rosamund sighed. 'There is nothing about this war which is remotely enjoyable.'

'Of course not; but we must learn to live for today. To take each day as it comes; to treat it as though it were our last, and to live it to the full.'

'Yes. I suppose so.'

Thierry leaned forward and kissed her gently on the cheek. Rosamund pulled away, shocked at the gesture she had not seen coming.

Thierry smiled at her. 'Sleep. We must try to sleep.'

'Yes, we must,' she answered reprovingly. She turned away from him and hunkered down against her backpack.

'*Dormez bien,*' he replied.

'*Oui, dormez bien.*' She realised that, without thinking, they had been speaking in English. It would not be long before that would become inadvisable.

Thanks to the exertions of the night, sleep came swiftly, in spite of the cold. When she woke, she found herself lying against Thierry. He was still fast asleep. Carefully she stood up and walked to the shattered window; a strong breeze was blowing at a length of sacking that had once been used as a crude curtain. The sky had cleared, washed clean by a deluge of heavy Highland rain, and the moon was rising. They had slept for long enough – at this time of year nights were short in the Highlands; they would need to crack on. As she looked out across the heather, she saw a single figure drop behind a distant boulder at the foot of the mountain. She turned, shook Thierry awake and then crossed to wake Eric from his deep and rumbling slumbers. 'We need to go,' she said urgently. 'And not northwards. Come on. We don't have much time.'

It was not an easy journey; the moon kept dipping behind scudding clouds and they had to frequently stop for their eyes to adjust to the darkness, all the while being aware that they might stumble across the 'enemy' and fail in their mission.

Then they reached a narrow chasm between two outcrops of granite. Eric Ridley went first, throwing his radio across the six-foot gap, making sure that it landed on a soft cushion of heather. They had encountered such obstacles before; this was just another one in their way. Eric leapt after his radio, landed, picked it up and threw it across his shoulder, making way for Thierry who sprang across the wide gap, rolled in the heather and got to his feet as though he had already undertaken parachute training. The two men moved on, their heads down, butting against the strengthening wind and the threat of a rising sun that would make clear their whereabouts to anyone scouring the terrain with binoculars. Rosamund, who had been some way behind them, reached the chasm and made to leap after them, but as she jumped, her foot caught in a snaking stem of heather. It held her fast for a moment before her foot twisted free and she slipped down the deep gully. She flung herself forward and both her hands instinctively reached out for support and grabbed a cluster of wiry, woody stems that hung over the precipitous edge on the opposite rockface. Dangling above the deep abyss, she fought for breath, knowing that the two men had gone on ahead and realising that to shout and attract their attention would also mean that she would give away their position to the 'enemy'.

For what seemed like an age, she fought the conflicting emotions that rattled in her head. Should she cry out and risk failure in their mission? Would it prove she was nothing more than a weak woman – a liability on any sortie involving physical exertion? And yet, if she let go the stems and fell to the bottom of the deep gully, she would at best break her legs and at worst . . .

Her heart pounding in her chest, she kicked her legs, the better to gain purchase on the smooth and slippery rocks. Damn! To have come this far, only to prove she did not have what it took after all . . .

Irritation and anger now crowded her mind and she felt tears of frustration spring to her eyes. And still she kicked, hoping that at any moment her boots might find purchase and she would be able to scramble out and catch up with Thierry and Eric. But every effort made her weaker. The sky was beginning to turn pale; the sun would soon be up and she would be discovered . . . what? Hanging there helplessly, or in a lifeless heap at the bottom of the deep gully? It would be the latter, for her arms were failing now and the twisted stems would soon slip from her grasp.

As all these thoughts raced through her mind, she heard a voice she knew. 'It is too risky. Stay where you are and look after your aunt.' It was Harry's voice. How right he had been. She should have stayed where she was. And proved him right? No! She could do this. No! She could not. She had tried and she had failed. She was a weak woman who would have been better off staying at home, running church bazaars and knitting mufflers.

She heard a voice again, but this time it was not Harry's. 'Grab my hand! Quickly! Grab my hand!'

It was Thierry. He was reaching down. But her hands were weak now; her arms screaming with pain. She was not heavy in herself, but with the added weight of her clothing, her boots and her backpack, it was all she could do to retain her grip on the twisted heather. Her head began to spin. Her vision of him was blurred, yet still she managed somehow to cling on, nothing more. She felt his hands tighten around her wrists, felt herself rising upwards as if to heaven.

Then all of a sudden she was lying prone on the heather, her chest heaving as she battled for breath, both men hovering anxiously over her. 'You're stronger than you look,' she murmured.

'And so are you.'

She detected a note of relief in his voice. And was there something else, too?

'Are you alright?' he asked. 'Can we carry on? It is not much farther now, and the sun is rising.'

Still panting, she nodded and stumbled to her feet. 'Just a little setback,' she explained.

'Is that what you would call yourself? A little setback?'

Rosamund swung her arm and slapped him across the chest, but she had no more breath to answer him further.

'You're a tough 'un, I'll say that for you,' said Eric, clearly impressed with her stamina. 'Not many girls I know would have managed that.'

'Thank you, Eric,' she managed. 'Nice to have a compliment.'

Thierry smiled. 'Nearly there.'

Two hours later they arrived at the rendezvous indicated on their map, undetected and triumphant. In spite of his incessant teasing, it was all Rosamund could do to resist giving Thierry a kiss there and then.

I am not sure now whether I really expected to get through the assessment. I knew I was determined, but so much of one's life is dictated by outside agencies and by abilities, which, until they are called upon, one does not realise one possesses. I knew then, and I know now, that I am relatively stubborn and determined, but that does not always translate itself into tenacity, for tenacity is different to stubbornness. Stubbornness can so easily turn into pig-headedness, whereas tenacity involves a degree of reasoning and flexibility – a way of surmounting difficulties by inventiveness and adaptability – two characteristics which I like to think that I do possess, thanks in no small measure to my experiences with the SOE.

It was at the end of our training at Wanborough when I realised that if nothing else happened to me during the war, at least I had come this far; I had made the effort, I had 'stepped up to the plate' – to use that dreadful modern expression – and proved that I had it in me to be the equal of those men around me – even if, on occasion, they had helped me through a bad patch. The men I worked with would, I hope, admit that there were times when I had helped them, too.

This 'give and take' between men and women is something that is often overlooked these days. I certainly regard myself as a feminist. I recognise that men and women have different strengths and weaknesses, but as individuals, rather than by gender. I am lost in admiration for those suffragettes who had the courage of their convictions – and the tenacity – to fight for the right to vote and for greater equality in many things.

Some argue that the situation has changed but little. I am not one of them. Yes, I have met men who were cruel and misogynistic, but I have also met men who are sensitive and considerate. I have met women who have been deceitful, bullying and as cruel as any man, and others who have been kind, supportive and generous of spirit. To suggest that any of these attributes are the sole prerogative of men or women is absurd. These are sentiments that will not endear me to some members of my sex, but they have been arrived at over a lifetime of experience and observation. I am old-fashioned, I know, but I have come to realise that the female sex has at its disposal an armoury every bit as effective as that of the male of the species; it is just that the weaponry involved is of a different nature to that of our male counterparts. It can be more subtle, perhaps – and some would say rather more surreptitious and calculating – but when it comes to achieving one's goal, it can be every bit as effective. As my friend Thierry Foustier would have put it: 'Vive la différence.'

Ah, Thierry. Now there was a man . . .

Chapter 15

WANBOROUGH AND LONDON

OCTOBER 1941

'To conquer without risk is to triumph without glory.'

Pierre Corneille, *Le Cid*, 1636

'You will be allowed home until you are recalled, which will, I have to tell you, be very soon. You will not reveal anything of your training, your whereabouts over the past few weeks, or the nature of the work you will undertake on your return.'

The station Commandant, Major de Wesselow, was emphatic in his instructions, despite the pleasant smile and the apparently relaxed demeanour.

Thierry, Eric and Rosamund sat in a row of chairs in the small briefing room at Wanborough. On the wall behind the Major a vast map of France showed the terrain in which they were soon to be working, and through the window they could see the walled garden and the Surrey landscape which had been their training ground for the past few weeks. Soon it would become nothing more than a distant memory; hopefully, a memory that would last a long time.

'You would be well advised to avoid the company of the persistently curious and those you think might be a security risk. You will be informed of your mission on your return. I suggest you explain to your nearest and dearest that they are unlikely to hear from you in the near future. It may be some time before you return home; in that respect you will be no different from the thousands of soldiers, sailors and airmen who are already committed in this war. Though your own work will be somewhat different to theirs, it will be every bit as vital.' He eyed the three recruits in front of him with curiosity. 'Any questions?'

There were none. His face wore a more serious expression as he added, 'You will no doubt have heard that many who go from here do not return. I would be misleading you if I contradicted that statement of affairs. But what I will say is that much of your success will be down to the way you handle yourselves, and the way you operate as a team. Be cautious, be careful, and think twice before lowering your guard to anyone. Learning who you can trust will be the difference between life and death. You will have to take risks, but make sure they are calculated risks.'

De Wesselow picked up his hat from the table and made to leave. 'Good luck,' he said. And then, looking at Rosamund, 'To all of you.'

Aunt Venetia was surprisingly understanding, but then Rosamund reminded herself that her aunt had already proved herself adept at keeping secrets.

Her return to Eaton Square did not last long. After just four days, she was recalled. The parting was a difficult one: Aunt Venetia felt she was in some way responsible for her niece's actions, and Rosamund was aware that she was leaving an aunt of indeterminate years to fend for herself with only Mrs Heffer on hand in case of emergency. But she had underestimated the steel of her Aunt Venetia who, on the surface at least, was impervious to fear.

'You are not to think of me at all. I shall be fine. I still have a house, thank God, and I have every intention of welcoming you back home when this dreadful war comes to an end. If not before,' she added hopefully.

'God willing,' murmured Rosamund as she gave her aunt a final hug.

'I shall not come out into the street,' said her aunt. 'Far too common to wave goodbye there.' She took both Rosamund's hands in hers. 'I don't like long goodbyes, my dear, so let's just say *"bon voyage"* and leave it at that, shall we?' She kissed her niece on the cheek, let go of her hands and turned to mount the stairs to the drawing room that would become her sanctuary. Halfway up she turned round to face Rosamund. 'You will take care, won't you?'

Rosamund nodded. 'I will.'

'Yes, well . . . goodbye.'

Her aunt continued to climb the stairs, unable and unwilling to turn around and reveal to the niece she had come to love so much the tears that were coursing down her cheeks.

Some agents were dropped off by boat, but we were to be delivered into France by Lysander aircraft. I have never been overly fond of flying, hence my reluctance to become an 'Atagirl' delivering planes, but I was not about to let that stand in my

way. If I had to be taken to France by water, then so would Thierry and Eric, for we had now been grouped together as a team or 'cell': Thierry as the Organiser, Eric as the Radio Operator, and myself as the Courier, which involved all manner of fetching, carrying, coming and going at the behest of instructions from above. We would operate independently of all other groups. To travel by water would take longer and would present more risks; I would have to get used to flying.

We were given new documents and new identities, as well as a code name for use in radio dispatches and for shorthand reference. After some discussion with de Wesselow, it was agreed that I was to be Christiane de Rossignol, code name 'Colette'. Clearly I had more than a little input in deciding on my new identity: I wanted, somehow, to feel that Celine would be with me, and since the name was so familiar, I felt it would be easier to assume than one which was totally alien to me.

Night after night I drilled these names into my brain, hoping that before too long they would become as natural to me as my own. We used our new names with one another – often calling them out just to make sure that our colleagues would turn around when addressed by them and ignore the ones they were born with. Thierry Foustier kept his own name but had the code name of 'Patrice', and Eric Ridley became Marcel Clemont, code name 'Hector'.

And so, armed with a new identity, I stepped out into a world that was as frightening as it was unfamiliar, all the while wondering if I would ever see again the world in which I had grown up; the world of rolling green valleys and tide-washed shores, a world of familiar sights and familiar voices, all of which I must now fight to reclaim.

Chapter 16

OCCUPIED FRANCE

OCTOBER 1941

'*Nos amis, les ennemis.*'
Our friends, the enemy.

Pierre-Jean de Béranger, '*L'Opinion de ces Demoiselles*',
1815

The Westland Lysander Mark III from Squadron No. 138 (Special Duties) was not, despite its affectionate nickname of 'the Lizzie', a comfortable aeroplane in which to travel. It had originally been built to carry one passenger in addition to the pilot, but its use as a means of transport for the SOE had resulted in its being adapted to take two passengers in its rear cockpit. It could fly only within a week of a full moon – the moonlight essential for navigation – and was painted matt black to assist in camouflaging it from the enemy.

The aircraft which transported Rosamund, Thierry and Eric took off from Newmarket – the short stretch of even ground that passed for a runway was situated alongside the racecourse and ranked as one of the smallest and most secret of the airfields used by the RAF.

It was the Lizzie's ability to take off and land in a restricted space which made it suitable for the transfer of agents into occupied territory, but it still presented an easy target for the German Luftwaffe, and many were shot down. In May and June of 1940, of the 175 Lysanders that were used in operations over France and Belgium, 118 were lost.

The pilot, equipped only with a map and a compass, would be guided in by no more than half a dozen torches held by members of the French Resistance positioned on the ground. If touching down proved impossible, then he would fly exceptionally low – another of the Lizzie's traits was that it could fly at low speed without stalling – almost hovering in the air, while the passengers stepped out from the aircraft in special padded suits and rolled across the soft earth, to be picked up by a ready-and-waiting ground crew.

It was a risky and dangerous operation, but one which offered a greater chance of the valuable Lysander being able to return to base without being brought down or captured. Competition for their use was eagerly contested by both the SOE and MI6 – the number of aircraft available at any one time was limited and would affect greatly the frequency and effectiveness of vital operations.

Eric and his radio transmitter would be the only passenger in the first of the two aircraft, which would set off ten minutes before that carrying Thierry and Rosamund. Care would be taken to make sure that each Lysander would take a slightly different route from the other.

The flight would take just over two hours, and for Thierry and Rosamund in the cramped and noisy rear cockpit, in their padded suits, movement was restricted and conversation all but impossible.

So this was it, thought Rosamund. All the talking, all the preparation and what was most likely to prove misplaced bravado, had led here. She was bundled into the back of a small and noisy aeroplane, which seemed to vibrate like a gigantic bee. Soon she would leave behind quiet, rural Surrey to be set down in a country she had never visited and which was occupied by enemy forces. Was she mad? How foolhardy was this? It had seemed the right thing to do, but now she was not so sure. Muffled up in her bulky flying suit, helmet and goggles, her pack by her side, she lay alongside a Frenchman she hardly knew, preparing to be dumped far from home among people who were just waiting to catch her out. And when they did? She shook her head, the better to clear it of unprofitable thoughts, as the Lizzie taxied briefly towards the end of the makeshift runway and with a roar, took off at precisely 1900 hours into the darkening skies. The aircraft tilted slightly on take-off, and she felt herself roll towards Thierry, who playfully pushed her back into position.

The time seemed to drag. She kept her eyes looking forward at the pilot – a map on his lap and a compass mounted in front of him. He glanced frequently at these two flying aids as the flight progressed and, once they were across the English Channel, never stopped looking to left and right, aware that there was a distinct possibility they would be attacked.

Rosamund was convinced that at any moment they would be shot down, but tried to be positive. Every minute that went by was a minute nearer to their rendezvous – a place known only to Thierry. More would be revealed to Rosamund and Eric on their arrival, but as the Organiser, Thierry was the one entrusted with the most information. The less his compatriots knew, the better for security should they be captured. But soon all that would change, and Rosamund knew that the moment would come when she would be forced to test her own courage to the limits. She thought of Aunt Venetia, and Celine and Devonshire, hopeful that such positive memories might strengthen her resolve.

They were descending now from their 8,000-feet flying height; the Lizzie's engine was making a different sound – a lower growl that indicated a lessening of speed and a reduction in altitude. Still Rosamund could see nothing. The pilot looked round and indicated to them that they should make ready to disembark. Would he be able to land, or would he simply slow down and force them to jump clear of the aircraft?

Raising her head slightly, Rosamund caught sight of a small cluster of lights – pinpoint beams that would guide the pilot in. The hatch was opened, she and Thierry released their straps, the pilot gave a thumbs up and Thierry tapped Rosamund on the shoulder. As the plane appeared almost to hover in a slow glide just a few feet above the ground, she stepped out and, remembering all she had been taught, rolled into a ball and came to rest after two neat somersaults on the soft, thick grass below them.

She scrambled to her feet to see Thierry land twenty or thirty feet away. Then, as the Lysander climbed into the skies, she heard the crack-crack-crack of anti-aircraft fire.

There was no time to wait and watch. Before she could check that the Lysander and its pilot were safely out of danger, a hand grabbed at her arm, turned her around and pulled her across the field towards the low hum of a small lorry parked at the side of the road. There was no opportunity to watch the aircraft depart; all she could do was hope and pray as she and Thierry were manhandled into the back of the farm truck and a tarpaulin thrown over them.

As speedily as its modest-sized engine and venerable age would allow, the truck grumbled away from the makeshift airstrip, now quiet and deserted, as though its previous incarnation had been no more than a dream.

No one spoke: not Rosamund, not Thierry, and certainly not the three figures sitting in the front of the truck as it bounced and rumbled along the rough country lanes of . . . where exactly? It would not be long before Rosamund would discover their precise location, and the daunting task that lay ahead of them.

I felt terrified, elated and, strange as it might seem, guilty at being part of such a covert operation – that I had not earned my right to such excitement. On reflection, I can understand that a combination of adrenalin and the will to live make a powerful cocktail, and I suppose such a cocktail acts as a kind of anaesthetic – masking the reality of a situation which, if fully understood, might lead, if not to hysteria, then certainly to some kind of breakdown or inability to function. Natural instincts produce complex states of mind, which are part and parcel of self-preservation.

The whole episode of flying into occupied France, landing and being bundled off without a word being spoken produced in me a kind of otherworldliness. I knew that whatever happened over the days, weeks and maybe months ahead, I must not be surprised, taken aback or discomfited. I must accept every eventuality and every twist and turn of fate as it presented itself and deal with it in the most level-headed and matter-of-fact way I could, however hard that might be.

Rosamund and Thierry were bundled out of the back of the farm lorry with as little ceremony as they were bundled in. They found themselves in an ancient barn that smelled of sweet hay and cattle feed – a fragrance that transported Rosamund straight back to Devonshire. As her eyes became accustomed to the dim light cast by a Tilley lamp, she saw that their captors (for that, somehow, is what they seemed) comprised two men and a woman.

The older man – short and portly with a plump, round face, drooping black moustache and a flat cap – seemed to be the leader of the small group and introduced himself in French. 'I am Henri Dubois.' He did not smile, but there was about him an air of relief, most likely as a result of their being safely landed and sequestered in the barn.

He lifted his arm (no mean feat since it was encased in the thickest serge jacket that Rosamund could ever recall having set eyes on) and gestured to his two comrades in arms. 'This is Paulette and Gaston.'

His two compatriots were much younger than he – in their early twenties, Rosamund guessed – the young man slender, gauche and nervous of meeting her eye; the young woman quite the reverse. Her dark hair was tucked into a headscarf, and she fixed Rosamund with her deep brown eyes as she shook her hand with a firmness of grip that somehow transmitted the message that, though young and female, she was not to be underestimated.

'You are hungry?' asked Henri.

Rosamund nodded.

'Come with me.' Carrying the lantern, he led the way to the side door of the barn, the large double doors having been closed smartly behind them. 'Your comrade arrived twenty minutes ago,' he informed them. 'Your aircraft got away; his was not so lucky. We saw it come down a few miles distant. But your colleague is safe.'

'And his radio?' asked Thierry.

'Safe, too.'

Their host ushered them across a farmyard and into a house which could just as easily have been on a smallholding in Sussex or Suffolk. Piles of old newspapers lined the small vestibule, and the paraphernalia of rural life was everywhere – a broken bridle hanging from a wooden peg, spoke-backed chairs around a scrubbed kitchen table and a piebald dog that did nothing more than slowly wag its tail as they entered; the whole room was lit only by the warm glow of oil lamps once Henri had extinguished the cold, white light of the Tilley lamp.

Eric sat at the table, nodding acknowledgement as they entered. On the other side of the room with her back to them, her hands in the sink, stood a small woman in a floral print dress. She turned to greet them, her facial expression betraying a wariness that would come to be customary in the days ahead.

'Welcome,' she said, without real feeling and, after drying her hands on a length of rough cloth, shook those of both Thierry and Rosamund. 'Sit down. I will bring you some soup.'

A russet-glazed earthenware bowl of crusty bread stood on the table, and Eric's cheeks were flushed, most likely on account of the half-empty glass of beer that stood in front of him as much as the thick, nourishing soup.

Henri motioned them to sit and removed his cap, revealing a thick thatch of dark hair. 'This is my wife, Madeleine, and these are our children.'

Thierry sat down and completed the introductions: 'I am Thierry; you've met Marcel' – he gestured in Eric's direction – 'and this is Christiane.'

Rosamund nodded a greeting, being unsure of the form at this early stage, and decided to leave all the talking to Thierry.

The conversation that followed was brief and desultory. Thierry and Rosamund ate their bread and soup, both declining a glass of beer. Both Gaston and Paulette nodded their good-nights and left the kitchen through a primitively planked wooden door which presumably led upstairs, and once the two new arrivals had finished their soup, the table was cleared and a map unfolded by Henri and laid across it.

'You will be here tonight and all day tomorrow,' he said, having taken a large gulp from his own tankard of beer. 'Tomorrow night we shall take you to the place where you will stay. This is a small village where newcomers are easily noticed. Your accommodation is on the edge of a town where you will be able to move around without causing comment. Is that what you were expecting?'

Rosamund looked across at Thierry, who nodded his approval. She could feel her body warming up now; the wholesome nature of the soup was taking effect.

Madeleine asked, 'You are tired?'

'No. I'm fine. The flight was not too long.'

'We are close – as countries,' added Madeleine. She seated herself at the table and picked at a small piece of bread. Rosamund noticed that in spite of the solicitous conversation, there was a pinched look about Madeleine's face. It was a characteristic that would become all too familiar over the weeks ahead.

'You two were lucky,' muttered Eric. It was the first sound they had heard from him since they'd arrived; he had clearly been shaken by the fact that his aircraft, along with its pilot, had been the first casualty of their operation.

'Yes,' confirmed Thierry. Then he turned to Henri and pointed at the map.

'Can you explain exactly where we are, and what is our situation? In terms of the local . . . er . . . population?'

'Germans, you mean?' asked Henri.

'Yes.'

'They come and go. There is a strong Gestapo presence in Montbéliard . . .' he pushed his plump finger into the middle of the map, 'and also around Sochaux, where the factory is situated.'

Thierry looked thoughtful.

'You will be based at a house here,' continued Henri, moving his finger to point to a small town three or four kilometres distant, 'in Fesches-le-Châtel. It was my brother-in-law's.' He glanced at Madeleine, who looked away, unable to meet his gaze.

'Was?' asked Thierry.

'He was killed. Last summer.'

'I'm sorry . . .'

Henri shrugged. 'We are in war; casualties are expected. Even if . . .' his words faded away.

Rosamund glanced at Thierry, who said nothing.

'But it is late,' said Henri, folding up the map. 'We will discuss things in more detail tomorrow. Now you must sleep. There is no haste to rise in the morning.' He lit the Tilley lamp once more and motioned all three of them to follow him through the same door the younger members of the family had used. Behind it was a steep and narrow staircase, which they climbed one behind the other, negotiating the sharp corners with their packs held in front of them – something that presented a particular challenge to Eric with his angular transmitter. They passed a door which led presumably to Henri and Madeleine's bedchamber and carried on upwards to another door at the very top where Rosamund assumed Paulette and

Gaston slept. Alongside it was a narrow section of tongue and groove panelling, its once-white distemper peeling away. Henri put his shoulder to the panel which, with some persuasion, swung back on hinges to reveal a loft space directly beneath the hipped roof. Throwing his portly body forwards, Henri climbed up into the space, before turning and pulling each of them up and over the ledge in turn. No one looking at the wall would have guessed that it held a secret; it was simply the end of the staircase.

Henri cast an eye over the room in the manner of a B&B owner seeking approval for his accommodation. 'You will be comfortable, I hope. And safe, too, until we can move you tomorrow night.'

'Thank you. It looks fine,' commented Thierry reassuringly, looking around at the sparsely furnished space, which contained three camp beds, each with a blanket laid over a thin mattress, and a pillow whose linen cover was crisp and white. They might be itinerant visitors, but Madeleine had standards that were maintained for all.

A washstand, a floral ceramic basin and a water-filled ewer stood against the wall below the apex of the roof, and on each bed was a different coloured towel. The lavatory on the floor below would be shared. Rosamund could not help smiling at this primitive but perfectly acceptable form of housekeeping.

Henri wished them goodnight, then turned to close the door, adding, 'We shall be up early – animals to feed – but you need not rush. We will speak later in the morning. There will be breakfast for you when you come down.' And with that he nodded politely and closed the panel.

'Well,' said Thierry. 'Here we are.'

Eric was already kneeling at his radio equipment. 'Better send a message,' he murmured, turning a dial and flipping a switch or two before tapping out in Morse code a brief missive that Rosamund was too tired to translate.

'Are you sure it's safe?' asked Thierry.

It was the first time that Rosamund had ever detected a note of unease in Thierry's voice.

Eric nodded. 'Fine, if we're brief. I checked with the farmer before you got here. And I'll change location every time I send a message so that we are more difficult to pinpoint.'

'Mmm. Let me know each time before you transmit. I don't want to take any risks. Now that The Outfit know we're here, they won't expect any more contact for a while, and that's just as well.' He turned to Rosamund. 'Better get some sleep.'

Rosamund was taking off her jacket. They would be sleeping in their clothes, but the loft was surprisingly warm and she discarded as much as was decently possible. Slipping between the rough blankets, she asked, 'You know what we are going to do, then?'

Thierry had taken off his own jacket and was unlacing his boots. 'I know what we are going to *try* to do, yes.'

Rosamund looked at him quizzically.

'Get some sleep. I'll brief you in the morning.' And with that, he turned off the Tilley lamp, which Henri had left behind, and bade both his roommates a goodnight.

Rosamund slept surprisingly well, and was woken around 7 a.m. by the sound of animals in the yard below, the bright sunlight glinting through a high narrow window at the apex of the end wall of the loft, and the smell of frying sausages – something she had not experienced in a long while.

Thierry's bed was empty and he was nowhere to be seen. Eric was invisible under a mountain of grey blanket, which rose and fell in synchronisation with the gentle snores that emanated from beneath it. Rosamund smiled, threw her towel over her shoulder and walked over to the washstand, splashing the water on her face and neck and rubbing herself dry with the coarse towel, which erased any remaining traces of sleep or torpor.

Folding the towel and replacing it at the foot of her bed, she pulled on her boots, pulled back the panel and, after making use of the communal facilities, descended the steps to the kitchen.

The sight that greeted her warmed her heart. Madeleine was standing against the window, which was flooded with early morning sunlight, pouring hot water into a coffee pot. The kitchen door was open, and through it Rosamund could hear the rustic vocalisations of chickens and pigs, a distant lowing cow, the sound of a broom on cobblestones and a shovel on a stable floor.

The table was covered with a blue gingham cloth and sported several plates and covered bowls. At one end, seated behind a generous helping of scrambled eggs, bacon and sausage, a steaming mug beside him, sat a beaming Thierry. 'Good morning, *mam'selle*!' he said. 'Look at this!' He opened his arms wide to indicate the early morning feast.

'Goodness!' said Rosamund. 'This is what comes of living on a farm – even if most of it does have to be rationed and distributed.'

Thierry gestured to a chair on the side of the table as Madeleine put the fresh pot of coffee on the table, along with crusty bread and a saucer of bright sunshine-yellow butter. Rosamund looked up at her appreciatively, as Madeleine said 'Eat!'

She did not need asking twice. 'I'm ravenous,' she murmured.

'Has Eric surfaced yet?' asked Thierry.

Rosamund shook her head, her mouth filled with warm bread and the most succulent sausage she could ever remember eating.

'Lazy bugger.'

Rosamund washed down the sausage and bread with a mouthful of coffee, then leaned back. 'I don't think I've ever tasted a breakfast as good as this one.'

Madeleine frowned and said, 'It is not every day we eat so well,' before turning back to the sink and washing the crockery that had been used by those who had risen a good deal earlier.

'Are Gaston and Paulette up already?' Rosamund asked the farmer's wife.

'Of course. They have work to do. They must earn their keep. Gaston is in charge of the cows and the pigs. Paulette looks after the horse and the chickens and . . . whatever else we have on our hands.' There was a mild note of severity in her voice, but she looked, thought Rosamund, like a kind woman who would be fair if firm with her offspring.

'Henri has a share of a tractor. He is out moving straw and hay for a while. He will be back soon.' Then she carried on with her chores and Rosamund with her breakfast.

It was another half hour before Eric emerged, looking as though he had not slept at all, though the snoring had indicated otherwise. 'Mmm. Breakfast.' He piled up his plate with sausages, egg and bacon, and began the serious business of putting them away.

Thierry shook his head as he watched. 'When you've finished we'll have a briefing.'

Eric said, 'Certainly, boss,' but did not look up from the serious business in hand.

Half an hour later, the three of them sat around the kitchen table poring over a detailed map of the area, as Thierry finally made clear the nature of their mission.

'We are here,' he said, pointing at a tiny dot on the map

adjacent to the snaking outline of the River Loue. 'And we are moving tonight to this village – Fesches-le-Châtel. It is around four kilometres from Montbéliard . . . here . . . and right next to Montbéliard is our target . . . here at Sochaux.'

Rosamund looked at him expectantly.

'Once we've sorted a few things out – met our contacts here, got the measure of them and satisfied ourselves that everything is lined up – we have a simple task to coordinate.'

'Which is?' asked Rosamund.

'Sochaux is where the Peugeot factory is.'

'Cars?' asked Rosamund.

'In peacetime, yes. But it has been commandeered by the Germans to make parts for tanks. It plays a vital part in the build-up of German armaments. Its output is considerable. Our task is to destroy it, or at the very least interrupt the manufacturing process and delay its restoration.'

Eric pricked up his ears. 'Explosives?'

'Yes. And incendiaries. Henri, along with some of his compatriots, has been acquiring the necessary supplies and equipment to make it possible, but there are several things we have to take into account.'

'And they are?' asked Rosamund.

'First, we don't want to risk lives – ours and those of members of the Resistance – if Bomber Command change their minds and decide on an air raid. Not only will they take out the factory, they will take us out, too.'

'Why can't they do that then?' asked Eric. 'Why do we have to do the job at all?'

Rosamund cut in. 'Because a bombing raid is too risky, presumably. The Germans will be guarding the factory with anti-aircraft guns and will bring down any planes that attack.'

'Exactly,' confirmed Thierry. 'Their record of hits around

here is exceptional. We've already tried and failed, with heavy losses. It will be easier to mount a local operation. The Resistance are already involved in sabotage to some degree – building faults into the parts – but that only makes the Germans more determined to punish those on the production line who are involved. By using an outside agency . . .'

'Us?' muttered Eric perfunctorily.

'Yes. That way it is safer for the locals.'

'But will we have their cooperation?' asked Rosamund.

'Some of them, yes; but obviously there are those who don't want to rock the boat. Those who consider that the war is lost already and who are prepared to tow the German line for their own safety and that of their families.'

'What about the factory owners? Where do they stand?'

'They are on the side of the Allies. They will help us but only if we can convince them that we can be effective, without implicating them, and that we have no ulterior motive.'

'How do we do that?'

'I don't know yet. It will take some kind of negotiation. These are early days.'

'But we can't take too long?'

'No. The sooner we can stop the production of tanks, the better for all concerned – except the Germans.'

Eric scratched his head. 'Do you have an idea?'

'Yes. I want – somehow – to contact the head of Peugeot and convince him.'

'Isn't that a bit dicey?' asked Rosamund. 'What if he gives us away?'

'Our intelligence shows him to be on our side. He doesn't want to keep helping the Germans and is complicit in the factory workers' sabotage operations. He knows we could send in bombers – in spite of our lack of success so far – and that a successful strike could wipe out his factory and most of his workforce. It's better for him – and the factory – if we can halt production with very little loss of life. We just need to convince him that such a thing is possible.'

'So you'll have to find a way of meeting him?' asked Rosamund.

'Yes, but first we have to meet the group of people we will be working with and see if we can trust them.'

'You mean, some of them might be working for both sides?'

'It's more than likely. When the enemy occupies your homeland, some people will do anything to get rid of them; others will appear to be doing so but when things get difficult . . .'

'When push comes to shove, as we say across the channel . . .' added Rosamund.

'Quite. There may be one or two who will blow with the wind, whose loyalty to the Allies – and to the French Resistance – is not as absolute as we would like. I hope that is not the case here and that Henri has done his homework properly, but you never know.'

'So this whole operation is risky?'

'Very,' confirmed Thierry. 'And then, when we've done the deed, we need to get out of here, and there will be no shortage of our friends in the grey uniforms who will try to stop us.'

Almost to herself, Rosamund murmured, 'I haven't seen one of them yet – a German, I mean.'

'Oh, you will, Rosamund, you will. And you'll have to get used to them. You're a pretty girl. Be careful.'

Chapter 17

FESCHES-LE-CHÂTEL

OCTOBER 1941

'A country like this . . . where every man is surrounded
by a neighbourhood of voluntary spies, and where roads
and newspapers lay everything open.'

Jane Austen, *Northanger Abbey*, 1817

Later that day the farm truck was pressed into service once
more, and Thierry, Rosamund and Eric were transported the
few kilometres to the house at Fesches-le-Châtel.

Again, Henri, Paulette and Gaston sat in the front of the
truck, while the three visitors bounced along the uneven roads
and tracks in the back, surrounded by the detritus of farm life
– a few bales of hay and straw, an assortment of shovels and
pitchforks, and lengths of rough sisal twine which hung in
tangled garlands from the metal hoops that supported the
ancient canvas cover.

In between scanning the countryside for landmarks that might
prove useful in the weeks ahead, Rosamund would glance at
the backs of their heads through the small and filthy window

at the rear of the cab. Partly due to the noise of the engine and partly due to the lack of clear visibility, it was impossible to hear the conversation of the three family members, not that it was either frequent or prolonged. But she would have been keen to know their thoughts on the three newcomers who had been billeted on them.

After half an hour the old truck pulled up sharply, but the rumbling engine that sounded like some bronchial old man continued to throb to its customary irregular rhythm. The forward motion had ceased so abruptly that it caused Rosamund's heart to pound. She told herself to get a grip. If she were to be alarmed at every sudden change of movement and circumstance over the next few weeks her heart would most probably give out before the operation was complete. She smiled ruefully at the very thought.

The tatty canvas flap was thrown up once more, and Paulette and Gaston motioned the three of them to get down from the truck. Rosamund looked around her. They were parked on a small apron of weed-covered gravel behind a low, barn-like extension to a tired, two-storey, lime-washed house. The small area of gravel was bordered by an overgrown quickthorn hedge on the other side of which a field of turnips lay listless in its autumnal livery.

Through the billowing haze of blue-grey exhaust fumes from the truck, Rosamund noticed the flatness of the landscape and the keenness of the autumn wind, which blew across the field in fitful gusts. The house was on the edge of the town – itself a jumble of assorted dwellings, some stone, some rendered and washed with pale colours, most roofed with mellow terracotta tiles. A church spire protruded from them in the distance. The overall feeling was of a small and unremarkable community that had hunkered down in the face of the chilly wind and the oppressive atmosphere of wartime occupation.

There was little sign of human life, but then it was early evening, and most of the inhabitants would be partaking of what modest rations they could assemble in the face of unwelcome privation.

Once they had disembarked, the lorry's engine cleared its throat and rumbled away with Henri at the wheel and Gaston beside him.

'We must go in,' said Paulette, with little expression in her voice.

The interior of the ramshackle barn proved to be much like that of its counterpart at the farmhouse where they had first been taken: a jumbled store of mud-encrusted machinery – much of it rusting – unidentifiable metal containers, old sacks, ropes and general agricultural debris. The air was thick with the tang of damp, decay and sour sump oil. At first, Rosamund wondered if this was where they were expected to live, but Paulette led the way to a door at the back of the barn into which she inserted a large rusty key. With some pressure, and biting of the lower lip on Paulette's part, the lock yielded and the creaking dust-laden door leading into the house itself was pushed open, revealing a pleasant whitewashed kitchen, warmed reluctantly by the dying rays of a lazy sun. A scrubbed pine table and four chairs occupied the centre of the room. On the table lay an assortment of provisions – a crusty loaf, a block of butter wrapped in waxed paper, various jars and unidentifiable parcels – which, no doubt, Madeleine had provided for their sustenance. Battered enamel pots and pans hung on one wall and a faded hunting print on another. A pile of logs stood alongside a blackened stove, and without a word, Paulette opened the front of the stove, took a box of matches from the pocket of her overalls and lit the ready-laid fire within its recesses.

Thierry and Eric pushed open another door and disappeared

through it as smoke began to billow out of the stove into the small kitchen. Rosamund raised her eyebrows, but Paulette assured her: 'It always does this, until the chimney is warm.'

It was the most that Rosamund had heard her say in the brief time that she had been in the girl's company. Paulette was, she guessed, slightly younger than herself at around eighteen or nineteen, but without doubt she was a capable sort, brought up – like Rosamund – on a farm, and schooled from an early age in looking after herself. Within a few moments, just as Paulette had predicted, the fug subsided and the fire began to draw. The watery glow of the setting sun was replaced with the glow of a crackling fire, and Rosamund was grateful for the much-needed warmth – both physical and spiritual – that it generated.

Thierry and Eric were upstairs now. She could hear their feet on the naked floorboards above her head. So this would be their home for as long as it took to complete their mission if, indeed, that mission was of a finite duration. Nothing had been mentioned in that respect, and Rosamund knew that she must harbour no hopes of returning home in the foreseeable future. It was a prospect she regularly tried to put out of her mind. An image of Aunt Venetia came into her head. Dear Aunt Venetia, who might as well be on the moon as back in London, which now seemed so very far away. She checked herself, and came back to earth. French earth.

'This was your uncle's house?' asked Rosamund, by way of making conversation.

'Yes,' came the brief reply. Paulette busied herself pulling the short calico curtains across the small kitchen window. The daylight was dying now.

'I was sorry to hear that he died . . .'

'Yes.' Then, realising that Rosamund was waiting for more,

she added with reluctance, 'It was hard – especially for my mother.'

'I'm sorry,' said Rosamund, again. She attempted to make reparation. 'It seems that we have all lost somebody. I lost my best friend. We had grown up together. She was killed by a bomb in the summer. Not very far from an air raid shelter.'

Paulette shook her head. 'Who would grow up in a war?'

'We have no choice.'

'No. Except to keep fighting.'

'Yes.'

Looking uncomfortable, Paulette briskly took down a saucepan from the wall, picked half a dozen large potatoes from a sack that stood on the floor by the sink, and set about putting together a meal. Rosamund took this as her cue to leave the room and explore the rest of the house. There was a small parlour with comfortable easy chairs, an old chest of drawers and a large mahogany mirror over the large inglenook where no fire burned as yet. The room felt cold and damp, the result, thought Rosamund, of being unoccupied for over a year.

She made her way upstairs and was relieved to find that there were two bedrooms – in one an unmatching pair of single beds and in the other a large double with an ornate white-painted iron bedstead. Thierry and Eric were already unpacking their modest belongings and putting them away in the two chests of drawers that sat on either side of the single beds.

'Is this one mine?' she asked, rather unnecessarily, pointing to the double bed in the room across the landing from them.

'Unless you want to share with me?' offered Thierry with a grin.

Rosamund felt herself colouring up. 'I'll resist the temptation,' she countered, and turned to enter what would pass for her sanctuary during their stay. She pushed the door so that it was part closed, and walked across to the small dormer window that looked out across the fields. It was almost dark now, and no street lights lifted the gloom. She shivered, opened her backpack and took out the few spare clothes she had, preparing to put them in the small cupboard at one end of the room. She was surprised to find some garments already hanging there. At first she thought they might have belonged to Paulette's uncle, but she soon discovered that they were women's attire.

There was a knock at the door and Paulette put her head round. 'My mother and I did not know if you would need some clothes. We had to guess your size.'

It was an olive branch of sorts, and Rosamund was grateful for it. She gestured towards the bed, motioning Paulette to sit, half expecting her to shake her head and retreat. But she did not. She came and sat on the edge of the bed while Rosamund arranged her few possessions in the cupboard and on the table.

'You are very brave,' said Paulette, quietly.

'Me?'

The girl nodded. 'To come here, to a foreign country and help us.'

Rosamund did not know how to reply. She shrugged and smiled. 'I have to.'

'No, you do not. You could have stayed at home. Safe.'

'I'm afraid it's not very safe at the moment. With the bombs falling. They do seem to have eased off a little, but I can't believe that will last.'

'No. But at least you were surrounded by your own people.'

Rosamund perched on the small chair opposite the bed and asked, 'What do you do? From day to day, I mean?'

Now it was Paulette's turn to shrug. 'I feed the animals . . . and help Papa on the farm.'

'But in terms of . . . ?'

'Resistance?'

'Yes.'

'I do what I am asked to do. And try not to be noticed.'

'By Germans?'

Paulette nodded, then added, 'And others. This war does not just divide countries from each other; it divides communities. Families even.' An aura of sadness surrounded her as she spoke. For the first time, Rosamund could properly take in the girl's appearance. The figure that was masked by the baggy overalls, drawn in at the waist with a thick leather belt, was slender of proportion but shapely. The hair peeping out from beneath the headscarf that retained it was dark and glossy. Rosamund suspected, from the modest amount on view, that it was long and lustrous. The face, though totally devoid of make-up, was pretty and delicate, the eyes a soft shade of blue – a fact, she could not help thinking, which would not have escaped Thierry's notice. For a fleeting moment she felt a pang of jealousy, then swiftly told herself not to be so silly.

'I shall need help,' said Rosamund. 'Learning things – where to go, what not to do, how to . . . carry myself.'

'Be busy,' offered Paulette. 'Look as though you are confident in what you are doing. Do not stand and stare. Avoid making eye contact. Just go about your business as though nothing has happened. Decide where you are going and what you are going to do when you get there. That way you will look purposeful and not attract attention.'

'Easy to say . . .' countered Rosamund.

'You will get used to it. The important thing is not to engage them in conversation unless you have to. Your French is so good that you will not stand out in that way to the Germans, who have lousy French anyway. But it is the locals who cannot always be trusted. Try to . . . blend in.'

'My friend was French. The one who was killed. Well, her father was, and we spoke French all the time when I was young.'

'I can tell.'

'You're very kind.'

Paulette smiled. 'It will make a change to have another female around the place. But be careful. It is dangerous. Everyone is suspicious. It is difficult to know who to trust.' She got up from the bed. 'I must go and prepare supper.'

'There's no need. I can do that,' offered Rosamund, aware that her own culinary skills were basic, to say the least.

'Tonight I will do it. You can take over tomorrow.'

'Of course.' She hesitated; then said, 'And Paulette . . .'

The girl turned. 'Yes?'

'Thank you. It's all a bit scary. I'm glad you're here.'

Paulette nodded. 'Me too.'

She closed the door behind her, and Rosamund sat on the bed. For the first time since her journey had begun she was gripped by raw fear; fear that she could almost taste. In spite of the presence of Thierry and Eric, she felt totally alone. Alone and in a foreign country where not all the natives were friendly, and where those who were not natives would be only too happy to torture and to kill her.

More than anything, I wanted to cry that night. To sob my heart out – for what I had lost, for what had been taken away from me, and for what I had committed myself to. Suddenly it all seemed so huge; the mountain I had to climb so insuperable. What could have possessed me, in a fit of misplaced bravado, to imagine that I was up to the task? I was just like Paulette. I should have stayed in my own country, as she had done – not that she had any option but to do so. At least at home I would have been among my own people. Here I was among strangers. How well did I even know Thierry and Eric? We had been thrown together by circumstances just a few weeks previously; hardly long enough to form a comfortable and trusting alliance, let alone some sort of bond. And yet I knew that I had no alternative but to trust them, for both of them had my life in their hands, just as I had theirs in mine. I think that is what galvanised me and prevented me from becoming a gibbering wreck. Paulette seemed to be so capable; she had learned to live with the fact that her own country had been invaded and occupied. Surely my own lot was not as unenviable as hers? I steeled myself to believe that I had a real responsibility to my own country, to help prevent an invasion from happening – or at least to keep the enemy at bay – in whatever small way I could. And at least I had the knowledge that Aunt Venetia, Mrs Heffer and Diana Molyneux were doing their own bit back home and would, God willing, be there when I returned. If I returned.

That first evening I thought so much about Harry. I wondered *where he was and what he was doing. I conjured up images of us meeting, and working together here, behind enemy lines, even though I realised that such a scenario was little more than wishful thinking. I had no idea where he was, and did not even know the country in which he was operating. But I also knew in my heart that I must be realistic and get used to the fact that I might never see him again. When that thought first crossed my mind, I felt unspeakably disloyal. Heartless even. But I would not be telling the truth if I denied that I tried to put him from my mind; to be realistic and to treat our brief liaison as something brought on by war, and which was unlikely to survive the hostilities for countless reasons.*

Then there was Thierry – handsome, dashing and, I suspected, completely unscrupulous where women were concerned. I noticed, too, that occasionally his hand would brush against mine when we were poring over a map, and he would ease me out of the way when he wanted to get to a door – placing his hands on my shoulders and moving me to one side. In those early days of knowing him I told myself that all this was par for the course for a Frenchman, and that I should not read anything into it. But at the same time I was aware of a certain frisson when such contact occurred. It unnerved me slightly, and I did my best to treat my thoughts as fanciful. Thierry was, after all, a French Count, sophisticated in spite of his apparently carefree approach to most things in life. I found him to be a sea of contradictions: one moment he was flashing a smile and a wink at Paulette, or brushing my cheek with the back of his hand on the pretext of removing a smut that had emanated from the smoky stove, the next he was the serious organiser of our small cell, explaining the intricacies of the local geography or the strategy we would employ to achieve our aims.

For those first few days in our house on the edge of the town, we did nothing more than venture out on foot, looking as though we were intent on our business as additional members of the local workforce brought in to help at the factory, all the while getting to grips with the lie of the land – the local shops, their proprietors, their opening hours, what they stocked and what they did not – so that we would not put ourselves in the position of appearing to be outsiders.

Yes, we were new to the town, but then so were others who had been brought in to add to the workforce in the nearby factories, not least the one that had originally produced cars for Peugeot.

After a few days, Henri stowed us in the back of the lorry and drove us past the Peugeot buildings, which now comprised the German tank factory. Quite suddenly our mission to sabotage the German war effort became very real.

Chapter 18

LONDON

NOVEMBER 1941

'Trust not him with your secrets, who, when left alone in
the room, turns over your papers.'

Johann Caspar Lavater, *Aphorisms on Man*, 1788

'You assured me that this cell was secure. I specifically asked you
to choose an operation that would avoid placing her in a situation
that was high risk.' Charles Belgate was the nearest he became
to being angry. He was sitting behind a large mahogany partners'
desk in his fifth-floor office in Baker Street. Outside, the view
over London was obscured by thick fog. It was early evening.

'It *was* secure.' Doris Kilgarth stood on the other side of the
desk, facing him. Her hands were clasped in front of her, and
she was doing her best to avoid wringing them – the better to
give the impression of being in control, when events would
suggest otherwise.

Lord Belgate picked up a buff file and waved it in front of
her. 'But according to this missive, nothing could be further
from the truth.'

Still he did not invite her to sit in the vacant chair set at an angle in front of his desk. It was a scenario which she knew indicated his supreme displeasure. Charles Belgate was a stickler for good manners. When a woman entered the room he stood up. He would not sit down until she did. On this occasion, not only was Doris kept standing, but His Lordship had remained seated as she entered. It did not bode well. But then, neither did the situation unfolding across the Channel.

'If I can't rely on you, Kilgarth, then who can I rely on?'

Lord Belgate dropped the file on the desk in front of her and finally – and impatiently – motioned her to sit. She did so, at the same time picking up the file and, once seated, examining the cover. EYES ONLY read the customary directive. Underneath it was written, in red italic script, 'The Scarlet Nightingale'. Doris's eyebrows rose, and she looked enquiringly at her inter-locutor. She did not say 'The name's a bit melodramatic, isn't it? A bit "Boy's Own Paper"?', but her expression made it clear she thought as much.

Charles Belgate waved his hand, the better to make light of the inscription. 'It is a personal thing. Her *nom de guerre* is Christiane . . .'

'. . . de Rossignol. The Nightingale; I know.'

He continued, '. . . and she always writes in red ink. It seemed . . . apt.'

Doris looked down and opened the front cover, then sat quietly, her expression betraying no emotion, as she read the closely typed sheet of paper within. It did not take her long to assimilate its contents. With slow deliberation she closed the file, leaned forward and placed it back on the desk with more than usual gentleness and care. 'This is all new.'

'It might be new, but it's reliable.'

'So it would appear.' Doris spoke slowly and purposefully,

looking more nun-like than ever surrounded by the wimple of white hair. 'When did it come to light?'

'In the last twenty-four hours. There's been nothing concrete up to now, nothing that we could be certain of – just the usual blips every now and then, usually put down to carelessness . . . or good luck on the part of Gerry, or of our French comrades who would buckle rather than fight.'

'But now?'

Charles Belgate stood up and turned to look out of the window. 'It seems that someone is on to them. The . . . misfortunes, you might call them . . . have been happening more and more frequently.' He turned back to face her. 'I want this stopped and I want Rosamund Hanbury, Ridley and Foustier—'

'You mean Colette, Hector and Patrice?'

There was a note of impatience in his voice now: 'Whatever code names you want to call them, Miss Kilgarth, I want them pulled out. Now.'

'But they've only just got there.'

'And they are in great danger.'

Doris was surprised. 'All our operatives are in danger. That's the nature of the job. We can't make an exception for this one.'

'Miss Kilgarth!' The tone was unmistakable and uncompromising.

'Look, sir, give me a few hours to make some enquiries. We'll try to get in touch with them. They've been quiet since their first message. But, even if we want to extract them, Lysanders are at a premium – MI6 are refusing to budge in terms of their requirements. Between the two of us, we're making unrealistic demands on the RAF. They simply don't have the capability.'

She paused, but read the look of earnest desperation on the face of her superior. 'To be honest, I'm not sure we could get them out quickly even if we tried. The only saving grace is that they are not far from the Swiss border, but if push does come to shove, then crossing that won't be easy. It might even be more difficult.'

Lord Belgate returned to his desk and slumped down in his chair. 'I should never have encouraged her. "Never mix business with pleasure" – that's always been my motto. Why the hell did I make an exception this time? I should never have got involved, and that's the truth.'

'As far as anybody is concerned, sir, you're not involved. Patrick Felpham is the one officially associated with this work, not you. As far as everyone here is concerned you're just . . .'

'Go on – say it: "A harmless old duffer who used to be a part of the service and who has now been put out to grass." Except that I haven't, have I? They've called me back in to "do my bit", though there are times when I really wish they hadn't. What do they think I do in this office?'

'They realise you are a good man to have around. A wise counsellor. A man of experience that shouldn't be wasted. But nobody will blame you when things go wrong.'

'That's of little consolation. I'm less concerned with my own reputation and standing than with the safety of someone . . . I've become rather fond of.'

Doris regarded him with a look that spoke volumes.

He responded swiftly. 'I know, Miss Kilgarth; I know. Unprofessional I might be, but I do feel a particular responsibility for . . . this operative. That's all.'

'And Lady Venetia?'

'And Lady Venetia, yes. Not that she will know anything about it. But I shall know . . .'

Doris offered an olive branch. 'You've been doing this a long time, sir . . .'

'Too long.'

'Don't reproach yourself for caring. We all care, even if we're not allowed to show it. All human lives matter, but we would not be true to ourselves if we did not admit that some matter more personally than others.'

Lord Belgate leaned forward on his desk. 'Do they matter to you, Miss Kilgarth?' he asked wearily. 'Really?'

She fixed him with her gimlet eyes. 'Oh yes. They matter. More than you know. I feel a great responsibility towards "my girls". That's how I think of them, you know. I have no family to speak of – a brother in a sanatorium, but he doesn't really know me. I have no children . . .' she paused and looked out of the window, then said softly, 'apart from the ones I send overseas to do our bidding. And so many of them never come back. I've lost more children in this war than anyone I know . . .'

A silence hung in the air. A silence heavy with sadness. It was broken after some moments by Lord Belgate: 'So you'll do your best, Doris?' he asked gently.

'Oh yes. I'll do my best, sir. I always do. But if I'm honest, I really don't hold out much hope that I can succeed. Our only consolation is that as yet no lives have been lost.'

'So far. But you and I both know that it's only a matter of time. When they've got all the information they think they can get, then our cells become expendable.'

'Such a waste,' murmured Doris, half to herself.

'Well, at least make sure they are on their guard. Let them know that the scenario is not as secure as we thought, that someone is probably on to them. He – or she – might not yet know precisely who they are, but it can only be a matter of time.'

Chapter 19

FESCHES-LE-CHÂTEL

NOVEMBER 1941

'The bright face of danger.'

Robert Louis Stevenson, *Across the Plains*, 1892

It had been a week since their arrival and Thierry, Rosamund and Eric were beginning to get the measure of the small town in which they had been billeted. For the most part, everyone went about their business in a quiet fashion, but there was, beneath the surface, an undercurrent of discontent which would occasionally manifest itself in the form of a brawl in a bar when some local youth found the status quo too much to bear or when an old-time resident had had too much to drink and found their bravado expanding as their circumspection shrank. These outbursts were usually stopped by other locals who would bundle out the offending parties, rather than waiting for the army of occupation to do the same with more severe consequences.

Rosamund encountered her first group of German soldiers within a few days of their arrival at the house in Fesches-le-Châtel.

I can remember the very first time I found myself confronted by the enemy. Thankfully I did not have to speak. Thierry had sent me on an errand – a simple one, to buy a loaf of bread. We used these 'errands' as a way of working out where the Germans gathered, where their depots were, that sort of thing, so that we could plan routes that, for the best part, would avoid encountering them.

I was coming out of the local boulangerie, heading across the road and walking the half mile back to the safe house, when I turned a corner and almost walked straight into a group of four soldiers, leaning on the wall and smoking. It was as if I had walked into the lion's den. For the briefest of moments I froze but, I hope, not long enough for them to think anything of it. One of them stood to attention and saluted – but not out of respect. Then they all laughed and one of them said, 'Good morning, fraulein; how are your buns?' in very bad French. I smiled and shook my head, attempting to make light of it, and I kept on walking, sure that they would stop me or follow me or . . . I knew not what. But they just laughed and let me carry on. I have never been so relieved to get back 'home' and shut the door. I wanted to cry, but I stopped myself. I realised that if such an innocent encounter was to unnerve me, then there was little hope of my being of any use to anyone in what was to follow.

I made a cup of strong coffee, sat down at the kitchen table (Thierry and Eric were in the barn talking to Henri) and swore to myself that from now on I would toughen up. When I look back on it, I can still feel a frisson of fear. You must remember *that up until that moment, 'the Germans' had taken on almost mythical qualities. They represented all that was evil in the world. No one who stayed at home would ever encounter them, except on newsreels where they were kept at a safe distance, where their malevolence was at arm's length, safety through celluloid. We felt the consequences of their actions in the Blitz, but we did not meet them face to face.*

What surprised me, I realised, was that they were just ordinary people, like us. Not creatures with three heads. That normality made them, in my eyes, all the more frightening.

I remember the encounter particularly, because it occurred on the day of the bad news. The news which very nearly caused us to pull the whole operation.

Rosamund came upon Thierry, Eric and Henri when she entered the barn at the side of the house to tell them she had prepared lunch. They looked especially grave.

'Has something happened?' she asked.

Henri looked across at Thierry.

'Let's eat,' he said, and they followed him into the kitchen.

'We have two problems,' he said, as he sawed off a slice of the crusty loaf and cut himself a chunk of goat's cheese.

'Only two?' asked Eric, attempting to make light of it. Thierry shot him a critical glance. Eric was, since their arrival on French soil, a man of few words who now undertook most of his communion with the world in a series of dots and dashes.

Rosamund waited. Henri kept his eyes on his plate of bread and cheese, as yet resisting the temptation to eat.

'Two major problems. The first is that we have to convince the owner of the Peugeot factory – Robert Peugeot – that it is in his interests, and the interests of his employees, to let us destroy one of his presses.'

'Just one?' asked Rosamund.

'It is the one that is most crucial to their war effort. It makes the turrets for tanks. Without it, they are – as you would say – "scuppered".'

'How do we know which one it is?'

'The manager of the factory will show us.'

'And how do we convince Monsieur Peugeot to let us do that? Surely it will reflect badly on him if he is seen to be colluding with "the enemy".'

'We have worked that out. Eric and I saw him this morning. Henri set up a meeting.'

'And he was happy for you to do it?' asked Rosamund disbelievingly.

'Oh, he took some convincing, of course. He is on the side of the Allies but he knows that if it appears he is sabotaging the work then there is a real danger that he and his workforce will be removed to Germany and used as forced labour. They build in deliberate faults as often as they can, but if they go too far the Germans will lose patience. I explained to him that if he allowed us to sabotage the press, apparently with no connection to him or to Peugeot, then we could stop the RAF bombing raids – the factory is one of their prime targets; they know what it is producing – and his factory and staff would be safer as a result.'

Rosamund's eyes widened. 'And did he agree?'

'Not without conditions. He wants proof that we are not *agents provocateurs* – and that we are who we say we are.'

'How can we do that?'

Thierry looked across the table. 'Eric came up with the idea.'

Rosamund looked questioningly at the radio operator.

'Yes, well. It seemed obvious, really.' Eric cleared his throat, and began the explanation. 'There is a relatively simple way to convince Monsieur Peugeot that we are indeed *bona fide* sabo-teurs and that we have no ulterior motive. As Thierry said, we need to be able to assure him that when we have completed our mission satisfactorily, that bombing will stop. He and his factory, and all those who work within it, will be safe, and there will be no recriminations.'

'So?'

Eric continued. 'I suggested that Monsieur Peugeot give us a phrase – a sentence, a quotation – that we can arrange to have broadcast on the BBC on a given day at a given time, and that will prove that we are British agents and that we mean what we say.'

'And did he agree to cooperate?'

'Eventually,' said Thierry.

'And can we do that?' asked Rosamund of Eric.

'We can. But I will have to insist that they take special care when they are decoding the message so that every single word is exactly as Robert Peugeot instructed.'

'Can The Outfit get the BBC to cooperate?' asked Rosamund.

'Oh yes,' said Eric. 'We have connections. I used to work there.'

Rosamund sat back in her chair. 'So when will all this happen?'

'Tomorrow night at 7 p.m. French time,' replied Thierry, 'provided Eric can get his act together in time.'

Eric shot him a withering look. 'I will be sending the message tonight. It will air twenty-four hours later. They won't let us down.'

Rosamund was curious. 'And what was the message? The quota-tion or whatever that Monsieur Peugeot wanted you to use?'

Eric frowned. 'It's here somewhere,' he said, rummaging through his trouser pockets and finally withdrawing a crumpled piece of paper. 'Yes, here we are.' He handed the note to Rosamund and she read it out loud:

'In 1815, Monsieur Charles-Francois-Bienvenu Myriel was Bishop of Digne.'

'Rather appropriate, don't you think?' asked Thierry. 'You recognise it, of course?'

'I'm not sure. It seems vaguely familiar. Victor Hugo?'

Thierry smiled at her. 'Very good. They are the opening words of *Les Misérables*.'

He was, she thought, rather patronising in his praise. Rosamund folded the note and handed it back to Eric. 'You'd better get on then,' she said, realising that perhaps she had sounded rather sharp. She shot a glance at Thierry.

'Yes. Off you go to your radio. Let us know how you get on.'

Eric left the table and went upstairs to transmit the message.

Rosamund took a sip from the glass of deep red wine that sat in front of her, musing on the fact that even in wartime the French still managed to lay their hands on a decent bottle. But then, she reasoned, it did not have far to travel.

She nibbled at a crust of bread and then said absently, 'You said there were two problems. What's the other one?'

Thierry glanced across at Henri who had been slowly eating his supper and barely looking up from his plate. 'We have, as you would put it in your country, a bad apple.'

'A bad apple? What do you mean?'

'Someone who is probably aware of Henri's role in the Resistance and who, if given the opportunity, could give us away,' Thierry elaborated.

Rosamund's eyes widened. 'How? I mean, how do you know?'

'Information from London – and confirmation from Henri.'

'So . . . do we leave? Now?'

'What do you think?'

'What *should* I think? If we are about to be arrested, shouldn't we get out of here?'

'Without doing the job?'

'But if we can't do the job? If we are stopped from doing the job?'

'We hope that will not be the case. But it is a risk.'

Rosamund looked across at Henri who looked up to meet her eye. 'It was small things at first,' he said. 'Things which could have been coincidences. Then we started transmitting false information, and when that was acted upon we knew that someone was intercepting our messages. We changed our tactics and our last transmissions were not intercepted. Now you have arrived we have stopped transmitting ourselves, but we all need to be careful.'

'Is it just radio messages then?' asked Rosamund. 'They have not identified who was transmitting them?'

'We don't think so. But we cannot be too careful.'

'You think someone knows why we are here?' she asked Thierry. 'Someone outside the family?'

'We are not sure. We think that certain people who are not sympathetic to the Resistance might be suspicious of Henri, so he is going to take a back seat for a while. He'll have no involvement. We'll operate from here independently of the farm. Henri will stay there and get on with . . . farming. Eric is an experienced radio operator; we'll have to rely on him to regularly change his frequencies and his locations to keep us safe.'

Rosamund pushed the glass away from her. Somehow it seemed irresponsible to enjoy a glass of wine under such circumstances. 'Be honest with me,' she said. 'How likely is it that we will be discovered?'

Thierry smiled at her. 'There is always a danger of being discovered,' he said. 'But if we are careful, and vigilant, then we might be lucky.'

Chapter 20

SOCHAUX

NOVEMBER 1941

'Courage is rightly esteemed the first of human qualities
because . . . it is the quality which guarantees all others.'

Winston Churchill, *Great Contemporaries*, 1937

The coded message was transmitted, as planned, by the BBC,
Robert Peugeot was consequently convinced of their credentials,
and one evening in late November, Thierry Foustier and Marcel
Clemont (aka Eric Ridley) set off for the Peugeot factory in
their battered van. They would park it a few streets away and
walk up to the factory gates with their accreditation as insurance
personnel, examining machinery and evaluating the cost of
maintenance. The plan had been gone through in meticulous
detail and the details rehearsed at the house much of the day
and late into the night; every possible eventuality was accounted
for.

The explosives, detonators and timing device had been provided
by Henri and left in a sack in their barn. They would not be
taken to the factory in the van, for fear of being discovered;

instead, they would be taken there on the train, carried in a holdall, by Rosamund.

It might seem cowardly on the part of my two male colleagues that I was the one to carry the explosives, and that I was made to go by train rather than travelling with Thierry and Eric in the van. But women travelling by train attracted far less attention than men. Yes, there was a chance that I would be stopped and searched, and if that happened, I knew that the game would be up and that I would be imprisoned or . . . worse. But this was the risk I would have to take. And you must remember that I was the one with the expertise when it came to demolition. Not that at Wanborough Manor I had realised just how useful that facility would become – or how soon it would be needed.

To be fair, Thierry was very unhappy about the arrangement, being a gallant Frenchman who felt that he should take the risk himself, but it was I who volunteered for the task and I who insisted that it was safer for me to take charge of them. After all, I would be the one to use them. Should anything go wrong with the setting up or timing of the explosion, I would have only myself to blame.

With the fear of discovery – and the previous interception of radio transmissions – it was decided that the three of us would operate with no further personal communication with Henri and his family. It was not that we did not trust them –

we did – but we were uncertain of the support of those around them, their friends, their acquaintances, and the watchful eyes of neighbours who might not be so well disposed to the activities of the Resistance.

In the days before the operation we kept ourselves to ourselves; Thierry had already arranged with the production-line manager where and when we would be met, and under what pretext we were to enter the factory.

Thierry and Eric would be insurance inspectors and I would be a bookkeeper, my bag filled – on first glance – with nothing more interesting than account books, even though what was hidden underneath them was more likely to set the world on fire, or at least part of a factory.

The train from Fesches-le-Châtel to Sochaux was small, airless and rattled along the lines in such a way that I thought there was a chance that my explosives would detonate before I reached my goal. If all I managed to demolish was a railway carriage I could become the unluckiest saboteur in the war. It was only a short journey, but it seemed to take an age. When finally we reached the station at Sochaux, I disembarked, clinging tightly to my bag, and walked to the factory gates, where I showed my papers to a uniformed security official. There were soldiers everywhere, rifles slung over their shoulders. The factory was just closing for the evening. On many days it worked through the night, the German army being desperate for more tanks to win the war, but on this particular evening some maintenance work needed to be done and the machines had to be switched off to undertake the necessary servicing.

I kept calm; my papers were examined and my face scrutinised. Then the guard pointed at my bag.

'Books,' I said. 'Account books.' I opened the bag and showed him the ledgers that lay within.

*For one moment, I was certain that I would be found out;
that the books would be removed and the bottom of the bag
examined. If that happened, it was all over.*

*The guard picked up a telephone and spoke, half in German,
half in French, to someone on the other end of the line. He
put down the phone, looked at me again and, after what seemed
like forever, my papers were handed back to me and I was
motioned through the gates. I was instructed to go with a man
in a grey coat and not, on any account, to leave his side. I was
in! Now, all I had to do was meet up with Thierry and Eric.*

*I was shown into an office – where any bookkeeper or
accountant would have been expected to be deposited. The man
in the grey coat departed and there I sat, ostensibly poring over
ledgers that made absolutely no sense to me and which, being
in a state of high tension, I could not see clearly anyway. But
I turned pages, and made what I hoped were, to anyone watching
me work, appropriate marks in column after column.
Occasionally a guard would walk past the office window and
glance in. I gave the impression of concentrating fiercely on my
task, all the while my mind racing.*

*After half an hour or so, when the workforce had all
dispersed, Eric put his head around the door. It was such a
relief. Eric was not the sort of person who generally inspired
elation at his presence, but on this occasion I can't tell you how
relieved I was to see him. He was accompanied by a short,
nervous-looking man of sixty or so whom he introduced as the
factory manager. He shook my hand and I remember it being
particularly sweaty. He was clearly every bit as nervous as me.
I picked up my bag and, leaving the ledgers behind on the desk,
followed the two of them out on to the factory floor.*

*The guards – and there were plenty of them, since the
factory was undertaking vital war work – were scattered*

around in small groups of two or three. I could see the closest group at the far end of the production line, at some distance from the particular machine we had targeted and were led to by the factory manager. Most of the machines were switched off, but there was still a hum of engine noise from those that were being tested after maintenance, enough to cause anyone who spoke to raise their voice above the din. This, mercifully, would cover any small sound that I made while undertaking my task.

Thierry was talking to three guards at the other end of the production line, keeping them occupied. I could see now why Eric had not been given that job, for Thierry's command of language – he also spoke German – clearly made him the best man for it. Though I would rather have had Thierry watching my back than dear, boffin-like Eric. But this was no time for such thoughts.

I realised that if I achieved nothing else in this war, now was the moment for me to prove myself. I should have been nervous – I was nervous – but something else took over as I looked up at the enormous machine whose diagrams I had been studying every evening in my room. So this was it. I had to get it right, and I had to be quick.

Down at the end of the factory floor Rosamund could see that Thierry had positioned himself facing in her direction, so that the guards' backs were turned away from her. The group was, she guessed, about fifty yards away from her. The machine in front of her, towering like some steel giant, was silent. She knew exactly where to position her charge, how to set the detonator and the timer. She acted swiftly, lifting the explosives from her bag with economic movements and concealing them in an aperture of the gigantic press where they would not be noticed should anyone make a cursory inspection before the machine was switched on early the following morning.

Feeling the beads of sweat forming on her forehead, she wiped them away quickly with her sleeve, intercepting them before they ran into her eyes and impaired her vision. She breathed deeply, inhaling an atmosphere heavy with the smell of oil and grinding steel. The whole operation took less than two minutes. She glanced up to check that Thierry was still occupying the guards, then, satisfied that all was as it should be, she switched on the timer and nodded at Eric and the diminutive factory manager who was now glancing feverishly from left to right and seemed, if anything, even more nervous than before.

Rosamund slipped the empty holdall under her arm and the three of them walked back towards the office as calmly as their nerves would allow. Safely inside, Rosamund picked up the ledgers and deposited them in the bag. Then, nodding at Eric, she picked it up and, escorted by their grey-coated accomplice, they made their way out of the factory towards the gate.

They were stopped once more by the security detail, at which point the grey-coated man turned on his heel and disappeared with all haste back to the factory. It crossed Rosamund's mind that if he were so inclined he could go straight to the guards, tell them what had happened and have them all arrested. And Thierry was still inside.

Eric showed his papers and, after some moments, was waved through the heavy gates. He disappeared, as they all agreed would be the case. It was safer to operate individually whenever possible; if one was caught, the others were to make no attempt to intervene. To do so would endanger any mission and risk even more lives than their own.

The guard on the gate – a thick-set, bull-necked individual wearing the grey German army uniform – took Rosamund's papers from her and pored over them with more than usual interest. He was not the same guard who had questioned her on her arrival. He was new to his shift. Keener. More alert. She suppressed any outward sign of nerves over the moments that seemed to last an age.

Looking up from her papers, he said, '*Bist du buchhalter?*'

Rosamund shook her head and replied in French, 'I'm sorry. I don't speak German.'

'You are a bookkeeper?'

'Yes.' She spoke as evenly as she could.

The guard pointed to her bag. 'Open it.'

Rosamund did as she was bid, aware that her breathing was becoming heavier. Many things ran through her mind – not least, was she sure she had removed any traces of the equipment she had brought in with her? Detonators! The spare detonators! They were still in the bag. It was too late. She had no alternative but to put the now open holdall down on the wooden counter in front of the guard and let him inspect the contents.

Her heart thumped beneath her coat as the guard began to lift out the books and ledgers. One after another, slowly and methodically.

Her head began to pound now. Three books, four books, until finally the bottom was reached. He lifted the bag from the counter and turned it upside down. Nothing fell out. The bag was empty.

Wondering what divine intervention had stepped in to protect her, Rosamund managed a weak smile, as if to show that she had expected nothing else.

The guard put the books back into the holdall, fastened it and handed it back. '*Guten abend, fraulein,*' he said, and motioned her through.

Rosamund walked purposefully out of the gates and down

the short road leading from the factory. She turned a corner and found herself in a deserted street flanked by a high brick wall, topped by barbed wire. She stopped, leaned against the wall and breathed deeply. It was done. She lowered the bag to the ground and stretched back against the brickwork, gasping for air as though it was her last chance to breathe. She thrust her hands deep into her pockets and felt – a detonator, one in each. It was all she could do not to laugh.

But there was no time to lose. She glanced at her watch. Four minutes. In four minutes she would discover whether their mission – and her part in it – had been successful.

She prayed that Thierry was clear of the factory, then she hurried on to the station, trying her best not to break into a run, and stood on the platform awaiting the arrival of the train. As it rounded the bend a few hundred yards away in a cloud of steam and smoke, she heard an explosion. At first she could not be sure that it was not the train itself, but the reactions of others on the platform told her this was not the case.

The relief Rosamund felt on opening the door into the kitchen of the house was palpable; especially when she saw Eric sitting at the table with a glass of red wine in front of him.

His eyes lit up at the sight of her. It was the first time she had noticed such a positive reaction. He smiled, raised his glass and said, 'You did it! I hung about outside to watch – from a distance, of course. Bloody mayhem it was. Cheers!'

'Where's Thierry?' she asked.

The door from the parlour opened and a smiling face came into view.

'Here!'

It was then that she burst into tears.

Chapter 21

FESCHES-LE-CHÂTEL

NOVEMBER 1941

'In her first passion woman loves her lover, In all the
others all she loves is love.

Lord Byron, 'Don Juan', 1818-24

There was no guilt as she lay in Thierry's arms, just a sense of
profound relief – and release. It was as if all the pent-up tensions
of the previous weeks and months had been set free.

She had not for one moment expected this to happen; never
imagined that she would give way to her emotions, even though
from their first meeting she had found him attractive. She had
never lain with a man before. There had been fumblings among
the hay with the occasional youth in Devonshire, but she had
reached the age of twenty still a virgin.

She had sobbed at her first sight of him coming through the
door into the kitchen – half out of relief that their ordeal was
over and the mission accomplished, but also because at that
moment she knew he was safe and that she cared for him more
than just as a comrade in arms.

He folded her to him as she wept, her body wracked with sobs. Eric took his cue and left the table, glass and bottle in hand, silently climbing the stairs to his room and closing the door.

As the tears subsided, she looked up at Thierry's face. 'I'm sorry,' she said.

'What have you to be sorry about?' he asked gently. 'You have done what you set out to do. Mission accomplished.'

'I know . . . it's just that . . .'

He stroked the back of her head as it lay on his shoulder. 'Shhh! You don't need to say anything. I understand.'

She lifted her face to his and they kissed passionately, each of them grateful for a chance to let their feelings show. Then he led her upstairs to her room, undressed her and made the gentlest of love to her.

I have tried many times to understand my actions that night. Tried, I suppose, to excuse myself for what happened. I was, after all, only twenty years old, I had just undertaken an operation – the magnitude of which most normal people would never be asked to equal – and my relief at its accomplishment, coupled with the fact that I had survived – I was still alive – pushed all other thoughts of morality aside. I had not been brought up to let my feelings show in such a way. Indeed, there were times when I thought I would never 'know' a man. But here I was, more alive than I had ever felt. Endorphins, we call

them nowadays – those chemicals that can produce in a body excessive 'highs' – combined with the feeling of elation, banished all normal inhibitions without thought.

And Thierry? I don't think I considered what would be going through his mind. It was as if we had been thrown together in some scene from a film, and the moment he wrapped his arms around me he might have been Clark Gable and I Katherine Hepburn. Fanciful? Maybe. Infatuation? Possibly. But until one finds oneself in that situation, it is impossible to understand entirely the motivation of either party.

All I knew was that I wanted to be loved so deeply that evening; loved by a man I had observed at close quarters for several months and who, in spite of his vacillations between cavalier insouciance and intense workmanlike powers of reasoning, I had come to admire and to trust.

To go to bed with him seemed the most natural thing on earth, and at that moment I gave little thought to the morning. He was the gentlest and most courteous of love-makers. There was no haste, no rush, no force involved, just an overwhelming sense of giving on both sides.

But when I woke up in the morning, I was alone. Thierry had gone and I was left to muse on the events of the day before as a watery sun crept in at the window. I lay for some time between the sheets of a bed that had witnessed me turning from a girl into a woman in the twinkling of an eye. A French eye; an eye that sparkled.

And then the guilt came into play. That sneaking, dawning realisation of the perils of being carried away in the heat of the moment, of not only giving oneself away, but of letting down others. Of letting down Harry. How could I have done so? What could have possessed me? The feeling of elation was replaced by one of shame and confusion. What had the

*encounter meant to Thierry? What had it meant to me, come
to that, and how would it affect our working relationship? All
of these conflicting emotions would now come into play on a
rotational basis as I reasoned with myself and examined my
motivations. But confused as my feelings were, I was determined
that I would not let the events of that night affect my ability
to play my part in the team. The best thing, it seemed, was to
pretend it had never happened. I wondered if Thierry would
do the same.*

It was on the following morning, after she had come down for
breakfast, that Rosamund witnessed a state of affairs she had
not encountered before – that of Thierry being angry. At first
she thought he must be furious with her for last night, but it
soon became clear that this was not the case.

'What more do they want?' he asked Eric.

Rosamund poured herself a coffee from the pot that stood
on the stove, and quietly sat down at the table. Her fair hair
was tied back and she wore a floral-patterned blouse under a
pair of drill dungarees that had been provided for her use by
Madeleine and Paulette. Her face, freshly washed in the basin
of her room, glowed with life. Her eyes sparkled.

Thierry glanced at her as she entered, and the sight momentarily interrupted his flow. 'Good morning,' he said, his face
breaking into the gentlest of smiles. 'Did you sleep well?'

'Yes, thank you. Like a log.'

'Like what?'

'Nothing. It's just a saying. I slept well, thank you.'

The niceties having been accomplished, and Thierry, having
gathered his thoughts once more, continued, 'It's bloody impossible. How the hell can we get a photograph?'

Rosamund was puzzled. 'A photograph of what?' she asked,

grateful to have something to take her mind off the confusion of thoughts that buzzed around inside her head.

Thierry shrugged and tossed a hand in the direction of Eric, an indication that the explanation would be left to him.

'The RAF want proof that the machine is out of action. If we can't convince them, then the bombing raids on the Peugeot factory will continue.'

'But that's not fair!' exclaimed Rosamund, realising in an instant that she might sound like a spoiled child. 'The whole point of the exercise was to prevent the factory being bombed, to put the press out of action without loss of life. And now they want to continue their raids?'

'It would seem so,' agreed Thierry, his anger subsiding as that of Rosamund grew.

Rosamund hesitated, searching for words. Eventually she said, 'So how can we prove it?'

Eric butted in. 'By taking photographs of the damaged press and showing that it cannot possibly be repaired.'

Rosamund slumped back in her chair. 'How on earth can we get those?'

Thierry, leaning against the sink by the kitchen window, took a sip of his coffee. 'Easy. We send you to the gate with a camera. You smile sweetly at the guards, say you are a journalist and ask if you can take a few snaps of the damage caused by the explosion last night. The guards bow courteously and let you in. You take the photographs, breeze out and we post them to London.'

Rosamund sighed. 'Very funny.'

Then Thierry said, 'Actually, I think there *is* a way.'

Eric and Rosamund regarded him quizzically.

'But I'm not prepared to put our team at risk again. This one is down to Henri.'

'I thought we were not involving Henri any more?' said Rosamund.

Thierry frowned. 'What is your saying? "Needs must when the devil drives"?'

'So what will you do?'

'Henri has contacts. Secure contacts. All we need is one of them to pose as an insurance man – he probably knows someone who really is in insurance – and for them to enter the factory, take the required photographs and give them to us to pass on. Henri will have to talk to Robert Peugeot, of course, and make sure it can be arranged. Peugeot won't be very pleased, having already taken the risk of allowing us in to . . . do the deed . . . but it will no doubt seem preferable to leaving his factory at risk from bombing raids.'

'When we had already assured him that it would not.'

'Exactly.'

'You think it can be done?'

'It must be. And when Monsieur Peugeot – and Henri – realise the likely outcome of failure to come up with the goods – and the consequent loss of life – I don't see how either of them can refuse. The biggest problem will be getting the job done quickly. We need to get out of here as soon as possible. The Gestapo will be stepping up their enquiries and it would be safer if we were away from here.'

Henri was a resourceful man; his position within the Resistance was respected and his contacts comprehensive. The required operative was located, Robert Peugeot was placated – as much as was possible – the 'insurance man' was instructed and dispatched to do the job, and the tension within the house for the duration of the exercise was palpable.

When, two days later, an envelope containing the required

photographs arrived, Thierry, Rosamund and Eric laid them out on the kitchen table and marvelled at the total success of the operation. It was clear that the damage to the tank press was irreparable; it would need to be replaced, and that would take weeks or even months.

Thierry was especially complimentary. 'Well done, Christiane,' he said to Rosamund. Then he added, 'You clearly are something of an expert when it comes to shaking things to their foundations.'

Rosamund blushed.

'Now let's get ourselves out of here. Tomorrow morning we leave early.'

Chapter 22

LONDON

NOVEMBER 1941

'And bold and hard adventures t' undertake,
Leaving his country for his country's sake.'

Charles Fitzgeffrey, 'Sir Francis Drake', 1596

Aunt Venetia was uneasy. She told herself she was being unreasonable; that such feelings were bound to be experienced when your nearest and dearest were posted overseas in a war. But there was more to it than that. Something in her waters told her all was not well. It might be intuition, it might be imagination, but it was not something she felt she could ignore. It had been a month since Rosamund's departure. A month of worry, uncertainty and silence. Of course she had not expected to hear any details; she was well informed enough to understand that secrecy – even among one's intimates who had inside knowledge – was a code that was strictly adhered to; especially when it came to the likes of Messrs Felpham and Belgate. Sir Patrick Felpham might appear to be a bit of an old buffer, but Venetia was aware that much of his bluster was nothing more than a cover – a means of putting off the scent anyone who might become too curious. How could anyone so seemingly otherworldly possibly have anything to do with the secret service? She had long since learned the futility of questioning the precise nature of his work – 'This and that, my dear, this and that' – but knew that he was involved in covert operations. It was also thanks to his good offices that certain provisions were more readily available to her than to other households – even in Eaton Square – provided she could be relied upon to host dinner parties that would help to 'facilitate connections', as he put it. The fact that he was something of a trencherman meant that such arrangements had an added advantage in these times of privation.

Charles Belgate was a different kettle of fish altogether. He was one of her oldest friends and before the war had held a senior position at the Foreign Office. But he was retired now, and just how serious or vital his role was in wartime intelligence or international relations, she had yet to ascertain. His acquaintanceship with General de Gaulle might be historic rather than current, but she suspected there was more to Charles Belgate's involvement that met the eye. She knew it was unlikely that she would find out the precise nature of such work – in that respect he was as adept as Patrick Felpham at deflecting enquiries – but he might at the very least be able to reassure her of Rosamund's safety. He owed her that at least. It would take all her charm and cunning, she knew, but she had not lived the life she had, among the people she had, without picking up on vibrations from time to time. She would winkle it out of him somehow; at least, that was her intention.

This was one of the reasons why she had arranged a dinner party. Not a large one – just a handful of friends who could be relied upon to 'get on' and who would make pockets of conversation that would distract the rest of the party when she found a moment to ask questions that were not for widespread debate.

The frequent bombing raids on London had subsided, and although life could not be said to have returned to normal, the nightly journeys to the air raid shelters were in abeyance, and people did their best to keep up flagging spirits of an evening with songs around the parlour piano, visits to the local pub or, in Lady Reeves's case, with a reestablishment of her 'little dinners'.

Mrs Heffer and her brother the allotment gardener – carrots and parsnips particularly good this year – had been pressed into service as usual, and Patience Westmacott – whose presence at the 'de Gaulle dinner', where she had buttonholed the *charge d'affaires* as though he were some recalcitrant shopkeeper, was still fresh in Aunt Venetia's mind – had been dragooned into service once more: her strident tones would be a suitable distraction for anyone intent on eavesdropping when Venetia found her moment to quiz Lord Belgate.

'The *placement*, Mrs Heffer; you have the placement?'

Mrs Heffer, with the patience of a saint, pointed to the red morocco-covered seating planner resting in its usual place on the small table beside the fireplace, so that guests, while warming themselves against the winter chill, could ascertain their place at table.

'Ah, yes. Of course. Must just check . . .' Aunt Venetia ran her eye over the slips of white paper arranged around the depiction of the oval table in last-minute scrutiny. It was the third time she had done so in the last hour, but then it was important that confrontations should be avoided, that good humour should prevail, and that all her guests should feel they were having a good time, the better to put them in the mood to relax and – perhaps – be more forthcoming than was the norm.

Satisfied that all was well (as indeed it had been the last time she had checked just twenty minutes ago), she enquired of her cook-housekeeper, 'And the claret?'

'Decanted. Four bottles. White wine in the cellar to be brought up just before the meal. Port and brandy in the drawing room. Ned will wait on.'

'Yes, yes, of course.'

Mrs Heffer's brother was pressed into service on these occasions, now that the Reeves household was run on a skeleton staff. He was not exactly a liveried footman, but he did wear his three-piece Sunday suit and employed a liberal amount of brilliantine to tame his unruly thatch, which, on a bad day, resembled an exploded Brillo pad. Ned Heffer's greatest attribute (aside from vegetable growing) was an ability to be totally unimpressed, however grand the company, and to say nothing throughout the evening. In this respect, he was a godsend to Lady Reeves.

Lord and Lady Belgate, Sir Patrick and Lady Felpham, Sir Basil and Lady Flynn (he a royal courtier, she a lady who lunched), Patience Westmacott and her brother Hamish, and the Hendersons – an elderly couple from next door, along with their bachelor son – made up the party of twelve, and it was not long before the log fire and a glass or two of Pol Roger warmed up the party sufficiently for there to be a lively buzz in the drawing room.

In spite of her underlying anxiety on this particular evening, Venetia Reeves was an experienced hostess, and not one to charge in like a bull at a gate when she needed information. Such a mission was to be undertaken with stealth and guile. She did seat Charles Belgate on her left but, as etiquette demanded, assiduously refrained from talking to him during the first course – one of Mrs Heffer's more adventurous soups – and during the main course and pudding kept the conversation light and innocuous.

The table was narrow enough to permit conversation across its width as well as between neighbours on either side, and before long Venetia could cast an eye around and see that the evening was moving along nicely. Sir Patrick Felpham was the only one whose attention was given wholly to the contents of his plate rather than to conversation, but then Venetia reminded herself that as well as a reflection on the quality of the meal, it was no doubt a useful ploy when it came to deflecting questions that he would rather not be asked. She smiled to herself and looked across at Patience Westmacott, whose dissertation on the relative merits of root vegetables in a wartime winter, while not fully engaging Sir Basil Flynn, had at least given him the chance to savour the 1929 St Julien in his glass. Ever the adept courtier, he nodded sagely from time to time and smiled distractedly, his mind no doubt elsewhere. Venetia sighed and hoped that she had not totally ruined his evening. At least the claret would be some consolation.

And then she rose and motioned the party through the double doors to the drawing room where good coffee and little cubes of Turkish delight (thanks to the intervention of HM Government) were served as the diners sank into the sofas and easy chairs ranged around the room, the log fire replenished with timber thanks to Ned's good offices.

Some twenty minutes after they had retired to the drawing room, Venetia saw her opportunity. Lady Flynn had risen from her seat next to the fire, where she had been engaged in conversation with Lord Belgate, and left to powder her nose. Spotting her opening, Venetia lowered herself into the space on the two-seater sofa. 'Ah, there you are!' exclaimed her quarry. 'I thought you were ignoring me.'

Venetia took the remark as a compliment. Clearly she had not been oppressively attentive.

'Oh, you have more important people than me to speak to,' she offered.

'Not true,' came the reply. 'How have you been? We haven't seen you for a while.'

'No,' replied Venetia. 'I've been battling on.' She tried not to sound too sorry for herself. 'Rather rattling around in this house, if you must know.'

'Yes. I suppose it is rather large. But useful. For entertaining and suchlike, eh?'

'So it would seem.' She paused. 'But I think my entertaining days are numbered.'

Charles Belgate looked concerned. 'Nonsense. Nobody does it like you . . .'

'Except Emerald Cunard and Laura Corrigan and Edith Londonderry and a whole host of ladies who do it rather better and on a much grander scale . . .'

Her companion sensed a change in mood and his face showed signs of concern. 'I thought you liked hosting these parties. Especially the ones that are really . . . useful?'

'I did, Charles; but I think my heart has rather gone out of it since Rosamund left.'

'I see. Yes, well, I can understand that. But the thing is . . . while the Cunards and Londonderrys of this world might host grander gatherings . . . er . . . present company excepted,' he said, winking and trying to make light of the subject, 'yours are really rather more pleasurable and every bit as useful.'

'You think so?'

'I know so.'

Venetia turned and gazed at the burning logs in the grate. 'Maybe my heart has just gone out of it.'

Lord Belgate reached out and took her hand in his. 'These are bloody times, Venetia,' he said softly. 'Don't let them get you down. We need you – I need you – to keep our spirits up but also to keep the wheels oiled. You may not think that what you do is important, but I can assure you that it makes a real difference to the war effort.'

'Oh, I'm not so sure,' said Venetia weakly.

'I'm telling you it does,' said Lord Belgate earnestly. 'If you hadn't had de Gaulle around that evening and made him feel comfortable, things could have been far more tricky than they turned out – and that's tricky enough. You underestimate your ability as a facilitator.'

Venetia saw her opportunity. 'Oh, that wasn't me; it was Rosamund. It was she who charmed him.'

Lord Belgate looked reflective and, thought Venetia, more than a little apprehensive. 'Yes, she did rather, didn't she?'

'I wish I knew where she was. This house is very quiet without her.'

'I can imagine.'

'That's why I'm thinking of moving away.'

A look of alarm crossed Charles Belgate's face. 'Where will you go?'

Venetia shrugged. 'Oh, I don't know. Somewhere away from the bombs. Somewhere smaller, where there are fewer outgoings. I'm sure you can find another hostess to take my place.'

'Don't even think of it. Come on. What can I do to help? There must be something that will make it easier?'

Venetia saw her opening. 'Well, if I had Rosamund back, that would help.'

She looked her dinner guest in the eye. 'I don't suppose you know where she is?'

Charles Belgate sighed. 'You know better than to ask me that, Venetia.'

'But you do know, don't you?'

The noble lord rubbed his chin, then took a sip of the brandy at his elbow. He set it down on the table and turned to face his inquisitor. 'She's been doing vital work, Venetia, that much I can tell you. She's been astonishingly brave and remarkably effective.'

Venetia nodded. 'I knew you'd know.'

Charles Belgate looked uncomfortable. 'Look, I can't possibly give you any details . . .'

'No. I understand that, but you can tell me that she is still alive. You can tell me that she's safe. Surely that isn't a state secret.'

Lord Belgate did not meet her eye. 'She is still alive,' he said softly.

'And safe?'

'At the moment, yes.'

'And what does that mean? Is she in danger?'

The look on his face was as stern as she could recall having seen it. 'Yes, she is in danger, but then all . . . operatives . . . are in danger. It goes with the job.'

Now it was Venetia's turn to take the hand of her companion. 'Get her out, Charles. Please!'

He regarded her with a look of concern. 'Venetia, everyone who goes to war takes risks – whether it is the Tommy-on-the-shore or Johnny-head-in-air. You're asking me to use our friendship to make a special case for one person. Much as Rosamund is a person I have come to care for – to feel close to, in a funny sort of way, thanks to her relationship with you

– I cannot use my influence, such as it is, to intervene on your – or her – behalf. It would be totally unethical, don't you see?'

Venetia thought for a moment and then said, 'Yes. Of course. It was wrong of me to ask.'

Charles Belgate patted her hand. 'Not wrong. Just . . . inappropriate. And totally understandable.'

'She's all I have left, you see, Charles. I've always thought of myself as a strong woman – I *am* a strong woman – but I've reached an age (rather older than you) where my appetite for battling on is not as durable as it once was. I'm weary of making do and mending, of conjuring up meals out of nothing (and I do appreciate your help on that front) and of doing it all in isolation, with only Mrs Heffer and her brother Ned for company. I mean, they're very willing, but hardly intellectually stimulating.'

Charles Belgate nodded sympathetically.

'Oh, I know I have these little dinner parties to amuse me, but they are quite thin on the ground now, and you, and lots of my other friends, are either too busy managing a war or else have moved out to the country.' She sighed heavily. 'I've really rather lost my appetite for it all. I know that's not what I should be saying when the rest of the country is knuckling down and fighting Gerry, but I'm really rather worn down by it, and the prospect of losing Rosamund when Celine has already been taken from us is more than I can bear. Do you understand?'

Her companion nodded. 'Yes, perfectly. And I sympathise, too. Our son Billy is up there somewhere in the clouds. I keep an eye on him, but it's a strain.'

'But he's a young man, Charles. Young men are meant to fight for their country.'

'And young women are not?'

'That's not what I mean and you know it. But there are other ways of fighting a war rather than being on the front line, and rightly or wrongly I really would rather that Rosamund was a little closer to home.'

Charles Belgate squeezed Venetia's hand. 'She did choose to go, you know.'

'Yes. I'm aware of that. And there was absolutely nothing I could do to stop her. Perhaps I'm just being selfish, Charles, but with her parents dead, I feel that I have a responsibility for her safety. My brother did entrust her to me, and although he is no longer with us, I do feel a responsibility to his memory. Maybe I should have been firmer—'

Charles Belgate cut in. 'Do you really think Rosamund would have listened? Do you honestly think you could have deflected her from her intention to "do her bit"?'

Venetia sighed heavily. 'No, I suppose not. But I just have a feeling that she might have bitten off more than she can chew. There's an unease in me, Charles, that I cannot suppress. Not just what you might call a "normal" worry. It's deeper than that. I have a distinct feeling that Rosamund is in mortal danger. She's young, Charles, and inexperienced in the ways of the world . . .'

'Like most of those who are fighting for this country of ours, Venetia. I often think that it is we older ones who should be out there on the front line. We've had a life. We are expendable. Why don't they put guns in our hands and send us off to war and let the young ones stay behind and enjoy what we have already experienced?'

'I've said the same thing to Rosamund,' said Venetia wistfully.

Charles Belgate smiled sympathetically. 'But it doesn't work like that, does it? Our reflexes would be too slow, our energy and stamina levels sorely lacking and it would all end in disaster.'

'I suppose so.' Venetia turned away from him and got up from the sofa. 'So I must just learn to live with it?'

Charles Belgate rose at the same time. 'Don't lose heart, Venetia. I'm sure Rosamund will come through. She's a resourceful girl and she has her wits about her. That counts for a lot, you know.'

'But will it be enough, Charles? That's what worries me. Her French is very good, I'll grant you. But when it comes to pretending to be someone she is not? Well, she's always been far too honest for that.'

Chapter 23

BAKER STREET, LONDON

NOVEMBER 1941

'Little thieves are hanged, but great ones escape.'

Seventeenth century proverb

'What do you mean the moment has come? What moment?'

Charles Belgate was sitting at his desk. In front of him, experiencing more than a hint of *déjà vu*, stood Doris Kilgarth.

'To get them out. Your "Scarlet Nightingale" and her colleagues.'

Her superior flinched in a moment of irritation born of fear and impatience. 'She is not *my* Scarlet Nightingale, as you put it. She is *our* Scarlet Nightingale.'

'Yes. Sorry. Well, it's confirmed. We know now they've been rumbled and that the powers that be have identified them.'

'Bloody hell,' he murmured. Then, almost to himself, 'Always listen to a woman's intuition.'

'I'm sorry?'

'Something that someone said to me recently.' He shook his head to clear it of extraneous thoughts, then asked, 'Do we know who gave them away?'

Doris Kilgarth frowned and shook her head. 'It's confusing. There are conflicting messages coming out from a couple of cells not too far away. They all operate independently but sometimes their paths cross – if not physically then in terms of information received.'

Lord Belgate motioned her to sit at the chair in front of the desk. 'Go on.'

'What is common to them both – or all three of them, it would seem – is that there is a leak. There have been a couple of occasions recently where we've had to relocate our groups pretty swiftly. We've been successful, but more by good luck than judgement.'

'And now?'

'Thierry Foustier's team – your . . . *our* . . . Nightingale and Ridley the wireless operator – managed successfully to put a vital piece of equipment at the Peugeot factory in Sochaux out of action. It's something we've been trying to do for ages but it was proving impossible. Anyway, the trio succeeded and even managed to get photographs to us showing the extent of the damage. It was quite something, I can tell you. There will be no German tanks produced at that factory for a while, thanks to their efforts.'

'I knew their mission was sabotage but I was unaware of the intimate details. It was a successful mission then?'

'Totally.'

'Is that why we have to get them out?'

'Partly. The Gestapo will be keen as mustard in that area now – sniffing out the likely perpetrators. Your Scarlet Nightingale and her bunch are an effective little team and we'd like to move them on to other operations – especially those involving sabotage. Young Rosamund has quite a flair for explosives by all accounts.'

'That would come as a surprise to her aunt Venetia,' murmured Lord Belgate.

'Sorry?'

'Nothing. Just a private thought. Her aunt has been on at me to get her back. I explained that I had very little influence and that if I intervened to extract every operative whose elderly relative worried for their safety, then I'd have no one left out there.'

'You didn't tell her that you'd already asked me?'

'No. Venetia doesn't really know how involved I am, anyway. She has her suspicions that I still have connections here, but that's all. I'm afraid I offered her little solace.'

'You didn't tell her that her niece is in danger then?'

'I told her that every operative is in danger.' He stood up and walked to the window, gazing out over the dreary winter land-scape of grey roofs and chimneys, soot-laden walls and piles of rubble, brightened only by the occasional red of a London bus snaking through the traffic. He turned around to face Miss Kilgarth: 'So what has happened to change things?'

'Operations like this one, that make a big difference, tend to give rise to extreme feelings, as you'd expect. Those who are annoyed by such success work harder to try and ferret out the perpetrators. There's a strong military presence around the factory – not to mention the Gestapo – but there is also a complex Resistance movement. The stronger the movement, the more sense it makes for the Germans to try and infiltrate it.'

'And you think they have infiltrated this group?'

'Somehow, yes. But we can't work out who the double agent is. Henri Dubois, who has arranged their accommodation, is one of our most reliable contacts.'

'Family?'

'Yes. A wife, a son and a daughter, all ostensibly onside.'

'Someone else then?'

'Possibly. We've done our best to keep our trio isolated from all other cells. We had hoped that only Henri and his family would know of their presence but . . .'

'Leaks?'

'Invariably. However hard we try. Someone sees a new face and asks questions of someone else who knows someone who . . . you know the sort of thing.'

'And you think we need to get them out?'

'Yes. And quickly. I'm making the necessary arrangements with the RAF. I want them airlifted by Lysander tomorrow night – provided we're not too late, and provided we can find an aircraft.'

'Do they know yet?'

'They know there's a danger they've been rumbled. I don't want to radio them again until everything is set up, not least in case our messages are being intercepted. We're in regular contact but at random, pre-arranged times and different frequencies and they know to keep changing their locations for transmission to minimise the risk of being intercepted. For now they've been told to lie low and keep out of trouble.'

'So they are aware of the imminent danger.'

'Yes.' Doris Kilgarth shrugged. 'It's a bit of a bugger, sir. They've only been out there a short time and they were doing so well.'

'Yes.'

'Still, if we can get them back safely from this sortie, we can set them to work somewhere else.'

'Yes.' Charles Belgate looked troubled. 'Will you tell her aunt that or shall I?'

A rueful smile flickered across Doris Kilgarth's face. 'We haven't got them out yet.'

Chapter 24

FESCHES-LE-CHÂTEL

NOVEMBER 1941

'If the Normans are disciplined under a just and firm
rule they are men of great valour, who . . . fight
resolutely to overcome all enemies. But without such rule
they tear each other to pieces and destroy themselves,
for they hanker after rebellion, cherish sedition, and are
ready for any treachery.'

William the Conqueror, attributed deathbed speech, 1087

A cold wind had sprung up, whipping across the fields and
tearing the turnip tops to shreds. The farmer had tethered a
couple of goats to the other side of the hedge that bordered
the barn where Rosamund, Thierry and Eric were billeted.

Rosamund looked out of her bedroom window. The sun was
only just beginning to rise, and it did so in the privacy cloak
of dense cloud. Perhaps that was the best kind of weather in
which to slip away, rather than in the blinding light of unsea-
sonal sunshine.

Those two days immediately after the operation passed in a kind of haze. Thierry said nothing about our encounter. I think that was what I expected. I had enough sense to hope that nothing further would occur – partly because I felt it would get in the way of our working relationship, might even put us in danger – but also because I had to cling on to the hope that Harry was alive and that my loyalty should be to him. But I do admit that I occasionally dreamt about Thierry – a flight of fancy, I suppose, for I felt that there was no harm in that. I worked hard at putting it out of my mind, though occasionally I caught Eric looking at me out of the corner of his eye. He never said anything, but he must have known what happened that night.

I consoled myself with the fact that Harry had made a declaration of love. But did that declaration still hold good? It had been made over a year ago and since then we had had no communication with one another. It all seemed so distant; such a long time ago. So much had happened in the interim. I wanted to believe that nothing had altered between us. In a way it was true, but then so much else had changed, and I could not assume that he would still feel the same.

Throughout my life I have always prized loyalty above all else, and I could not help but feel that on that one night in the heat of the moment I had let Harry down. Thierry was with me every day; Harry was . . . I knew not where. I was not even certain that he was alive. All these thoughts would whirl in my head until I reached a stage where I had to banish them and live for today. I found myself in a foreign country, in danger of my life and reliant on a handful of people I had known only a few months. It was an unnatural state of affairs, and I reasoned that I could not be expected to function rationally under such circumstances. It was, I suppose, an easy way of excusing my behaviour, but that behaviour would very soon be tested.

Rosamund washed, dressed and descended the narrow staircase to the kitchen. She was the first to do so and, after starting the fire in the stove with dry kindling and logs, set the kettle on the hob and patiently waited for it to boil. It would, she knew, take quite some time. Perhaps they should not wait, but just set off as quickly as possible. Where to? That much information Thierry had not yet imparted. Their main task accomplished, the trio must now make good their escape, before the net closed around them. Oh, why did the other two not wake? Thierry had explained the night before that they must leave under cover of darkness, and it was now almost light. Perhaps he and Eric had drunk more Scotch whisky than was good for them. They had offered her a glass but she had declined, in spite of the fact that the Dubois family had insisted that they should celebrate their achievement. Paulette had brought round the bottle – there was seldom any to be found in France – and left it on the table with a note. Thierry had smiled and said it would be churlish to refuse. She looked at her watch. It was half past seven.

Rosamund tapped her fingers impatiently on the pine table. She could leave it no longer. She must wake them. She climbed the stairs and knocked on the door of their bedroom. No answer. She called, 'Thierry! Marcel!'

Still no answer. She opened the door and saw both men fast asleep in their respective beds. She walked over to where Thierry lay and shook him. Still he did not wake, and his breathing was slow and deep. She shook him again and again until eventually he was roused from his deep slumber. 'What? What is it?' he murmured.

'We need to be away. It's light already.'

'Mmm?' He looked befuddled.

Rosamund walked over to Eric's bed and shook him. He, too, took some moments to come round. 'Where am I?' he asked, in English.

Rosamund admonished him for this slip, and through a thick cloud of confusion, he asked in French, 'What happened?'

Thierry was now holding his head and frowning. 'Christ! What was in that Scotch? I only had a couple of small glasses.'

Rosamund's eyes widened. 'Can you see me?' she asked.

'Of course I can see you,' said Thierry, clearly irritated at the question, but also at his own inability to fire on all cylinders.

'How many fingers?'

'Too many,' he muttered. Then: 'Bloody hell! They put something in the Scotch.'

'Who did?' asked Eric.

'Whoever left it.'

'Paulette left it,' said Rosamund. 'Oh, my God!'

She rushed across to the window and drew back the calico of the curtains to take a better look at the dawning day. It was then that she saw the small gathering of men in the corner of the field. Farm workers came and went on a daily basis, but they seldom stood in groups like this one unless they were being charged with some collective task. Somehow that did not seem to be the case here. Something told Rosamund that all was not as it should be.

'Oh, no!' she murmured.

'What is it?' asked Thierry.

'Come and look – if you can see straight.'

Rosamund pointed to the group of men, perhaps fifty yards away. 'What do you make of that?'

Thierry peered through the window. 'Just farm workers, I suppose.'

'Are you sure?'

He looked again, and then his body tensed. 'No. Not just farm workers. There are three soldiers in the middle of them. Gestapo.'

'Something up?' asked Eric as he stumbled out of bed.

'Is your transmitter safe?'

'Stowed in the eaves. It should be.'

'Nothing we can do then. Except . . .' Thierry turned to Rosamund. 'Put your coat on. At least we can get you out of here.'

Thierry threw on some clothes as Eric endeavoured to do the same, then he ran downstairs, motioning Rosamund to follow him.

'Take the shopping basket and make as if you are going down to the *boulangerie*. You should be able to keep them at a safe distance as you pass.' He turned to Eric who was rubbing his eyes in an attempt to focus more clearly.

'Eric? You can go out a couple of minutes after Rosamund has left. Come on, man! Walk alongside the field under cover of the hedge. Keep your eyes open – if that's not impossible – watch their movements at a distance and come back here in an hour if the coast is clear. It may be nothing, but it is much better if we split up.'

Rosamund took down her coat from the back of the kitchen door. Her heart was beating rapidly. 'When shall I come back?'

But she did not hear the answer. It was masked by a hammering on the door.

'Aufmachen! Aufmachen!'

Thierry glanced at both his companions. There was no way out. Without saying any more, he opened the door. Three members of the Gestapo were blocking the way. Two were carrying pistols and a third a machine gun.

'Gentlemen, good morning! What can we do for you?'

Chapter 25

FESCHES-LE-CHÂTEL

NOVEMBER 1941

'They rose in dark and evil days.'

John Kells Ingram, 'The Memory of the Dead', 1843

'*Ihre Papiere bitte.*'

'Papers, yes, of course,' replied Thierry in French. 'Christiane, Marcel, your papers for the gentlemen, please.'

Rosamund caught a glimpse of the three implacable faces over Thierry's shoulder. Their uniforms bore the insignia of the Schutzstaffel. A shiver went down Rosamund's spine, though she fought hard to look unperturbed. All three of them stepped back to retrieve their papers, and as they did so, the three uniformed men walked forward into the small kitchen. They did not take off their hats, steely grey with shining peaks, above which shone the sinister motif of the Waffen SS – a silver skull, surmounted by a spread eagle, its talons grasping the all-too-familiar swastika. It was the first time Rosamund had seen it up close.

She glanced at Thierry and Eric as they climbed the stairs, but none of them spoke. They parted at the top and walked into their separate rooms. Rosamund had already packed her bag, which sat at the foot of her bed. She fished into the pocket inside it and pulled out her identity card and papers, then she turned towards the door and began to descend the stairs ahead of Thierry whose belongings were not yet packed, thanks to the unexpected effects of the previous night's whisky. Who could have been responsible for its contamination, for that was obviously the case? The Dubois family, or some outside agency? She thanked God that she herself had declined to join them. At least she had managed to keep a clear head; she would certainly need it now.

She handed her papers to the member of the trio who seemed to be the most senior. He was tall and gaunt with piercing pale blue eyes that transmitted a coldness she had rarely experienced before. His insignia showed him to be an Obersturmführer; the other two were of more junior rank – Untersturmführers, if she had remembered correctly from her training. The senior officer stowed his pistol in his holster, all the while fixing her with that icy gaze, while the other two retained their weapons and looked around them suspiciously as if expecting an attack from some hidden force. It never came.

'Christiane de Rossignol?'

Rosamund nodded.

'Where are you from?'

'Dijon.'

'Your occupation?'

'Bookkeeper.'

The officer smiled, but it was a cold smile that did nothing to dispel the chill that pervaded the room. 'You were at the factory in Sochaux the night of the explosion?'

Rosamund's heart pounded, but she did not let her anxiety show. 'Yes. I left just before it happened.'

'Convenient.'

'Lucky.'

The officer shot her a cynical smile. Rosamund was reminded of the wolf in *Little Red Riding Hood* – an image that was swiftly dispelled when she reminded herself that this was far from a fairy tale.

'Why were you there?'

'I was asked to go over some figures. In the accounts. There was a discrepancy in the costings for maintenance of certain pieces of equipment. I was asked to check and see where the mistakes had been made.'

'And were you able to find them?' The face was expressionless; the voice shot through with sarcasm.

'Yes. It was a simple oversight; nothing very complicated.'

'Explain it to me.'

Rosamund felt cornered. Why had she taken on the guise of a bookkeeper? She, to whom figures might as well be a foreign language. In measured tones, she heard herself say, 'The contra account column had been confused with the bought-in ledger. The two had been transposed, and if you knew where to look, it was easy to see how the two could have been confused.'

There was a long pause, in which the world – or this small part of it – appeared to stand still.

The Gestapo officer broke the silence. 'And then you left?'

'Yes. I was checked in and checked out. You will discover that from the records at the factory checkpoint.'

The officer's stare became, if anything, even more menacing. 'It is because of the records at the factory checkpoint that we are here, Mademoiselle de Rossignol.' He rolled his tongue around the name with unnecessary relish, then closed the identity card and folded up Rosamund's papers, but he did not hand them back. The two junior officers stood by, mute and unmoving as the interrogation progressed.

Where was Thierry? thought Rosamund. What was taking him so long?

'How long have you been in Fesches-le-Châtel?'

'We all came here a few weeks ago,' said Thierry, interrupting. He was downstairs now, his papers in his hand.

The officer's expression remained impassive, but there was a renewed note of irritation in his voice as he remarked, 'I was asking the young lady. And you are?'

'Thierry Foustier.'

'Your papers, please.'

Thierry handed them over.

The officer unfolded and scrutinised them, saying, without looking up, 'There are three of you?'

'Yes,' answered Thierry. 'Marcel will be down in a moment.'

'All living in the same house?'

'Yes.'

'How so?'

'We have been put up here while we work for the Peugeots. Christiane is an accountant, Marcel and I work for the insurance company.'

'So you are here to assess the damage done to the factory?'

'We came here before that,' explained Thierry calmly. 'To look at the machinery and make evaluations. We are a small part of a much larger team.'

'Oh, I don't doubt that. I think that is the first honest reply you have given me.' The senior officer turned to his two subordinates. 'Search the house. Leave no . . . how do they say in English?' he asked pointedly. 'Ah, yes: "Leave no stone unturned" . . .'

Thierry and Rosamund remained silent and gazed ahead blankly, determined to give nothing away.

'And where is your friend? The third member of the party. Marcel, you say his name is?'

'Yes. He'll be down in a minute,' confirmed Thierry. 'I'm sure he's looking for his papers. You caught us by surprise.'

'I am sure we did. But then, that was the intention.'

The two Untersturmführers, still armed, split up – one pushing past them towards the small sitting room, the other mounting the twisting staircase in the direction of Eric. It was only moments later that the uncomfortable silence was shattered by the sound of breaking glass, followed by a deafening crash as an unidentifiable object sailed past the window behind them. It was followed by Eric Ridley, who landed safely and then rapidly took off across the fields.

The officer who had clearly found nothing of interest in the small sitting room, ran back into the kitchen. The senior officer, no longer impassive, motioned him to run in the direction of the commotion as his SS colleague – clearly unwilling to follow Eric's example and exit via the upstairs window – came running down the stairs shouting, *'Funksender! Gebrochen!'* and shaking the machine gun which had jammed and consequently saved Eric's life.

Thierry glanced sideways at Rosamund, but neither of them moved.

The senior officer, now in possession of incontrovertible proof that all was not as it purported to be in the house of the three newcomers to Fesches-le-Châtel, flashed Rosamund a brief smile. 'Does your friend always leave the house in such an unorthodox fashion?'

Still the two captives said not a word. It was clear that Eric, aware that his wireless transmitter was hardly likely to remain undiscovered, had followed the instructions given at Wanborough Manor and done his best to render it useless before endeavouring to make an escape himself. If his compatriots were to be arrested, then he was the only one with any chance of escaping with whatever information he had been unable to transmit.

Thierry and Rosamund stood motionless under the watchful eye of the senior officer, who now had his pistol trained on them. Outside the cottage they heard shouts, followed by rapid gunfire. The machine-gun carrying officer had clearly managed to un-jam his weapon and open fire on the retreating form of Eric.

Silence followed, during which the three figures in the kitchen were as still as if they had been turned to stone. At length the kitchen door burst open and the junior officer reappeared. The senior officer regarded him questioningly. The subordinate shook his head. '*Ich konnte ihn nicht fangen.*'

Rosamund and Thierry looked at each other once more. This time Thierry smiled. As he did so, the junior officer slammed the butt of his weapon into his ribs. Thierry crumpled to the floor and Rosamund instinctively bent down to help him. Not that she remembered doing so. The butt of the machine gun was brought into service once more – this time on the back of Rosamund's head. The rest was blackness.

Chapter 26

LONDON

NOVEMBER 1941

'When sorrows come, they come not single spies,
But in battalions.'

William Shakespeare, *Hamlet*, 1601

Having no children of her own, and with her only sibling insti-
tutionalised, Doris Kilgarth invested in her female operatives
rather more emotional weight than she knew in her heart to be
advisable.

When the news came through that Rosamund – along with
the Frenchman Thierry Foustier – had been apprehended by the
Gestapo, her heart sank. It was not simply that she dreaded
informing Charles Belgate of the situation, but that she felt
personally responsible for the young woman's safety. She had
lost too many operatives over the past year, and losing this one
wounded her deeply. She saw in Rosamund Hanbury something
of herself as a young woman. The very thought might leave the
likes of Lord Belgate incredulous, for there was little physical
similarity between the two women, but Doris recognised in

Rosamund a steely determination and a swiftness of apprehension that she herself had possessed in those early days in the service.

Granted, the freshness of approach and the youthful zeal had diminished somewhat over the years, but the determination to succeed had never faltered. If Rosamund Hanbury were to lose her life . . . well, it was not something Doris wished to contemplate right now, even though such a possibility constituted a real and present danger.

Rather than confront Charles Belgate in person, she had taken what she knew to be the coward's way out, and had the decoded Top Secret memo delivered to him that morning. It was brief and to the point:

EYES ONLY

Patrice and Colette arrested
Hector at liberty or killed
No further information

She wondered how long it would take between the dispatch of the memo and the summons to his office. The answer was seventeen minutes and thirty-two seconds.

At first he did not speak. Doris had become accustomed to the sight of her superior's back as he surveyed the various restorative activities in Baker Street below. Today she had longer than usual to take in the exquisite cut of the pinstriped Savile Row suit, the polished brogues and the crisp white shirt collar that sat exactly half an inch above the suit and half an inch below the thinning grey hair that steadfastly remained on the head of this government mandarin.

When, eventually, he did turn round, she saw that his face

was drained of what little colour it usually possessed. In all her years in the service, she had never seen Charles Belgate display any high emotion other than indignation at another's procrastination, or irritation at some slap-dash piece of work.

He cleared his throat and asked evenly, 'Any further news?'

'No, sir. I'm afraid not.'

'Bloody awful business.'

'Yes, sir.'

'And after such a good job at the factory.'

'Yes.' Doris Kilgarth felt that the less she said the better, but knew that she would not escape without some form of inquisition.

'The information is reliable, I suppose?'

'I'm afraid so, sir. It was the last message that Marcel – that's Eric Ridley – managed to transmit before the other two were apprehended.'

'And he is at liberty or killed. Which?'

'Impossible to say. He sent the message and then would have destroyed his wireless transmitter and endeavoured to make his escape. Whether or not he succeeded, we don't yet know. He wanted to inform us that at least he was making an attempt to extricate himself from the situation.'

'That's a tactful way of putting it,' muttered the peer, only half to himself.

'All we can do is wait.'

'I suppose so.'

'I think I should warn you, sir, that it might be a long time before we get any news, if, indeed, we get any news at all.'

'Yes, Miss Kilgarth; I know how it works,' he said.

There was a complicit silence between them, then Doris asked, 'Do you ever wonder how we manage to carry on doing this, sir?'

Her boss spoke levelly: 'Every hour of every day, and most especially right now. But if it were not us, then it would be some other poor soul and I wouldn't wish it on my worst enemy.'

'No.'

'It's the age, you know.'

'Sir?'

'The age of those we send out there – often to their deaths. How can we do it, Doris? Tell me that. How can two old folk like us – you are younger than me, I know – but how can we send men and women . . . boys and girls, really . . . off to die in a foreign country when they've never had what amounts to a life?'

Doris tried to force a smile. 'It's not always the case. Some of them achieve great things and return safely.'

'Great things, eh? Like blowing up factories?'

'Yes.'

'Sordid, I call it. Not great.'

'But if they didn't, wouldn't the results be even more . . . sordid, as you put it?'

'Perhaps.' He turned once more to the window, as if looking for some kind of sign. 'I've fought too many wars, Doris, and that's the truth. I've no appetite for it. No appetite at all. Talking of which, I have to see Venetia Reeves tonight.'

'One of her suppers?'

'No. A visit to the theatre.'

'Something nice?' She blanched at the triteness of her question.

Lord Belgate turned back from the window. 'It couldn't be more inappropriate.' He winced and then said, '*Blithe Spirit*, at the Piccadilly.'

'Oh.'

'Yes. Anything remotely like "blithe" my spirit could not possibly be.'

Doris turned to leave, but paused a few feet from the door.

Charles Belgate noticed her hesitation. 'What is it?' he asked as she turned to face him.

'I don't know whether I should say this. I don't know whether you will want to hear it, or whether you will think I have acted irresponsibly.'

Charles Belgate's expression remained impassive. 'Go on.'

'I've sent a message to Hawksmoor.'

Chapter 27

PICCADILLY THEATRE, LONDON

NOVEMBER 1941

'It's discouraging to think how many people are shocked
by honesty and how few by deceit.'

Noel Coward, *Blithe Spirit*, 1941

'Charles! How lovely to see you! Come in, come in!'

Venetia Reeves was standing just inside the open door of her
box at the Piccadilly Theatre, her shoulders swathed in fur and
her ample bosom shimmering with sequins. In her hand was a
crystal flute half filled with champagne. She was having a reviver
– the sort of evening she needed to get her through the misery
of war. All too often now she found herself enveloped in gloom
– a state of affairs not helped by the fact that her niece was no
longer present to jolly her along, and Mrs Heffer's capacity for
scintillating badinage was somewhat slender.

Charles Belgate smiled bravely. He would have to choose his
moment carefully. This was not the most appropriate environ-
ment in which to break bad news, if, indeed, he were to find
what amounted to an appropriate opportunity.

'Champagne! Goodness!' he offered valiantly.

'Of course. We need to take our mind off things, don't we?' It was a statement which he found difficult to dispute.

'You know the Flynns . . .' she gestured in the direction of the fellow occupants of the box, who nodded and smiled a greeting. Charles looked over the edge of the box at the packed stalls below. 'Quite a house,' he mused.

'Yes. And Mr Coward's in. With . . . oh, what's the name of that strange woman? The one with the short, dark hair. Funny.'

Charles Belgate looked in the direction of Venetia's gaze. 'Beatrice Lillie?'

'That's her. And look who's next to her.'

'Mmm?' he asked absently.

'Look who's sitting next to Beatrice Lillie.' She nodded again in the direction of the star of stage and screen.

'The Mountbattens,' he murmured. 'And the Duff Coopers.'

'And Pamela Churchill. Look! Right next to them! Well . . . when it comes to social climbing, that woman has a very long ladder.'

Charles Belgate could not help but smile. The worries of the war may well have dented Venetia's customary insouciance but not her appetite for gossip, and at moments like this she proved that it was alive and well and living deep inside, just waiting for an excuse to slip out.

'Venetia, really!' he admonished her.

'Well, Charles, I'm all for a bit of colour in life, and I do enjoy the trappings of an advantageous marriage myself, but Pamela Churchill leaves me standing. You know she's packed it in with Randolph and is now angling for that Harriman fellow from America. Shameless! Quite shameless!'

Charles Belgate was unsure as to the seriousness of Venetia's remark until she winked at him and added, 'Isn't it wonderful!'

He laughed a little. It was a long time since he had done so, but deep in his heart he felt deceitful, as though keeping the news of her niece's welfare from her was somehow dishonest. He would tell her when the time was right, and that moment, he had to admit, might well not come tonight. If only his wife were here; she would jolly him along. Her own 'war effort' had taken her to some church in the city, helping the homeless. But then Lady Belgate was not privy to a fraction of her husband's knowledge; that was the nature of the game. His game. His wretched game. He endeavoured to put the discomfort out of his mind for the duration of the play at least.

The curtain rose on the scene of an English drawing room with French windows open to the garden and a log fire burning in the grate. A maid entered with a drinks tray, and for a while at least, Lord Belgate would attempt to escape the sordid world in which he lived and disappear into that Arcadian image of English country life . . .

'Wasn't she good?' asked Venetia, applauding gently as the cast took their curtain calls.

'Which one?' asked Charles.

'Kay Hammond. So pretty. So elegant.'

He noticed that her face bore a trace of sadness, in spite of the fact that she was complimenting the actress. 'Are you alright?' he asked.

'Oh yes. It's just that . . . well . . . she reminded me a little of Rosamund. She has the same hair; the same spirit of mischief about her. The same sort of sparkle.'

'But she was a ghost,' offered Charles, and then he could have bitten off his tongue at his insensitivity.

'Yes. There is that, too.' The audience was still clapping

enthusiastically as Venetia turned to face him. 'Do you think we will ever see her again, Charles?'

She raised her voice to get over the sound of the applause.

'I hope so, Venetia. I do hope so. I am doing all I can to get her home safely, I promise.'

He had given up hope of coming clean, and the fact that he had to speak over applause made it easier, rather than more difficult. It was as if the edge was taken off it. To talk of something so serious at a moment of wild elation on the part of an audience gave him more courage than if he had had to talk softly in a silent room. He could see, too, that since their last conversation about her niece, Venetia had somehow steeled herself for what she perhaps considered the inevitable: that Rosamund might not return. Charles knew that beneath the often frivolous exterior, there beat the heart of a realist. Venetia was, in spite of outward appearances, a resilient soul. She would, on occasion, find the ground snatched from under her, and wobble a little, but she would refuse to be downcast for long.

The applause had died down now, to be replaced with a merry buzz of conversation as the audience began to leave the theatre.

'Marvellous,' said Sir Basil, congratulating his hostess and kissing her on the cheek before he and Lady Flynn took their leave. 'Really took us out of ourselves.'

Venetia picked up her fur wrap and handed it to Charles, who draped it around her shoulders before picking up his own overcoat and Homburg.

'We were talking, you know, just before she left, and I said that I thought older people should fight – do you remember me telling you that? I offered to man a Lewis gun, but she just laughed.'

Charles looked at her sympathetically.

'When did we grow old, Charles?' asked Venetia as they descended the stairs. 'When was the turning point?'

'I don't think there is a particular point, Venetia. Not really. It creeps up on us gradually and we only notice it after the event. One day we are . . . well . . . blithe spirits, without a care, the world stretching out in front of us, and the next we are over the hill and past it. Except that you and I know that we are not; that we are simply older and maybe just a little wiser.'

'You think so?'

'Not always, no. Sometimes I wonder if I have learned anything on this bumpy journey. But I am certain of one thing . . .'

They had reached the pavement now, and Charles shepherded Venetia to her waiting car, with only a fleeting thought about a petrol allowance and how lucky his hostess was in that respect. Lucky, and careful, for he knew she used it only rarely, to cheer herself up, she said, and to show resilience in the face of adversity. He continued his conversation through the open door as his hostess settled herself into the deep leather of the Daimler.

'I will not rest, Venetia, until I have sorted out this bloody mess. There are many young people risking their lives out there, and I am concerned for them all. But there is one in particular for whom I feel a personal responsibility. I'll do my best to get her home in one piece, and that's a promise.'

He closed the car door, raised his hat and smiled as the car purred away from the pavement. He knew in his heart that he had made a promise he would find extraordinarily difficult to keep.

Chapter 28

GESTAPO HEADQUARTERS, MONTBÉLIARD

EARLY DECEMBER 1941

'Sweet is revenge – especially to women.'

Lord Byron, 'Don Juan', 1818-24

Obersturmführer Schneider and Unterstürmfuhrers Koch and Neumann had transported their captives to the imposing pillared building that had become their headquarters in this part of occupied eastern France. The two had been photographed, had their fingerprints taken, been stripped of their clothing and given grey canvas pyjama-like suits, and locked in separate cells, each equipped with nothing more than an iron bed with a thin ticking-covered mattress and a rough blanket, and in one corner a bucket. There they were left for three days and fed only meagre rations. They had ample time to contemplate their fate while Schneider awaited the man charged with their interrogation. His arrival was not met with any jubilation on the part of Obersturmführer Schneider. Quite the reverse.

*

Otto Koenig listened attentively, his brow furrowed, his eyes barely blinking. 'And you think they were responsible for blowing up the Peugeot factory?'

'Almost certainly.'

The conversation took place in German, but Koenig would be able to question them in French and also in English; he spoke all three languages fluently.

'And you have questioned Robert Peugeot?' he asked.

'Yes,' confirmed Schneider. 'He denies all knowledge of their true identity, and we can't really pursue the matter further on that front. If we arrest him, we will likely have a mutiny on our hands. We need to keep the factory in production. As it is, it will be several weeks before the damaged machinery can be repaired.'

As usual, an uneasy atmosphere surrounded the two men – Schneider, in a smart Gestapo uniform, Koenig in a nondescript grey suit and tie. Schneider, blond, angular and Aryan, was not a fan of Koenig, who was tall, dark and lean, his face – despite his relatively young age – etched with the woes of the world and overlaid with the sort of inscrutable expression that made it clear he would never give anything away. Perhaps that's why he was considered so good at his job. As far as Obersturmführer Schneider was concerned, Otto Koenig was a necessary evil. He would have preferred to do the interrogating himself, but conceded that the other man's linguistic skills far surpassed his own.

'You questioned Henri Dubois this morning,' Scheider stated. 'It seems our three friends had been staying with him before moving on to the house where we arrested them, and that, too, is owned by a member of his family. What did we learn from him?'

'Nothing very much until his wife turned up,' replied Koenig.

'And then?'

'A little more.'

'She came in of her own accord. Why?'

'To save her husband.'

'How could she do that? If he is a member of the Resistance, he must pay the price.' There was no hint of compromise in the Obersturmführer's voice.

'She offered us additional information. More important information.'

'On the two prisoners?'

'Yes.'

'Why so?'

'In the hope that we would release her husband in exchange for them.'

Schneider sneered. 'She is obviously under a delusion. Where is Dubois now?'

'In a cell.'

'And his wife?'

'In another cell.'

Schneider smiled. 'So we have all four of them.'

'Yes.' There was little expression in Koenig's voice.

Schneider seated himself on the throne-like chair behind the imposing carved mahogany desk, silhouetted like some deadly spider against the large scarlet flag with the swastika at its centre which hung on the wall. Schneider enjoyed the grandeur of his position, from the uniform itself to the trappings of rank – the desk, the office, the insignia and the respect which he imagined these accoutrements accorded him in the eyes of his subordinates. He motioned Koenig to sit opposite him in a smaller and less imposing chair. 'Why are you here?' he asked.

'You know why I am here, Herr Obersturmführer.'

'I know we value your languages, Herr Koenig, but you are

not always here. You appear only on certain occasions. I am curious to know why.'

Koenig looked impassive. 'I come here when I am requested to do so by your superiors.'

The remark was not lost on Schneider, but he ignored the intended slight and pursued the line of their original conversation. 'What happened to the third member of the party? The wireless operator.'

'We assume he got away. He may not get far. We have look-outs posted at railway stations. But he has his papers so . . .'

'He may give us the slip?'

Koenig shrugged non-committally.

'And the wireless itself?'

'Damaged beyond repair.'

'We cannot learn anything from it?'

'I'm afraid not. It suffered rather badly on its journey from the top floor to the ground.'

Schneider disregarded the modest attempt at humour, rose from his chair and tapped the desk. 'So why did Madame Dubois come to the aid of her husband? This is very unusual. It is unlike members of the Resistance movement to give each other away, and they know we do not bargain.' He paced the floor, his hands behind his back, tapping one against the other as he tried to understand the motives of the husband and wife.

Koenig explained, 'It seems she had been talking to the wireless operator. Asking him about his wartime experiences.'

'And he was forthcoming?' There was a note of incredulity in Schneider's voice.

'Madame Dubois seems to have a secret supply of Scotch whisky . . .'

'Does she? I wish I did,' responded Schneider drily. 'Even I find that hard to come by.'

'She managed to discover that he was in the British navy, and that he was deployed on Operation Catapult in the Mediterranean.'

Schneider stopped pacing and turned to face Koenig. 'He told her that?'

Koenig shrugged. 'I suspect he was lulled into a false sense of security. He had been flown into France to work with the Resistance; he would have regarded her as a colleague. She was hospitable. Plied him with whisky. He may not have told her very much, but that was enough for her.'

'Enough for what?'

'Madame Dubois had a brother in the French navy.'

'So?'

'When France was occupied by German forces, the bulk of the French navy was assembled at Mers-el-Kébir in Algeria. Admiral Darlan assured Churchill that he would never hand over French ships to the Germans, but Churchill felt that he could not risk the safety of his country on the word of the French Admiral. On the third of July 1940, he ordered the British navy to open fire on the French fleet. Operation Catapult. The French ships were either irreparably damaged or sunk and more than a thousand French soldiers and sailors were killed.'

'What has this to do with our prisoners?'

'Madame Dubois's brother was one of those killed. She felt that the man who has escaped – so far – was one of those responsible.'

'An eye for an eye?'

'So to speak, yes.'

'So she betrayed all three?'

'It would appear so. She sent her daughter to the safe house with a bottle of whisky. She had put some sleeping powders in it so that, having enjoyed her hospitality by way of celebrating their triumph, they would still be in the house when you and your officers turned up. She knew they had planned to leave early and so saw that as a way of delaying them until you arrived.'

'And all because . . .'

'She was very close to her brother; she feels his loss keenly and cannot forgive the British navy for being responsible for his death.' Koenig remained silent for a moment and then said, 'Will you release Madame Dubois and her husband?'

Schneider looked incredulous. 'And let them go back to their old ways – sabotaging factories and harbouring the enemy?'

'You have a reason.'

Schneider laughed. 'What possible reason could I have for releasing two people who are self-confessed members of the Resistance? I would be a laughing stock.'

'Not if you did so for tactical reasons.'

'What do you mean?'

'The other members of this cell will know that you are going for larger fish. It may encourage the Dubois, in other instances, to betray more outsiders – more of those who come to join the cause.'

'To save their own skins?'

'Possibly. But those they betray will probably be more skilful, more valuable to you – if your action today precipitates their cooperation.'

Schneider sat down again in his imposing chair and leaned back, steepling his fingers. 'You are very persuasive, Herr Koenig. But why do I think you have an ulterior motive?'

Otto Koenig shrugged. 'It is not up to me, Herr Obersturmführer. I simply offer a point of view.'

Schneider tapped the table. 'Very well. Against my better judgement, I will let the Dubois go, after first putting the fear of God into them and letting them know we will be watching them.'

'If I might suggest, Herr Obersturmführer, you might find it more . . . profitable . . . to let them go with good grace. If they think they are being watched and monitored, they are less likely to make careless mistakes – mistakes which might lead you to further arrests.'

Schneider shook his head. 'You have all the answers, Herr Koenig. All the answers . . .' He got up from his desk. 'Untersturmführer Koch will bring the two . . . British? . . . prisoners to you. Make sure you find out exactly who they are and what they were up to, will you?' Then he smiled and spoke in English: '"There's a good chap!" That's what they say, isn't it?'

Chapter 29

INTERROGATION ROOM, GESTAPO HEADQUARTERS MONTBÉLIARD

DECEMBER 1941

'Questioning is not the mode of conversation
among gentlemen.
It is assuming a superiority.'

James Boswell, *The Life of Samuel Johnson*, 1791

The room was bare except for two steel-framed chairs set at either side of a heavy wooden table fixed to the floor with stout steel braces. On the edge of the table at one side was a button, which could be pressed to summon assistance. From the ceiling, a single light bulb hung on a twisted flex. The only other source of light was a small, barred window high up in the wall of this basement room; too high to accord a view of anything except the dark and leaden sky.

Thierry Foustier was manhandled through the door by a uniformed guard and thrust into one of the chairs. The guard then retraced his steps back to the door, slammed it shut, turned the key in the lock and stood to one side, his hands behind his back, his gaze directed up at the source of the watery light that failed to dent the gloom cast by the grey-painted walls of the cube-like interrogation room.

I have very little recollection of what happened after the Gestapo came. I think I was hit on the head; I was certainly concussed or, at best, disorientated by my experiences. I remember nothing until waking up in a grey-painted cell in what I assume were Gestapo headquarters; though to this day I have no idea where they were or how I got there. I was on my own in a tiny cell with only a bed and a bucket by way of creature comforts, though the very phrase now sounds laughable.

My clothes had been taken from me and I was dressed in what I can only describe as drab grey pyjamas. It was bitterly cold that winter, and I had to pull the blanket about myself for anything approaching warmth. The food (if you can call it that) was dreadful – dry, crusty bread – usually quite old – and grey soup made from I know not what. And water, in very small quantities. I tried to make it last, but soon realised that anything I left for later would be removed, so whenever I heard the key in the heavy lock, I wolfed down what I could before it was taken away. To be honest, I had very little appetite, though I knew I must drink to keep hydrated and that if I did not eat, I would have little strength if the moment ever came when I would need it to effect an escape. The very thought, I knew, seemed ludicrously optimistic.

In spite of the dreadful circumstances, I managed to smile to myself and promise that I would never again question the contents of Mrs Heffer's soup, which was, in comparison, ambrosia. Not that I was likely ever to be in that situation again. Eaton Square might as well have been on the moon, so far away did it – and my former life – seem.

I do not know how many days I was kept there on my own and left in silence. I do know that whenever I tried to sleep I would be woken up for no reason at all, then left once more. I understand, looking back, that this was part of the process of trying to break us down. I say 'us', because I could only assume that Thierry was going through the same sort of experience, though I had no idea if we were in the same building or if we had been separated or, indeed, if he were still alive. There was no physical torture meted out to me at that point, though at any moment I knew that I might be hauled out and subjected to heaven knows what. We had been warned in our training that the Gestapo were adept at extracting information by physical force, if mental torture did not yield results. Sometimes, from distant cells, I could hear the heart-rending screams of other prisoners. I tried to block my ears, but the sounds were harrowing in the extreme.

In the quieter times I had plenty of time to think, though I cannot say that my thoughts were rational. I avoided letting myself imagine what physical discomforts I might be subjected to – what other prisoners were going through; I knew that such conjecture would not only be a waste of time but might also result in some kind of mental breakdown. Whatever happened, I had to be strong – in mind if not in body. And yet I would see strange apparitions and dream nonsensical dreams whenever

I did fall asleep, which was certainly not frequent enough to allow me to feel rested.

When I was awake and my modest nourishment brought about some kind of rationality, I wondered if I would ever leave the place alive. It surprises me now that the thought did not make me hysterical, but I like to think that as well as my training at Wanborough, my natural resilience, and what I confess is a certain bloody-mindedness fostered by the series of events I had encountered as a girl and as a young woman, had proved to me that there was nothing to be gained by losing my grip, and everything to hope for if I retained it.

I think now that although these thoughts might have got me through, they were, to say the least, a touch on the optimistic side. But if I were not optimistic, if I did not believe that I might escape this dreadful place, what would be the point in carrying on?

I made myself think of Devonshire, and the beach and the sea. I remembered the feeling of sand between my toes, and could almost taste the sweetness of Semolina's jam sandwiches and savour the tang of salt air. Any moment from those happier days that took me out of myself for just a brief while I clung to. I talked, in my head, to Diana about boys, to Aunt Venetia about clothes and to Celine about everything. I heard her telling me to buck up and stop being feeble. What was I worth if I gave up so easily? I felt her brush running through my hair, and her breath against my cheek, and as we talked, so she began to slip away from me, and then the pain of her loss became just too great and I talked instead to Harry. I tried to feel his arms around me and to gaze into his eyes for reassurance. We sat together and gazed at the waves – at our lovely life force, the sea. There were times when I found it hard to see his face clearly, and then I would shake my head and make myself remember. Then Thierry's face would appear. It was all so confusing.

I had little sense of night and day, for the sky outside the tiny window seemed always to be devoid of much in the way of light. Then the moment came when I heard the key in the lock, my cell door opened and I was bundled out by two uniformed Gestapo officers. My heart had never beat so fast and so loud. I was determined that if I were being marched off to be shot, I should say absolutely nothing and would remain outwardly calm and impassive. Deep, deep inside, I was screaming.

Thierry Foustier sat on the chair at one side of the table, gently swaying. He tried to imagine what would happen next, but realised the futility of the exercise and cleared his mind of everything except the desire for a good meal and a glass of wine. Eventually, even those profitless thoughts were expunged and he sat, trance-like, awaiting the arrival of his interlocutor. He had been brought here twice already and left alone for an hour before being marched back to his cell. Would this time be any different?

After half an hour, a brief knock heralded the arrival of . . . what? Another march back to the cell? He had heard of the techniques the Gestapo used to undermine their prisoners. The guard turned around, inserted the key in the lock and pulled open the heavy metal-lined door. A tall, thin man in a grey suit entered. In his right hand, a clipboard; in his left, a fountain pen. He sat down quietly at the table and nodded at the guard.

'You may go.' The instruction in German.

'But sir . . .'

'*Auf Wiedersehen.*'

Otto Koenig preferred to interrogate prisoners on his own,

without the distraction of another body in the room. It was against protocol and regulations – there would be no protection against personal assault – but he insisted on such conditions and reasoned that any disturbance could be reported with a press of the button on the table.

Koenig looked at his clipboard and asked in French, 'Thierry Foustier. Is that your real name?'

'It is the one I was born with.'

'I'll take that as a yes.' The tone impassive; the expression unperturbed. He released several papers from his clipboard and shuffled through them in an unhurried fashion. 'Your papers indicate that you work for an insurance company.'

'That is what I told your officer. The one who came to the house.'

'They are very good.'

Thierry looked critically at his inquisitor.

'They are very good forgeries.'

Thierry remained impassive and said nothing.

'You realise the seriousness of your situation?'

Again, no reply.

'Your compatriot, Marcel Clemont . . .'

A flicker of recognition crossed the Frenchman's face.

'Ah, yes. You see, we know his name. Or, rather, we know the name that appears on his papers, but we doubt that is his real name.'

Thierry's face resumed its blank expression.

'And the young lady working with you . . .' he looked down and sifted through the papers on the desk, 'Christiane de Rossignol . . .' He looked up again and smiled. 'Her papers say she is a bookkeeper.'

Thierry shrugged. 'That is for her to say.'

'How long have you been working together?'

No reply came.

'How do you know Henri Dubois?'

Again, no reply.

'I have all the time in the world, Monsieur Foustier, but it would be easier for both of us if you cooperated. My patience is endless but that of our Gestapo comrades is very limited. If you do not tell me what I need to know – what *they* need to know – they will find themselves forced to use what they rather elegantly call "enhanced interrogation techniques" as a means of extracting the necessary information, rather than the simple means of sleep deprivation that I prefer to employ. Answer my questions or you can look forward to a long and undisturbed sleep in the company of the angels.'

Thierry smiled but remained mute.

Koenig realised that little information would be forthcoming, but hour after hour he kept up the tirade of questions – sometimes asking them in soft, cajoling tones, sometimes raising his voice and shouting – all the while endeavouring to break the reserve of his prisoner.

Then, suddenly, and without warning, Koenig leaned across the table and put his face up close against Thierry's ear. 'Over the next few hours, several things will happen. You will go where you are taken without fuss and without asking any questions. Is that understood?'

Unsure of the meaning of such a statement, Thierry leaned back in his chair and regarded his interrogator with a questioning stare.

Koenig now spoke in a whisper and in English. 'Trust me, Patrice.' Then he pressed the button on the desk. The key turned in the lock, the guard entered and Koenig instructed in German: 'Take him back and lock him up. I will see him again later.'

'So soon, sir?'

'It has been . . .' he glanced at his watch, 'four and a quarter hours. I have what I need for now. I will see the woman next.'

The guard left, and Koenig pushed the door closed and waited for his next captive to appear.

When Rosamund entered the interrogation room, Otto Koenig had his back to her. He was facing the opposite wall and looking at the papers he held in his hands. It was not until the guard had left the room and the sound of the turning lock echoed across the space and reassured him that they were alone, that he turned round and faced her.

Rosamund's eyes widened and her lips parted as she clung to the edge of the table to steady herself. For what seemed like an age, she stared at the man in front of her without saying a word.

'Christiane de Rossignol?' he said evenly.

Rosamund nodded gently but still did not speak.

'I am Otto Koenig. Please sit down.'

As she sank into the chair only moments before her legs gave way, all manner of contradictory and confusing thoughts raced through Rosamund's mind. She tried in vain to work out why on earth the man who was about to interrogate her should be Harry Napier.

Chapter 30

INTERROGATION ROOM, GESTAPO HEADQUARTERS, MONTBÉLIARD

DECEMBER 1941

'Four be the things I'd been better without:
Love, curiosity, freckles and doubt.'

Dorothy Parker, 'Inventory', 1937

Despite his confidence that such was the case, Harry Napier glanced at the door to reassure himself that they were alone. He allowed himself the merest glimmer of a smile before asking levelly and in French, 'Your papers say you are a bookkeeper. Is this true?'

Rosamund opened her mouth to speak, but found that no words came out, so dry was her mouth. She cleared her throat and managed a weak 'yes.'

'And you were checking the books at the Peugeot factory on the day of the explosion?'

'Yes.'

'But you had nothing to do with the events of that evening?'

'No.' Rosamund swallowed, her mind racing. What was happening? Why was Harry here? Why was he interrogating her on behalf of the Gestapo? Whose side was he on? Was she hallucinating?

He continued, glancing at his papers for information. 'The factory machinery was badly damaged. Production has had to be stopped while one particular piece of equipment is replaced.'

She sat perfectly still as he spoke, watching his every move and concentrating on his every word with growing incredulity.

'It would take someone of extreme courage to undertake such work,' he said pointedly. 'Someone very brave, not to say fool-hardy.'

Rosamund sat mesmerised, her head spinning.

'And yet you say you had left the factory before the explosion happened?'

'Yes.'

'Very wise. You must have been some distance away when you heard the noise.'

'I was at the station . . .' she heard herself say, on automatic pilot.

'Your mission accomplished?'

'I was only checking the books; I told you.' Her fear and confusion were now mixed with rising anger, and Rosamund had to fight to stop it taking over, to prevent it from affecting the level tone of voice she was struggling so hard to maintain. It was as if the two of them had been cast in some strange role play, like those she had undertaken at Wanborough when they had tried to make her and her compatriots crack under the strain. They had conjured up all kinds of scenarios in those days of training, taught you how to behave in the face of enemy interrogation, but they had never intimated that such an experience might involve being questioned by someone you had, up to now, trusted and thought of as being on the same side. Should she ask him what was going on? Should she admit to knowing who he was, or was this part of some elaborate charade that she was meant to go along with? She wanted to burst into tears, to say it was all so unfair, to ask him how he could do this to her, how he could have deceived her, but her innate resilience – fuelled by the anger and confusion – prevented her from doing so.

'I have nothing to say,' she declared in as confident a tone as she could muster. 'I have told you all I know: that I am a book-keeper and that I was asked to go to the factory to check over some anomalous figures. I located the particular discrepancy, corrected it and left.'

Her interrogator sat down opposite her. 'And have you always had a head for figures?' he asked.

Rosamund sat transfixed. Harry knew she had not. He knew that Diana Molyneux was the one with the numerical skills and that she, Rosamund, was useless at anything involving mathematics. Words were her thing, not calculations and codes and confusing series of digits. She wanted to hit him, to scream, 'Why are you doing this to me?' Instead she dug her nails into the palms of her shaking hands, the better to conceal her feelings.

'I don't think you are a bookkeeper at all, Mademoiselle de Rossignol,' he said evenly. 'I think you are something much more important. I think you have talents and abilities far in excess of simple accountancy. It would not surprise me at all that you were capable of great courage, that you were possessed of considerable intelligence and that someone had recognised your worth and offered you a position that would make use of your sensibilities and your unique gifts. Am I right?'

The words dried up. Rosamund stared at him incredulously. What could she possibly answer? He had ranted on at her –

sometimes quiet and cajoling, at other times raising his voice and getting impatient at her lack of cooperation. There were moments when she thought she was going mad; that this was all a mirage – her mind playing tricks thanks to the lack of nourishment. Now, after what seemed like an age, the conversation ceased.

He got up, walked around behind her chair and put his hands upon her shoulders. She thought at first – just for one brief moment – that he was going to reassure her that all was well, like Harry would have done in former times. But as the hands rested, so the fingers began to press together into her flesh. The shock made her cry out. 'You're hurting me!'

He did not stop. Instead he squeezed harder, then abruptly withdrew his hands from her shoulders and put them around her neck . He squeezed again; even harder this time. She thought she would choke; she found it hard to breathe. She was on the verge of blacking out when he released his hands and said, 'You are lying, Madamoiselle de Rossignol. You are not telling me the truth! This will not end happily.' Her captor walked back around the table and lowered himself into the seat facing her, fixing her with a piercing stare.

Rosamund experienced a feeling of nausea mixed with terror. Who was this man? He was not the Harry she knew, and certainly not the one she had loved. Harry glanced at his watch, then took a notepad from his pocket, wrote something on the topmost sheet of paper, tore it from the pad and slid it across the table towards her, pointing to the words he had written.

Rosamund looked down at the familiar hand which she had not set eyes on in months, and at the words to which it pointed. Her vision was blurred, not just because of his apparent attempt at strangulation, but also through lack of sleep and meaningful nourishment. Straining her eyes, she managed to make out the message he had scrawled upon the piece of paper before he hastily removed it and returned it to his pocket: 'Trust no one but me. <u>Remember</u>.'

She looked up and met his eyes. A moment later he pressed the button on the table and the key rattled once more in the lock.

The instruction in German was brief and to the point. 'Take her away.'

Rosamund glanced over her shoulder as she was frog-marched out of the room. All she could see was Harry Napier – or Otto Koenig – which was he? – looking down at his papers and screwing the top back on his fountain pen.

'You want to do what?' Schneider asked Koenig in a disbelieving tone of voice.

'I want to interview them together. To see how they react with one another. I think I can get more out of the man by the way I treat the woman. Bring out his protective instincts.'

'It is highly irregular.'

'But then so are your "enhanced techniques of interrogation", Obersturmführer.'

'But effective.'

'Sometimes; not always.'

It was getting late. It was dark outside now, and Schneider had an assignation he did not want to forgo. She was a particularly promising French cabaret performer who had aspirations. He glanced at his watch. 'You will have to have a guard present.'

'You know I prefer to operate on my own.'

Schneider's voice betrayed his irritation and impatience. 'Yes, Herr Koenig, I know that, but in this instance I insist. You will have an armed guard inside the door at all times, and another one outside. Understood?'

Koenig shrugged. 'If you wish.'

'I do wish. I don't like this, Koenig. Since you have failed to get anything out of them they should be taken to the room at the far end of the basement and . . . helped to talk by other means.'

'If I've still failed when I have questioned them this time, then you may do so.'

'I will do so when I feel like it, Herr Koenig. Don't forget who's in charge here. You may have the blessing of certain powers to which I'm not privy—' he curled his lip in distaste, his face taking on an almost pantomimic sneer '—but when you come here to Montbéliard, in the absence of a Sturmbannführer, I call the tune. I wear the uniform. Is that clear?'

'Perfectly, Obersturmführer Schneider.' The words were spoken evenly without a hint of sarcasm, though Schneider was aware that such sarcasm was implicit in the delivery.

Schneider walked to the door of his office, opened it and called, 'Neumann!'

The subordinate Neumann appeared within moments, clicked his heels and offered the Nazi salute.

'You and Koch will take the two prisoners down to the interrogation room. They are to be questioned together.'

Neumann raised his eyebrows.

'Yes, I know it is not how we normally operate, but Herr Koenig thinks he can get more out of them that way. One of you will be inside the room – and armed – at all times. You will take it in turns – one inside and one outside the door. If Herr Koenig fails to discover anything more interesting than their hobbies and their ages, then you will take them down to the special room and see what you can achieve there. Is that clear?'

Neumann saluted, turned on his heels and went off in search of his fellow officer.

'And now, Koenig, I'll leave you to your task. Should nothing of interest transpire this evening, I shall be contacting my superiors tomorrow and recommending your removal from post. You record to date has hardly been what I would call glittering.'

'That is a little unfair, Obersturmführer. You will recall the two prisoners last month . . .'

'What is that famous saying, Herr Koenig? One swallow does not make a summer? Another English aphorism, I think. And this time, it is an accurate one. Good evening.' With that he motioned his interrogator to leave the room, then closed the door quietly behind him.

Harry Napier leaned against the wall outside Schneider's office and breathed deeply. On the other side of the huge mahogany door he could hear the Obersturmführer readying himself for his evening out, humming a snatch of *'Zigeuner, Du hast mein Herz gestohlen'* to himself. The thought of Schneider partnering his conquest in a tango was something that turned Harry's stomach. He glanced again at his watch. There was barely enough time. He set off in the direction of the interrogation room, down the single flight of winding and dimly lit steps to the basement, where the smell of damp and decay was overpowering. He remembered the garden shed from his childhood where his grandfather grew mushrooms, the windows blacked out with hessian, the atmosphere cloying and foetid. He shivered involuntarily and quickened his pace, rounding the corner at the bottom of the steps and walking along the whitewashed stone corridor. He glanced in the direction of the door at the very end, behind which resided the instruments of torture to which his captives would be subjected should he fail in his task.

He averted his gaze and, arriving at the door of the interrogation room, pushed it open. The room was empty. He looked up at the small window. It was pitch dark outside, and the cruel bright light of the single bulb that hung above the table stung his eyes.

There was a commotion in the corridor outside, and a scuffling as Thierry and Rosamund were bundled into the room and prodded towards the chairs with the barrel of Untersturmführer Koch's Beretta submachine gun. Both of them were handcuffed.

Neumann nodded at Koch who took his position outside the door, closing it and locking it after him. Neumann looked warily at the two prisoners – then at Harry – before positioning himself in front of the door, facing the three figures who were now his captives. His gun carried diagonally across his chest, he allowed himself a gentle smile, confident in having the upper hand.

There were still only two chairs in the room, now both positioned on one side of the table; Harry paced the floor on the other side and began his interrogation once more.

Rosamund glanced at Thierry. It was the first time she had seen him since their arrest; the first time she had been certain of the fact that he was alive. Her senses were heightened at the discovery. Thierry, too, had a light in his eye that had hitherto been absent, but the two sat calmly and quietly as the questions and statements rattled out from Harry, who kept up a continued flow of conversation that hardly warranted interruption.

He paced up and down in front of them and Neumann for half an hour, then glanced at his watch and said to Neumann, 'I would like some water, please.'

Neumann turned toward the door, and as he did so, Harry pulled a pistol from his pocket and held it to Neumann's temple, pinning him to the cold steel door. *'Waffe runter!'*

Neumann dropped his gun and Harry fished inside the guard's right hand pocket. Nothing. Then the left. Nothing. Finally, pressing the barrel of his pistol even harder against the German's temple, he pushed his hand inside the guard's breast pocket and found what he was looking for: the key to the handcuffs. 'Careless,' he murmured. Then he turned and tossed the key at Thierry who caught it, unlocked Rosamund's handcuffs then motioned her to do the same for him.

Now Harry spoke in French: 'Thierry, take the gun. Christiane, look away.'

As Rosamund did so she heard the sound of metal on bone and turned to see Neumann slump to the floor.

There was a thump at the other side of the door and Koch asked, '*Ist alles in Ordnung?*'

'*Alles OK,*' replied Harry. '*Ich musste Gewalt anwenden.*'

Harry turned from the crumpled body and began to drag the heavy table across the room until it was against the outside wall. Leaping up on to it, he pulled at the metal grille in front of the small window. It came away easily and he pushed open the swivelling pane. 'Amazing what you can achieve with a screwdriver and a spanner when you're not being watched,' he muttered.

Thierry flashed him a smile. 'Clever,' he said, as the two of them lifted Rosamund up on to the table and pushed her out through the window. Harry motioned Thierry to follow, then picked up the submachine gun and passed it to him before raising himself up and squeezing through the small aperture.

He heard a groan beneath him as Neumann began to regain consciousness. There was no time to spare.

'Keep close to the wall,' Harry instructed. They had come out into a street, not a compound or a yard, for the Gestapo headquarters had not been built as a detention centre but as an imposing public building. They flattened themselves against the smooth and elegant stonework and within seconds an old truck rounded the corner and pulled up beside them. 'In!' said Harry, motioning them to the flapping canvas at the rear of the lorry, and with little pause the truck took off down the road with its three passengers rolling around among straw and sisal, hardly able to believe they were free.

It had all happened so fast, and as the lorry careered through the streets of Montbéliard and out into the French countryside, the sense of urgency did not abate. None of the three was anxious to speak first, and the noise of the ancient engine and the rattling sides of the lorry made any kind of intimate conversation impossible. As a result they remained mute, holding on to the sides of the rickety vehicle as it bounced down lanes and tracks, finally coming to a halt on the edge of a field. The engine was switched off and the silence that followed was deafening in its intensity.

It was Harry who spoke first. 'Now we wait. Hopefully not for long.' Rosamund looked at Harry, then glanced across at Thierry, aware that she was in the company of the two men for whom she harboured the strongest feelings she had ever experienced. Love. Yes. But how had that love changed? Could she still love Harry when ... when, what? He was working for the Germans? But he had rescued them. What did that mean? It was all so confusing. And Thierry. The man at whose side she had come through all this. He had no idea of Harry's true identity. As far as he was concerned, a German called Otto Koenig had engineered their escape. As these thoughts spun and collided in her head, the droning sound that Rosamund had not heard since their arrival in occupied France began to fill the air.

'Quickly!' said Harry. 'Out!'

They tumbled over the tailgate of the truck and on to the frosty turf of the field. In the haste and bustle of their escape, Rosamund had quite forgotten about the cold, which suddenly seized her in its vice-like grip. She began to shake, and as she did so she saw the flares being raised up on the makeshift runway as the Lysander came in to land.

A figure leapt out of the cab of the lorry and shepherded the trio to one side of the field, wrapping a sheepskin jacket around Rosamund's shoulders.

She looked up and saw that it was Paulette – the daughter of Henri and Madeleine Dubois.

'Thank you! Thank you so much!' she said in heartfelt appreciation.

'I am sorry for what happened. It was not my mother's fault. She has not been well. We do not all feel as she feels. Please, please forgive her.'

Rosamund looked at her, confused and dazed by words she could not begin to understand.

'Quick! You must go!' urged Paulette, pushing Rosamund towards the now stationary aircraft whose engine was still running and whose pilot was gesturing out of the cockpit window for them to make haste.

'Thierry!' Rosamund turned to her companion and held out her hand.

Thierry shook his head. 'There is only room for two,' he said. 'I have more to do here.' He stepped forward and gazed into Rosamund's eyes, then gently kissed her on one cheek before stepping back and putting his arm around Paulette's shoulder. The look Rosamund saw between them told her all she needed to know. She turned and looked pleadingly at Harry.

'You first,' he said, lifting her through the opening underneath the plane.

Then he hauled himself up as the Lysander began to gain speed. It was already airborne as his legs disappeared from view and the door was bolted shut.

As the few bright flares of the foreign field faded from view, a rattling series of cracks rent the air around them. Involuntarily, Rosamund reached out and clasped Harry's hand. After barely half a minute, the anti-aircraft fire ceased and the feverish whine of the engine was all they could hear as they gained height and speed. Rosamund let go of Harry's hand and turned away, clasping her arms around her body in a vain attempt to stay warm as they headed out towards England and home.

Chapter 31

NEWMARKET TO LONDON

DECEMBER 1941

'France has lost a battle, but France has not lost
the war!'

Charles de Gaulle, 1940

From the tiny airfield at Newmarket they were shepherded to
a waiting car and driven straight to London. Conversation
during the flight had been impossible thanks to the noise; now
they were faced with a two-and-a-half hour journey in the back
of a spacious Rover. Neither of them wanted to be the first to
speak; Rosamund because she was unsure of their status after
the events of the last twenty-four hours, Harry because he was
afraid of saying too much or not enough.

Eventually it was Harry who broke the ice. 'Are you alright?'
'What do you think?' she replied.
'Confused?'
She sank down into the sheepskin jacket and pulled herself
tighter into the corner of the back seat. 'Totally.'
'I'm not surprised. It's a lot to take in.'

She shot him a look that reminded him of the depth of his understatement. 'I mean, what are you?'

Harry nodded in the direction of the driver and said, 'It's difficult to say.'

'I'm not surprised,' she murmured, understanding his reluctance to talk in the presence of a third person, but also letting him know that she was far from convinced of his transparency.

'I do what I have committed myself to do,' he said, in an attempt to help her understand his position. The attempt failed.

'Well, that much is clear,' she retorted, aware that she was beginning to sound like a petulant child. In her mind the confusion had not abated. How could it? She replayed over and over the events of her time at Gestapo headquarters, and asked herself every imaginable question. Had he known where she was all the time? Had he been involved in planning her operation, or was it all news to him? Was their meeting in Montbéliard purely coincidental? Had he been as shocked to be confronted by her as she was to be interrogated by him? What was his relationship with the Gestapo? It was certainly official and sanctioned or he would not have been there, would not have been given charge of English prisoners. Or had the Germans been fooled into thinking that he was a traitor to his own country? What did she mean 'been fooled'? Perhaps he *was* a traitor to his own country, and now here she was, in the back of a car, being driven to operational headquarters in his company. Would they ever get there? Would he spring yet another escape attempt? Would she be expected to cover for him? How could she?

Question after question rattled through her mind, and there was not a single answer to any one of them.

'I know what you must be thinking,' he said.

'Do you?' she blurted out. 'I find that hard to believe, when I hardly know myself.'

'Be patient. It will all become clear.'

'Oh, I do hope so, because at the moment I can't understand you at all.'

The rest of the journey passed in uneasy silence; Rosamund thinking that nothing he could say would make up for the confusion and lack of trust she felt enveloping her, Harry because he had so much he wanted to explain and yet knew he could not – partly because of the presence of the driver, but also because there were things she could never know and that he was certain she would not understand.

The car disgorged them under a large stone portico, where several men in suits were ready to escort them inside. At the doorway they were separated: Harry was taken down one corridor and Rosamund down another. He glanced over his shoulder at her as she was hurried away, but she did not look back.

They were kind enough to allow her a bath as soon as she arrived, and to give her a good meal and some clothes. She had forgotten what shoes felt like, her naked feet having been so cold for so long – a fact ameliorated only slightly by the blankets that had been offered to them in the back of the official car. The warm water and stockings allowed her circulation to return slowly, but having warmed up, she began to be overtaken by a supreme sense of tiredness exacerbated by lack of sleep and lack of nutrition. Her body cleansed and clothed and her appetite sated, she was taken to a room for the expected debriefing session. The two men seated at the desk – one rotund and ruddy of complexion, a clone of Sir Patrick Felpham, she thought; the other tall, thin and balding with rimless spectacles, the popular image of an Oxford don

– were kind and solicitous. She was asked if she wanted anything. Tea? What passed for coffee was not worth drinking, they said. She declined either, still full from the surprisingly generous and unexpected plateful of meat and vegetables that had been offered on her arrival.

They listened carefully and wrote notes continually as Rosamund described in detail their arrival in France, the people they worked with and the operation they had undertaken at the Peugeot factory. She was congratulated on the effectiveness of her demolition capabilities, and told that her work made a great contribution to the war effort.

The short, portly one allowed himself the satisfaction of explaining that the replacement press which the Germans had been transporting to the factory by barge had been sunk by the Resistance, not only further delaying the production of tanks, but also blocking the canal to other traffic. 'So, you see, your work continues to be of use.'

Rosamund nodded and smiled weakly. It all seemed so far away now. It had occupied her every thought for so long and now it was just history. She felt strangely deflated, even though the two men were endeavouring to convince her of the impor-tance of her role.

They asked about the Dubois family. Rosamund told them as much as she knew about Henri, Gaston, Madeleine and Paulette – the image of Paulette with Thierry's arm around her as they bade her goodbye dwelling uncomfortably in her mind's eye as she tried hard to avoid tainting her description of events with personal prejudices. She had not seen that coming, not at all, but did her best to gloss over the fact. It was of no concern to her interlocutors, surely. She was uncertain at this moment of just how much concern it was to herself.

In a few moments of silence as they were recording her

answers, she asked, 'What is it about the mother – Madame Dubois? Is there something I don't know?'

'Why do you ask?' enquired the tall, thin inquisitor.

'Because Paulette apologised for her mother's actions as she saw us on to the plane.'

The portly man glanced at the tall, thin man who looked thoughtful for a moment and then asked, 'What do you know about Hector . . . er, Eric Ridley?'

'Our wireless operator?'

The thin man nodded.

'He managed to escape. The Gestapo arrived and he went upstairs in the house to get his papers, but also to disable the radio.'

'The radio was in the house?'

'Yes. Thierry had always told him that it was safer to hide the radio elsewhere, but I think Eric had had some trouble with it and had been working on it in his room. That's why it was there. Usually it was kept at a distance to avoid linking it with us.'

'Yet another instance of Ridley's misjudgements . . .' murmured the short, portly one.

Rosamund regarded them both quizzically.

The tall thin one volunteered the information, explaining about Eric Ridley's role in Operation Catapult, and the fact that he had shared that confidence with Madeleine Dubois, whose brother had been among those killed at Mers-el-Kébir. He explained about Madame Dubois exacting her revenge, and why her daughter – thought to be a reliable contact – had found it necessary to apologise.

'But how do you know all this?'

'We have our sources, Colette – Miss Hanbury – that is our business.'

'And do you have proof?'

'Our sources are reliable,' confirmed the tall, thin one.

'I see.'

Then he offered an olive branch. 'It is a good thing that you are not partial to Scotch whisky, Miss Hanbury. Otherwise you, too, might have woken up late, and the radio would have been discovered and . . . heaven knows what else.'

'Yes,' murmured Rosamund absently. She wondered why they were asking her questions when they seemed to know the answers already. Then she asked, 'Do you know what happened to Eric?'

The two men exchanged another glance.

'Can you tell me?'

'Not good news, I am afraid,' said the short one.

The tall one cut in. 'I am afraid he was captured at the railway station in Pontarlier.'

Rosamund waited for further information. When none was forthcoming, she asked, 'Is he alive?'

'He was taken to Besançon – an internment centre. A concentration camp.'

'No!'

'We are led to believe he was executed . . . by lethal injection.'

Rosamund felt her stomach turn. One hand shot to her mouth. 'Oh no. No, no, no . . .' she gasped. 'Not Eric . . . he was so . . .'

'Careless, I'm afraid,' said the tall one, not without compassion. 'He was a good man, just . . .'

'Too trusting,' added his colleague.

Rosamund felt her anger rising. 'Is that a bad thing? Is it a mistake to trust people? Where are we if we don't trust those around us, those we work with? Those who are meant to be on the same side? Like Harry Napier.'

'Hawksmoor,' said the tall, thin one.

'Sorry?'

'Your code name is Colette; Harry Napier's is Hawksmoor. I think we can trust you with that information.'

'But what is he? I mean, whose side is he on?'

The short one was quick to answer. 'He is on our side, Miss Hanbury, most decidedly. But sometimes we have to infiltrate the enemy camp, and for that we need very special operatives who have very particular skills. Not just languages – which Hawksmoor has – but also an ability to—'

'Be two-faced?' Rosamund could not prevent herself from blurting it out.

'Be able to convince the enemy that they are of more use to them alive than dead.'

Rosamund shook her head. 'But isn't he betraying you by working for them? Surely he gives them information . . . ?'

'He does, you see,' added the tall, thin one. 'We carefully monitor the situation and feed him the information we want passed on. We – or, rather, Hawksmoor – makes them think he is useful.'

'So *they* trust him, and *you* trust him, but surely only one of you can be right?'

'I quite understand your point of view, Miss Hanbury, but as you remember from your training, the only person one can really trust is oneself. It is as well to be suspicious, to some degree, of the motives of others, especially when your well-being – your life, even – is in their hands.'

'Yes,' replied Rosamund bitterly. 'I am beginning to realise that.'

Chapter 32

LONDON

DECEMBER 1941

'And Christmas morning bells say "Come!"
Even to shining ones who dwell
Safe in the Dorchester Hotel.'

John Betjeman, 'Christmas', 1954

For several minutes they could not speak, but stood clasped in each others' arms on the doorstep. Aunt Venetia's tears of joy trickled down Rosamund's neck, as her own sobs wracked her body and she inhaled the long-forgotten perfume of her aunt – a fragrance that spoke of home and safety, even in war-torn London.

Then there was Mrs Heffer to greet, whose huffing and puffing and apron wringing did little to mask her own emotions, and her brother Ned, whose eyes crinkled at the sides with pleasure. He did not make so bold as to hug his employer's niece, but he did pat her gently on the shoulder and say it was good to have her back.

Later, seated in the drawing room – whose creature comforts

now seemed absurdly luxurious to Rosamund, who had become used to the rustic privations of occupied France – her aunt eyed her up and assessed the situation more comprehensively.

'Well, for a start there is nothing of you. Look at you: thin as a rail. Haven't they been feeding you?'

Rosamund could not suppress a sardonic smile. 'Well, no, actually. The occupying forces are not renowned for their culinary expertise and generosity – at least not to their prisoners.'

Aunt Venetia shook her head. 'Oh my goodness! You were taken prisoner. I don't believe it. '

Rosamund's face took on a more serious expression. 'No. I can't believe it either.'

'Is it really as dreadful as they say?'

'Oh yes. And worse.' Then she said, 'Let's not talk about it. Not now. Not ever, probably. It's not something I want to rake over. And, anyway, there's a lot I can't – mustn't – tell you. I've probably said too much already, so please don't breathe it to a soul.'

'No. No, of course. I'm sorry to ask only . . . it's just so wonderful to have you back, that's all; the best possible Christmas present. You've been gone a long time and I've been so worried . . .'

'I know. Three months is a long time in war. Especially in winter.' She looked out of the window and across the square. The plane trees were devoid of leaves and a cold wind whipped the bare branches to and fro as if to confirm the inhospitality of the weather.

'And Harry? Have you any word of him?'

Rosamund turned back from the window and smiled weakly at her aunt.

'Oh, I know. You're not allowed to say.'

'No.'

'Such a pity. I had high hopes for you two but . . .'

'Shall we change the subject?'

'Yes, of course. Dinner. Would that be a better conversational opportunity?'

'Lovely. Though I'm not sure I could eat much; I'm rather out of practice.'

'Well, you'll have a day to recover your appetite. I've invited the ones you know best – Lord and Lady Belgate – for supper tomorrow night.'

'Oh, and please not Sir Patrick Felpham! I don't think I could bear to watch him troughing his way through a meal. I'd probably throw up.'

'Rosamund! As it happens I have not invited the Felphams. I thought the Belgates would be company enough. Charles has been very helpful, you know; very concerned about your welfare.'

'That's kind.'

Aunt Venetia put down her cup and saucer. 'There are a lot of people who love you, you know. You may have lost a few along the way, but there are enough of us left who value your talents and your personality.'

'Gosh! You sound like a judge in a talent contest.'

'Don't be cheeky, Rosamund. It's time you learned to take a compliment gracefully.'

Rosamund sighed. 'I'm sorry. I'm also a bit out of practice when it comes to compliments.'

Her aunt smiled indulgently. 'Don't worry. We'll nurse you back to health. Only . . .'

'Yes?'

'I know I'm not allowed to ask, but . . .'

'What?'

'Will you be going back?'

Rosamund looked away. 'I don't know.'

An uneasy silence prevailed until her aunt said, 'Well, you're here now; that's the important thing. And I'm sure they are not going to need you between now and the New Year, so let's just make sure we have the best Christmas ever, shall we?'

'Yes, let's. And would it be alright if I slipped out for a while this evening? To catch up with Diana Molyneux?'

'Of course. You're home now, Rosamund. I'm so glad you're here, but I don't want to make you a prisoner.'

'Believe me, Auntie, this is nothing like a prison.' Then, softly to herself, 'And I should know . . .'

The meeting had been hastily arranged over the phone. Diana had another engagement – a Christmas drink with colleagues – which she swiftly withdrew from having heard her friend was back in town, and they agreed on the small restaurant in Maiden Lane where they'd met before, though Diana warned Rosamund that the five-shilling meal was not what it used to be.

Rosamund arrived there first and was shown to a white-damask-covered table in a booth beneath posters of the Moulin Rouge, which seemed faintly disrespectful at a time when France was merely a shadow of her former gay self.

All around were diners hopeful of a more generous meal at the start of the festive season, though their aspirations were tempered by the single menu fastened to a board propped up on an easel which promised much in terms of elaborate script but delivered little in the way of roast turkey and figgy pudding, in lieu of which were substituted rabbit and carrot cake.

Diana arrived ten minutes later and, glancing around the restaurant, failed to recognise her old friend until Rosamund said softly at her elbow, 'I'm here', at which Diana threw her arms around her and repeated the actions of Aunt Venetia.

Rosamund was beginning to appreciate the fondness that an absence could bring about, especially when that absence involved a degree of risk.

Slipping off her coat and throwing her handbag on to the bench seat opposite her friend, Diana launched into conversation without apparently drawing breath.

Rosamund marvelled at her appearance. Diana's face glowed underneath her lustrous dark hair and she wore a tight-fitting crimson dress – 'I've found this darling little woman in South Molton Street. You really must meet her; very quick and hugely reasonable. And Billy likes what they do for me too.'

'Billy?'

'Billy Belgate. Oh, of course; you didn't know. We've been going out for a while. I still can't quite make up my mind about him but he's very sweet. Short and sweet, I suppose.' Diana simply bubbled with enthusiasm before pausing for breath and saying, 'But I'm rattling on, Ros. It's only because I'm so relieved to have you back, not because I can't talk about anything but myself. Forgive me. It's been so long!'

Rosamund did her best to stifle a giggle, and then realised that it had been a long time since she had felt able to laugh.

'Tell me! Tell me what happened,' insisted Diana, and then, realising that she was making an unrealistic demand on her companion, 'I mean, as much as you can.'

Rosamund explained in the vaguest terms about having been part of an operation in occupied France, and having got back safely, which had not been the case with all of her compatriots.

'God! We're so lucky to have you back!' Diana leaned across the table and squeezed Rosamund's hand. 'We must order. Are you happy with whatever they suggest?'

'Of course. I've always liked rabbit. And carrot cake.'

'And Harry?' Diana asked. 'Any news of him?'

At this Rosamund's eyes began to fill with tears, and she found herself unable to speak.

'Oh God!' said Diana. 'Don't tell me he's been killed.'

Rosamund shook her head and reached into her handbag for a lace-edged handkerchief, which smelled of Aunt Venetia's perfume. It was nestled beside the letter Harry had written to her before she had left for France. She was not sure she wanted it now, but had not the heart to remove it and either destroy it or hide it away. To do that would be to pretend that nothing had ever happened between them, and that would be just too much to bear.

Diana waited patiently for the explanation that she hoped would come.

'He's very much alive,' confirmed Rosamund.

'Thank the Lord for that!' exclaimed Diana. 'Have you seen him?'

'Oh, yes; I've seen him.'

Diana sat wide-eyed, waiting for further elaboration.

Rosamund added, 'I can't tell you much; you know that.'

'Yes, but if you can't trust me, who can you trust?'

'That's just the point; I don't know who I can trust any more.'

'You can trust Harry, surely? When did you last see him?'

'Yesterday.'

A white-aproned waiter came to the table to take their order. Diana blurted out quickly that they would be happy with the rabbit, along with two glasses of something alcoholic, which they were clearly going to need.

'Beer, madam?'

'Beer will be fine.' Having dismissed the waiter as speedily as her good manners would allow, Diana leaned forward in her chair and confirmed, 'You saw him *yesterday*?'

Rosamund nodded and blew her nose before replacing the

handkerchief in her bag and returning to the conversation. 'Oh, Diana! I hardly know what to think any more.'

'Now look! You and I both work in a business where the least said the better. It's a business where we learn never to tell anybody anything. But now and again we have to let things out to somebody – in whatever vague terms we care to couch them – or we'd simply eat away at ourselves and pop off.'

The explanation was so very Diana-ish that Rosamund was forced to smile and ask, 'How can you eat yourself away and pop off at the same time?'

'Don't nitpick. You know what I mean.'

Rosamund took a deep breath. 'What do you think of people who work for both sides?'

Diana raised an eyebrow. 'Double agents?'

Rosamund nodded.

'It all depends.'

'On what?'

'On which side has their loyalty.'

'But how can you tell? I mean, how can you tell which side they would be on if . . . if . . .'

'If push came to shove?'

'Yes.'

Diana leaned back in her chair as two glasses of foaming beer were put in front of them. Reading the situation, the waiter departed swiftly. 'You would have to know the person well enough to trust that they were on the right side.'

'The right side being the side you were on?' asked Rosamund.

'Of course.' Diana raised her glass and waited for Rosamund to do the same, before saying, 'You don't know how relieved I am to have you back. I felt responsible for you in a funny kind of way.'

Rosamund took a sip of the rich, bitter beer, which hit the

back of her throat and instantly lifted her spirits. 'Gosh! That's good,' she murmured.

Diana continued. 'Double agents aren't all bad, you know. They are usually extremely clever – they have to be to survive – and some of them are also particularly brave.'

'Brave? Cowardly more like, having all their options covered.'

Diana shook her head emphatically. 'No. Not necessarily.'

'Go on then; convince me. How can a person possibly be brave if they work for both sides?'

'They are brave if they are asked by the side they really believe in to infiltrate enemy territory and pass themselves off as disaffected in order to gain the confidence of the enemy, with the aim of passing back information to the side they are really on. That makes them far more patriotic and brave than someone who simply operates for one side. They put their life at risk; if the enemy ever discovers that they are not what they seem, they will face certain death, probably after a dreadful ordeal at the hands of their captors. The Germans don't just pop you in a prison for the duration of the war, you know; they have means – ghastly means – of extracting the information they want.'

Rosamund looked at Diana meaningfully and said, 'I know.'

Diana was about to launch off again and then noticed the expression on her friend's face. She sat perfectly still for a moment. 'Oh my God!' There was a pause, before she added, 'You've been there, haven't you?'

'Yes.'

Again, Diana reached across and clasped Rosamund's hand. 'I am so sorry. I had no idea. Was it hell?'

'I wasn't tortured, if that's what you mean.' She thought of Harry's hands around her neck and shuddered. 'At least not much. I escaped before they got round to that. But, yes, it was as close to hell as I've been, if you discount losing my parents and Celine.'

'I feel so crass. So stupid. Ros, I am so sorry, I never really thought . . .'

'It doesn't matter; really it doesn't.'

Diana lowered her voice and spoke in a whisper. 'But Harry. Are you saying he's a double agent?'

Rosamund looked down at the table. 'You know I can't say that.'

'Yes, I know you can't say it. But I know that you could think it.'

Chapter 33

LONDON

CHRISTMAS 1941

'We have to distrust each other. It's our only defense
against betrayal.'

Tennessee Williams, *Camino Real*, 1953

She could not recall ever seeing Lord Belgate look so happy –
like a favourite uncle who is the life and soul of the Christmas
party. His face had lost its customary pallor and he was enjoying
a particularly fine glass of Taylor's vintage port at the end of
the meal, which, by Mrs Heffer's standards, was exceptionally
gastronomic – roast chicken and roast potatoes followed by
apple pie and cream.

They had retired to the drawing room, and Rosamund was
sitting on the sofa next to the man responsible for her wartime
travels as Lady Belgate and Aunt Venetia were discussing the
latest news on the domestic front, in particular the lack of
decorative Christmas wrapping – prohibited thanks to attempts
by His Majesty's Government to save paper.

'I'm giving National Savings Certificates to all my friends in the hope that they will take the hint,' said Lady Belgate.

'Very patriotic,' commented Aunt Venetia.

Charles Belgate glanced at his wife and smiled. 'She does her bit,' he confided in Rosamund. 'Though not quite as well as you have done yours.'

'You know then?'

Charles Belgate nodded. 'I know everything. Now.'

'But you won't tell Aunt Venetia? The details, I mean.'

He looked at her sideways and said, 'In our business we don't tell anybody anything, do we?'

'No. Of course not. Silly of me; only I don't want her to worry about me, that's all.'

'I think you're a little late for that, Rosamund.' He patted her hand. 'We all worried about you.' Then, anxious that his tactility should not be misinterpreted, he added, 'Some of us felt particularly responsible.'

Rosamund smiled and took a sip of her wine. 'You weren't really responsible, you know. I am my own person. I can make my own decisions.'

'Yes, but it was I who encouraged you in that direction.'

'You opened my eyes to what I could do. Yes, it was dangerous, but if I hadn't gone, then I would have stayed here feeling powerless and guilty at letting others take the risks, and that's no way to endure a war.'

'They also serve who only stand and wait. That's what Milton said.'

'Yes. But Milton was blind and I am not blind to everything that goes on around me.'

Charles Belgate could feel the conversation begin to take an uncomfortable turn. 'Well, there you are. You're back safely, that's the most important thing – for your Aunt Venetia in particular. And for me.' He smiled at her and she could see the genuine relief in his face.

'Can I ask you something?' she enquired.

'Of course. Anything you like.'

'Hawksmoor.'

Charles Belgate's eyebrows rose, and then he said, very slowly, 'Yes?'

'He is what I think he is, isn't he?'

The old man frowned. 'Now what am I supposed to say to that?'

'I need to know, that's all. I need to know that he is not . . .'

'A traitor?'

Rosamund nodded.

Charles Belgate put down his glass and said, 'Shall we go for a stroll to the window? I don't suppose we shall see much but we'll be out of earshot over there . . .'

The two of them rose and crossed the room to the tall, wide windows that by day offered a view over the war-battered countenance of Eaton Square. Lord Belgate eased the curtains apart slightly and gazed out over the darkened scene, devoid of street lights, and said, 'The essence of our operations is secrecy; you know that. The less each of us knows, the better for national security.'

'But some of us know more than others,' cut in Rosamund. 'And, having hopefully proved our worth, we want to be sure we are not misinterpreting things.'

'Just so. Point taken. Harry Napier – Hawksmoor – you should know, is not a traitor. He had perhaps the most difficult job in my department. I say "my department" without any claim to ownership, since I am retired, and as far as the rest of the world is concerned, I fill my days doing not very much. But

I help where I can. Felpham is the front man and I am nothing more than a backroom boy, really.

'Hawksmoor was asked to undertake the most dangerous of missions – to pass himself off as a disaffected British national with a fine grasp of languages who was prepared to work for the Abwehr – German intelligence – while in reality reporting back to us any information he managed to obtain. He did not have to accept the role – in fact, I did my best to discourage him. He's a sound chap with a promising future in front of him. Felpham was adamant that because of his unimpeachable character and his linguistic facilities, he was the only man for the job and so I bowed to his wishes. Hawksmoor insisted that he was prepared to take the risk – not least to his reputation.'

'Who knows what he has been doing?' asked Rosamund.

'Only those who need to. But I have to tell you that his previous boss is very impressed with him.'

'You mean the man in charge of the royal stamp collection?'

'No. I mean the man who *owns* the royal stamp collection. The King.'

'Oh. I see . . .'

'Now he's back, of course, and it is unlikely he will be able to continue in the role, thanks to the nature of his escape.'

'You mean, because he got me . . . us . . . out . . . ?'

'He felt that he could not carry on doing the job he was commissioned to do and see someone he . . . had feelings for . . . lose her life. Anyone who is captured and who they know to be guilty of sabotage rarely escapes death. It's as simple as that.'

'So he blew his cover in order to save me?'

'Couched in such dramatic colloquial terms, yes.'

'And you don't regard him as a traitor?'

'My dear girl, I regard him as one of the bravest and most

patriotic men I have ever met. A man who is prepared not only to risk his life for his country but also his reputation. Those who operate on both sides are generally considered to be of dubious probity and not especially trustworthy. Hawksmoor knew all this and yet, when it was explained to him what he could achieve – by passing false information to the enemy – he chose to put his own safety and honour on the line. A man who does that is either damned stupid or exceptionally brave. I don't see Harry Napier – er, Hawksmoor – falling into the former category. Do you?'

Rosamund shook her head. She stood silently for a moment, looking out of the window across the darkened square, then asked, 'Is Sir Patrick Felpham annoyed?'

'That one of his best agents pulled out of a valuable mission in order to save a single operative? Yes, he is a bit. But he also realises that someone who manages to do that sort of job and still retain a degree of humanity towards the people around him deserves respect.'

'What will he do now?'

'Hawksmoor? Well, his days as a double agent are probably over. As you put it, his "cover is blown" – certainly in that neck of the woods. We can still use him in a desk job, of course, though I suspect that he will not be terribly happy at the prospect.'

'So I've really rather scuppered his chances?'

'You may have scuppered his chances of doing the job he did, but you are also probably the person who saved his life. In the same way that he saved yours. I'd say you were pretty even, wouldn't you?'

'Perhaps. I'm not really sure.'

'The hawk and the nightingale – always an uneasy relationship,' murmured Lord Belgate.

'I'm sorry?'

'He is Hawksmoor and you are Christiane de Rossignol. Because of your penchant for red ink, I always referred to you as "The Scarlet Nightingale". Silly, really. Blame it on an old man's romantic nature.' And with that he rose, kissed her on both cheeks, gathered up his wife and bade Rosamund and her aunt a fond farewell.

Chapter 34

LONDON

APRIL 1942

'For whatsoever from one place doth fall
Is with the tide unto another brought.
For there is nothing lost that may be found, if sought.'

Edmund Spenser, 'The Faerie Queene', 1590

Christmas came and went in rather an anticlimactic fashion, the initial elation of survival and the seasonal festivities gradually giving way to a feeling of settled resignation, though that resignation was not without its share of gratitude.

Much to her aunt's relief, Rosamund was offered a job translating documents in Baker Street, and while she originally would have baulked at such a pedestrian pursuit after the heightened atmosphere of the operation in Sochaux, she was happy to endure the quiet life – for the foreseeable future, at least.

In her room at night as winter turned slowly and reluctantly into spring, she would play over the events of the previous few months, which had now begun to take on an air of unreality.

She wondered what they were all doing now – like Thierry

and Paulette, for instance. Were they together? Had they known each other for some time, or was their closeness something which had developed with unexpected rapidity? How could Thierry continue to operate in France now that he was known to the Gestapo? He would have a new identity, and new papers, of course – the Resistance were adept at arranging that – but he would have to change his appearance. She tried to imagine him with a beard, and then stopped herself from taking this futile exercise any further. She told herself to regard the whole event – including their night of passion – as an episode in her life that was now closed. It could be learned from, of course – it *must* be learned from – but in spite of its intensity, it was over and unlikely to be repeated.

Then her thoughts would turn to Eric; dear, straightforward Eric, who had been too trusting for his own good. An honest-to-goodness Lancastrian whose idea of a good meal was a mug of sweet tea and a pork pie. Poor Eric, who had imagined, to his enduring credit, that everyone on the same side would have the same goals and a degree of loyalty to those with whom they served. She remembered laughing at his down-to-earth senti-ments and being baffled by his ability to send the most complex messages by, as he would put it, 'twiddling his knobs'. His communication skills had not let him down, but something else had – his openness and trusting nature. How dreadfully unfair.

Frequently Rosamund would wake up in a cold sweat, having heard in her sleep the screams that emanated from the room at the end of the corridor in Montbéliard. She would be fighting for breath and her nightdress wringing wet, and the only way to banish the visions was to change her clothes, sit down at her dressing table and write something in her journal; something so divorced from war and conflict that it took her mind off the sordid realities of the past few months. The red ink, too, was brighter on the page than the black or blue-black variety and did its own bit to lift her spirits. Not so much a Scarlet Nightingale now, she thought, but a rather dowdy flightless bird with an uncertain future.

As a nod to Celine and the future together they had been denied, she wrote short stories set in France. Not war-torn France, but a peaceful France where the sun shone and the sea glistened on the southern coast. In the France of her imagination, there was a villa with a garden that ran down to the Mediterranean sea – a rocky garden through which palm trees and aloes, oleanders and olives pushed their brave stems to bask in the summer sun. Crickets hummed their song in the warmth of midday, and above the baked earth the air was redolent of lavender and rosemary. There were parasols and awnings and leisurely meals in the company of handsome young men, most of whom were tall and dark and slender and . . . oh, how she missed him.

She would frequently find her pen poised above the page, her eyes staring into the middle distance as she thought of Harry and wondered where he might be and what he was doing. Then she would get up and cross the room to her bed, slipping between the sheets and using the imagery of the man who had saved her life as a comforting distraction from the more disturbing products of a fevered imagination.

She had not liked to ask where Harry was or what he was doing, and she doubted that anyone would tell her if she had. Lord Belgate never mentioned him again; never mentioned the events that had so dominated her life. It was as if the vow of silence had been renewed; hear all, see all and say nothing. All she could console herself with was the fact that Harry knew where she lived and would contact her when the time was right if, indeed, it ever was. But right for whom? For him? For her? She had hardly been encouraging on their journey back from France. In the back of that large black car she had made her feelings quite clear. How could he possibly assume that she would want to see him again? And then, one day in April, a letter arrived at 29, Eaton Square. Rosamund recognised the handwriting, and took the small envelope up to her room and laid it on the window seat. She stared at it for fully half an hour before opening it carefully with a paper knife, then unfolding and reading the single sheet it contained:

My Dear Rosamund,

You have probably forgotten about me after all this time. I gather you are now office bound. They wanted to do the same with me, but I am afraid I resisted and am about to be sent on another mission where I am hopeful of not being recognised. If you felt you could see me before I went, I would be so grateful. I know you thought so little of me on our return to Blighty after our last encounter, but I hope that time has healed the rift somewhat and that you realise that my motives were all for the best. The last thing I wanted to do was hurt you – either physically or emotionally. I worry that you may never understand that.

If you can meet me in that little French restaurant at the end of Maiden Lane on Thursday evening – say at around 6.30 p.m. – we could have a quick catch-up before I depart.

I expect nothing of you, but did not want to leave on bad terms and without saying goodbye.

Yours, as ever,
Harry

She did not think twice about meeting him. She just hoped he had not given up on her. Walking to the restaurant, she could remember the last time she had felt so apprehensive, although that was for completely different reasons.

He was already there when she arrived, sitting at a table in the corner. He was the same Harry, but his face was more careworn than she remembered; more tired and weary. And then when he saw her, his eyes lit up and he smiled, giving her hope that she was not alone in her sentiments and that, perhaps, he still harboured some warm feelings towards her.

He stood up, leaned over the table and kissed her on the cheek. She handed her hat, coat and gloves to the waiter and sat down opposite him.

For some moments neither of them spoke, each looking at the other as though in some kind of trance.

Then he said, 'I was not sure you would come.'

'I was not sure you would ever ask me to,' replied Rosamund. 'Not after the way I spoke to you when we came back from France.'

'It was difficult,' he offered. 'You didn't know what was going on. And when I had to hurt you . . . simply so that they did not suspect . . . I thought I would rather give up and just confess. But I knew that was not the way to survive – for either of us. I had to make sure that as far as you were concerned, I was Otto Koenig.'

Rosamund did her best to lighten the moment. 'Not a favourite name of mine: Otto. What made you choose it?'

'It was chosen for me. Along with Koenig.'

'Rather appropriate bearing in mind your former employer.'

'Very quick of you. Yes. But I can't say I felt like either an Otto or a King . . .'

'Ours not to reason why . . .' she murmured.

'No.'

The waiter arrived with two glasses of wine.

'Goodness!' said Rosamund.

'I thought you wouldn't mind,' said Harry. 'I twisted their arm and when they found out it was for you – well, a lady – they managed to find something half decent in their depleted cellar.'

'It will set you back a bit,' said Rosamund, thinking out loud.

'Oh, you're worth it.' Harry grinned.

'You think so?'

'I know so.' He raised his glass. 'Here's to . . .'

'What?' she asked.

'Whatever you want it to be.'

They both took a sip of the wine and Harry remarked, 'Not bad. Better than beer . . . or water.'

'It's very nice,' said Rosamund. She was nervous of spoiling the moment, of saying the wrong thing. It was still not clear whether Harry was simply saying goodbye or . . . something more.

'So you are going on another mission,' she said softly.

His look was apprehensive. 'Yes.'

'In spite of . . . the way the last one ended.'

'I couldn't bear the thought of being stuck behind a desk.'

'You could have joined a regiment,' she said, then stopped short, worried that she had implied he was in some way cowardly.

Harry did not acknowledge the unintentional slight, but said, 'I offered to, but they wouldn't hear of it. Said I had talents they could still use.'

'But at a desk.'

'Yes. So I struck a deal with them and they found me . . . well, a job that would let me travel.'

Rosamund took another sip of the rich red burgundy. 'And I don't suppose you'll tell me where?'

Harry shook his head. 'You suppose right.'

'But surely you will be at risk after what happened in Montbéliard? Won't they be looking for you?'

'I won't be going back to France. I'll be going to Germany, and I'll have a change of identity – and appearance. You'd be surprised what a beard can do for a man.'

'Don't joke!'

'I'm not joking, I'm afraid. I have trusted contacts, which is why I have to go rather than anyone else.'

'You really are a glutton for punishment, aren't you?'

'Not really. I just know I wouldn't be able to live with myself if I call it quits now and push a pen for the rest of my life.'

'Funny.'

'What do you mean?'

'I can't think of anything better than pushing a pen for the rest of my life. Though not behind a desk in some government department.'

'Where then?'

'In the south of France.'

Harry smiled. 'Are you serious?'

'Completely. I've been writing. Short stories. I have this dream that one day I will be writing them in a villa in the south of France.'

Harry leaned back in his chair. On his face there was a look of surprise, bordering on disbelief.

'What's the matter?' asked Rosamund. 'What's so odd about that?'

'Nothing; nothing at all. It's just that . . . I didn't expect you to say that.'

Rosamund smiled. 'I'm glad I can still surprise you.'

Harry looked thoughtful. 'The Frenchman, Thierry Foustier. What was he like?'

'Officially or unofficially?'

'Both.'

'Officially, very efficient, very focussed, quite inspiring.'

'And unofficially?'

'Very dishy, very French and . . .' she shrugged and hesitated as if searching for a suitable description.

'Is this where I stop asking questions?'

'Probably, yes.'

Harry smiled. 'I don't mind.'

'Liar.'

'Well, yes, I do mind but . . . I don't blame you . . .'

'For what?' she asked, with a note of mock annoyance in her voice.

'For surrendering to his charms.'

'Well, thank you for that. I'm very grateful.' There was an admonishing tone in her voice, which served to hide her embarrassment and guilt at having, in Harry's words, 'surrendered to Thierry's charms'. At least she knew now that he would not be shocked to discover that such was the case. She felt a weight lift, and regarded Harry's attitude as a kind of tacit forgiveness for anything that might have happened in France.

'What do *you* know about him?' asked Rosamund.

'Not much. I know that he had a bit of a reputation as a lady's man.'

'And where is he now? Do you know?'

Harry shrugged. 'Out there somewhere, being someone else, as I shall be soon.'

Rosamund saw the light in his eyes. 'You're quite determined, aren't you?'

'Yes. Does that surprise you?'

'Oh, I've become used to you surprising me.'

'Can I surprise you again?'

'How?'

'By asking you to marry me.'

Rosamund simply did not see it coming. Before she could answer, he added, 'If you can forgive me for what happened in France. And if you don't think I am the lowest of the low who bats for both sides and whose loyalties are divided. I can only tell you that my loyalties are indeed divided, but they are divided between my country and you.'

Now it was Rosamund's turn to sit back in her chair and listen wide-eyed as Harry continued: 'It's a long story, but not as long as it could have been. Normally it takes an age to infiltrate their intelligence system. My route was speeded up because we had an agent in France who had been passing us good information. But he had had enough. He wanted out. We couldn't countenance losing the valuable information he was passing on. So he introduced me as a fellow disenchanted Brit who could see which way the wind was blowing and who wanted to be on the winning side. I was given the identity of a known British dissident – English mother, German father – with all that amazing paperwork and background details that only our department can produce – and airlifted into Germany. The Abwehr interrogated me and I managed to convince them of my loyalty to the cause. At first they were suspicious, but The Outfit managed to concoct a scenario where I could prove myself. I was to sabotage an important British target – the De Havilland factory. I then provided photographic evidence of my success and that was enough for them to believe I was on their side.'

'And the damage?'

'All mocked up. The factories carried on producing. Then the Abwehr realised that thanks to my languages, I could be more use in interrogating suspected traitors to the Nazi cause. This suited The Outfit because it meant I would be privy to more information.

'During all this there was never a moment when my patriotism wavered – in spite of the best endeavours of the Abwehr. And there was never a moment when my love for you faltered. The thought of one day being with you kept me going, and then when Doris told me that you had been captured – at least I figured that it must be you from the name and the mission – I knew I had to do something. I managed to sideline the man who had been charged with the task and take his place, but I couldn't see how I could get through it all without completely blowing it, not only because of the bloody Gestapo, but also because of you. What would you think? What *could* you think? Suppose you blew the gaff because you thought I was a traitor? But there was no way out for me and I knew I would have to find some way of getting you out of there alive. So I made up my mind that whatever happened I would do my damnedest to help you escape.'

Rosamund leaned forward and put her hands over his. 'And you did.' She looked into his eyes. 'And then we flew home in a plane and got into a car and I refused to speak to you.'

'You weren't to know. As far as you were concerned, you didn't know whether I was Otto Koenig or Harry Napier.'

'I should never have doubted you.'

'Don't be too hard on yourself. You had been locked up for days and deprived of food and sleep; I could hardly expect you to greet me like an old friend and throw your arms around me. Now that would have been interesting. I'd like to see what Obersturmführer Schneider would have made of that.' He paused. 'But you haven't answered my question. Will you marry me?'

'Of course I'll marry you, Otto or Harry or Hawksmoor or whatever your name is. Like a shot I will marry you.'

'In spite of the fact that I have to go away again?'

Rosamund squeezed his hands between hers. 'Must you?' she

asked, with the hint of a break in her voice. 'If I say "yes", won't that make you stay?'

'There's one last thing that I can do.'

'And nobody else can?'

'Not really. Nobody else knows all the ins and outs. It's nothing dramatic. Just the tidying up of loose ends. It shouldn't take long, and then I'll be back for good.'

'So how long do we have together before you go?'

Harry lowered his eyes. 'A week.'

'Oh God! I wait all this time for you and then all I have is one week?'

Just six days after our reconciliation, Harry and I were married at Caxton Hall registry office in London. Aunt Venetia tactfully went to stay with friends and gave us the house to ourselves. We had one beautiful night alone at 29, Eaton Square. I will never forget it. Not ever. It was filled with so much love on both sides – things were forgiven and misunderstandings clarified. We were starting the rest of our lives with a clean slate – knowing each other's strengths and weaknesses, and asking no more of each other than honesty and kindness and the purest kind of love. I gave Harry the letter I had written in reply to his own, and he promised to keep it with him always. The following morning, with tears in my eyes, I saw him off at King's Cross Station. I waved and waved until my view of him was lost in the steam and the smoke. It was the last time I saw him.

Chapter 35

LONDON

JUNE 1942

'Let aeroplanes circle moaning overhead
Scribbling in the sky the message: He is dead.'

W.H. Auden, 'Funeral Blues', 1938

It was two months after Harry had left for Germany that Lord Belgate broke the news of his death at the hands of the Gestapo. One day later he resigned from his post. No one saw Rosamund for days. Not Diana, not Mrs Heffer, not her aunt Venetia, no one. Trays were left untouched outside her door, until, one day, anxious to check that her niece had not attempted anything foolish in the light of her loss, Aunt Venetia hailed a local window cleaner and had Ned Heffer climb his ladder to look through Rosamund's bedroom window. The curtains were drawn, but one of the windows was open slightly and Ned was able to part the fabric and report that the body lying on the bed showed signs of life. Faint signs, but signs nevertheless.

There was no funeral. There was no body. At least when her

parents and Celine had died, they had some kind of closure. Rosamund had none. Her husband of twenty-four hours had been taken from her in the cruellest way possible.

The sense of *déjà vu* was palpable. She had been here before, but this kind of bereavement was different. She had previously lost people she loved, but now she had lost not only a person she loved, but the only being on earth with whom she had ever been 'in love'.

She understood that now, as she compared her feelings for Thierry with those she had for Harry, and knew, immediately, that they had little in common. Her passion for the Frenchman, who was undeniably attractive, was provoked and heightened by circumstances and a common bond. Now that bond existed no more, the feelings had subsided; their shallowness and evanescence clearly evident. But her love for Harry had endured throughout her time in France, and would continue for as long as she lived. Of that she was certain. In no one else's company had she ever felt so secure, so complete and so elevated. In the few brief times they were together, she had hung on Harry's every word, noticed every twitch of his facial muscles, drowned in the oceanic greenness of his eyes. And now he was gone. How could it be possible to love someone so much, so deeply, after such a short relationship? But love him she did, and the grief at their parting was so profound that she could not even manage to weep. Her heart simply tightened in her chest; her jaw ached from being clenched.

Rosamund's emergence from solitude, when it came, took Aunt Venetia by surprise. She came downstairs from her bedroom at 11 a.m. one late June morning, her hair tied back, her face pale and clear of make-up. 'I thought I'd go for a walk,' she said.

Aunt Venetia could only say softly, 'Good idea.' And then,

by way of adding to what might pass for normality, 'Would you like a little lunch on your return?'

'That would be nice. Thank you.' The small voice was so without strength or feeling that Aunt Venetia found herself unable to say any more. She simply watched as Rosamund pulled on a jacket and left by the front door.

She cared not where she walked, for her eyes were unseeing and vacant. But some unknown force willed her on. She walked and walked, all the way to Hyde Park, where the green of the grass and the sparkle of the Serpentine demonstrated that life outside her own shrunken world was still going on.

She sat on a bench beside the water, and for the first time since Harry's death, with her face buried in her hands lest others should see her grief, she wept uncontrollably. For a full half hour, her now-frail body wracked with sobs, and as she shed her tears, passers-by looked away respectfully, imagining – correctly in this case – that yet another loved one had been lost to the war.

A distant clock chimed the hour and, without looking at her watch, she rose, wiped her eyes on her sleeve, and walked back unseeing to Eaton Square.

Slipping off her jacket in her room, washing her face at the basin and doing her best to subdue the rawness of her reddened eyes, she walked downstairs to the dining room, where a neat table for two had been set in the window. Aunt Venetia was already there and looked up and smiled at her charge, motioning her to sit opposite. On her plate was an official-looking letter. Rosamund put it to one side and took a triangle of toast from the small silver dish, from which she took the tiniest bite.

'Aren't you going to open it?' her aunt could not resist asking.

Rosamund shook her head and murmured, 'Probably from work.'

'But it doesn't look like work.'

Rosamund pushed the envelope across the table. 'You open it.'

Aunt Venetia took her butter knife and slit the flap of the envelope neatly from one side to the other, then she unfolded the two pages within and read their contents silently. Her perusal concluded, she did not fold up the letter, but pushed it towards Rosamund. 'It's not from work, it's from Harry's solicitor. Your solicitor . . . Mrs Napier.'

The tears sprang once more to Rosamund's eyes as she said, 'No one's ever called me that. I don't suppose anyone will now.'

'Of course they will,' said Aunt Venetia. 'That's who you are.'

'Still?'

'Always. Well, until . . .'

Rosamund shook her head. 'Always. There's no "until".' She dabbed at her eyes with the lace-edged handkerchief that Aunt Venetia passed across the table, and tried to focus on the letter. She read both pages in silence and then looked up and said, 'Did you know about this?'

'I knew about its existence, but I did not know whether it was still in the family. Harry's family have had a house in the south of France for years. I suppose it would have come to Harry when his parents died.'

'I see now why he looked surprised,' murmured Rosamund, her eyes unfocussed and her mind elsewhere.

'Sorry, dear?'

'Before he left, I told Harry that all I wanted to do one day was to live in a house in the south of France and write novels.'

'Well, now you can!'

'Not now!' she said wearily. 'There's a war on.'

'But afterwards,' said her aunt reassuringly.

'You think there will be an afterwards? Do you think this war will ever end? Do you think we might actually win?'

Aunt Venetia laid down the soup spoon she had just picked up with the intention of sampling Mrs Heffer's latest culinary flight of fancy and said matter-of-factly, 'Of course we will. Thanks to people like you and Harry. You are in the throes of grief, Rosamund – deep, impenetrable grief. But that grief will ease, believe me. It will never pass away entirely – to hope for such is unreasonable and unrealistic. But when it does subside a little, you will find a way of carrying on. We all do. We have to. The alternative does not bear thinking about.' Aunt Venetia dipped her spoon in the rich brown broth, tasted it, and laid it down once more. 'And neither does this soup,' she muttered before continuing: 'If we do not approach life positively, if we succumb to the naysayers and the defeatists, then we might just as well throw in the towel now, because such negativity becomes a self-fulfilling prophecy. I am not a triumphalist, or a tub-thumping jingoistic warmonger – I had great reservations about Mr Churchill's approach at the beginning of this ghastly war, you may remember – but I cannot and will not be bowed down by a bunch of thugs who want to rule the world by bully-boy tactics. The only way to beat bullies is to stand up to them, and that – as you have discovered – is often painful and can have tragic consequences.'

Aunt Venetia had got into her stride now, and Rosamund found herself leaning back in her chair as the tirade continued.

'When others in this country are determined to fight for the people and the land they love, it ill-behoves the rest of us to tell them they are wasting their time, that the struggle is not worth the reward. They deserve our loyalty and our admiration; anything less is insulting and I for one will not countenance such appalling behaviour and . . . bad manners.'

Rosamund felt the tears springing once more to her eyes. 'Oh Auntie!' she said. 'You are wonderful!'

Her passion spent, Aunt Venetia slumped back into her chair. 'Well, there we are. I've said my piece. I'm sorry if I was a little too emphatic but . . .'

'No. Don't apologise. I'm sorry I'm so defeatist at the moment. It's just that I did love Harry so very much and I simply can't believe I am not going to see him again.'

'I know, I know.' Aunt Venetia leaned over and stroked her niece's hand as it rested on the table. 'We'll get there, you and I. We just need to stick together. And one day – as the song says, "when this lousy war is over" – we shall find your house in the south of France and move in.'

'You think so?'

'Oh, yes, dear. It was what Harry wanted, wasn't it?'

'Yes.' Rosamund smiled. 'I think it was.'

Chapter 36

VILLA DELPHINE,
SAINT-JEAN-CAP-FERRAT

'You can love someone so much . . . but you can never
love people as much as you can miss them.'

John Green, *An Abundance of Katherines*, 2006

EPILOGUE

*Although he never came home, Harry has lived on in my heart
and will continue to do so. In life, if one is lucky enough to
love as I have loved, and to have been loved equally deeply in
return, then one is truly blessed.*

*I had always thought that true love must take time to
mature, and in some cases that is true. I have seen enough
brief and passionate affairs to know that such heightened
emotions seldom last. But there are also relationships that*

are founded on something greater; a common bond that is stronger than mere passion and not always easy to define. Shared values, a shared sense of humour and a willingness to work at a relationship are all vital, but there must also be a spark – an indefinable element – which might not be in any way physical. It is not so much chemical as spiritual: the purest, the deepest and the most all-consuming love. I have known it, and while losing it might be the most harrowing thing on earth, to have experienced it is something that I would never wish to forgo.

My aunt and I discovered that the house in the south of France, in spite of being occupied by German and Italian officers during the war – its garden becoming overgrown and its swimming pool turning into a pea-green pond filled with fallen leaves and litter – had been watched over by an elderly couple next door. They had – by some means or other – managed to prevent it from becoming a complete ruin.

On the one flat and cultivatable area at the top of the rocky slope, I think they grew food for the war effort, rather as we – Ned Heffer in particular – supported 'Dig for Victory'. Mrs Heffer and her brother retired to a tiny cottage in Broadstairs after the war, where she is still probably making her special soups. Now that the war is over, she must be enjoying a limitless supply of unlikely ingredients.

Harry did not leave a lot of money – the villa here was his main asset – and Aunt Venetia had only a long lease on 29, Eaton Square, which ran out just after the war. So as a result, we threw in our lot together. We moved to the Villa Delphine in 1948, having had one or two alterations made. My aunt was rather elderly by this time and spent much time in bed, but she was as sparky as ever – most of the time railing against the injustices of life. I never imagined that she would want to leave Eaton Square, but having lived through the war and experienced some of the bitterest winters in living memory, the prospect of a milder climate appealed to her – and she had several friends with houses down here, vacated during the occupation but reclaimed afterwards, and so her social life could continue.

She still held court from time to time; we had her 'little dinners' on the terrace, where she could still feel as though she was facilitating all kinds of diplomatic liaisons which no one was unkind enough to suggest were not remotely necessary.

She was a great strength and solace to me in the years after Harry's death, and in a funny sort of way I feel close to him here, and close to the spirit of Celine, who talked so many times about the beauty of this part of France. How I would love to be able to show it to her. I cannot look at the sea in its summer aquamarine glory without thinking of the engagement ring upon her finger.

As Aunt Venetia predicted, I have come to terms with my loss – in some way, though not completely – and I am grateful for the brief time I had with Harry, whose honour and loyalty I continue to champion, even though there are one or two people who have suggested that his activities during the war were questionable. I know for a fact that he was brave and selfless and loved his country every bit as much as he loved me. There are few certainties in this life, but that I know to be one of them.

Aunt Venetia died peacefully in her sleep in her ninety-first year and is buried in the Protestant cemetery in Cannes. I feel that somehow I have turned into her over the years; I have certainly channelled her spirit and zest for life. When all I wanted to do was die, she taught me how to live, to enjoy life to the full, to take each day as it comes, to not be embarrassed about treating oneself, and to help others wherever possible (and if that involves a nice dinner and fine wine, so much the better. Yes, I think I have definitely turned into my aunt . . .)

As for Thierry, I heard no more of him until one day a caller arrived at the Villa Delphine, and asked for Christiane de Rossignol. It was many years since anyone had called me that. Jonathan, an English boy who had worked for us at the villa since leaving school, came out on to the terrace overlooking the sea where my aunt and I were enjoying afternoon tea – my morning's work (I always write in the morning) having been completed.

'A gentleman to see you, madam,' he said, indicating the open French windows. I walked through them into the drawing room, and there he was; the same Thierry I had said goodbye to more than ten years before. He looked just the same. He had a few more wrinkles, perhaps, but the tanned complexion, the smile, the floppy hair and the piercing blue eyes were all as I remembered. He was wearing a crumpled cream linen suit and an open-necked shirt that perfectly matched his eyes.

'Hello,' I said, in English.

He smiled that smile and just for a moment I was back in Fesches-le-Châtel looking at him across the breakfast table. In a split second, the years fell away and it all came flooding back – the quickening of the heartbeat, the fluttering in the stomach, everything.

'You came back to France?' he said.

'Yes. I came back.'

'But you did not tell me.' He looked crestfallen.

'I didn't know where you were, and anyway, there didn't seem any point.'

He shrugged. 'Why not?'

'Oh, I think you know.'

He smiled again. I sat down in a chair and motioned for him

to sit in the one opposite, then found myself talking just to stop myself from thinking too much about feelings I had put behind me. 'How is Paulette?'

'Paulette?' He looked genuinely puzzled, and then the penny dropped. 'Ah, Paulette! Yes. I think she is well. She is married now, I believe.'

'You did not stay together?'

'Alas, no. It did not work out. We were happy for a while and then . . .'

I could imagine the rest, but could not resist asking, 'And you? Are you married?'

'Me?' He laughed. 'No. I am not married. I am, how do you say, a free agent?'

Now it was my turn to smile. 'And you like it that way?'

Again the shrug, the outstretched arms, palms upwards and the mouth turned down at the corners in a resigned expression. 'I fear that when you have loved someone special as deeply as I have, all other comparisons pale into insignificance.'

'Your English gets better and better,' I said, and found it impossible not to smile.

'And you, Christiane? Did you marry your English hero?'

'Yes, I did.'

'And were you happy?'

'We were very happy. For twenty-four hours.'

Thierry looked puzzled.

'He went to Germany the day after we married – his decision – and he was killed two months later.'

'Merde.'

'Yes.'

'And you have not . . . ?'

'No, I have not . . . '

323

His face relaxed a little and the smile began to creep back. 'So you are single once more?' he enquired.

'Technically, yes. But practically, no.'

He tilted his head to one side, the better to ask the unspoken question.

'I live here with my aunt – she is outside on the terrace. I look after her now . . . and she looks after me.'

'But that is such a waste!'

Now it was my turn to shrug.

'Do you remember how it was? Between us?' he asked. 'The spark! The night of passion? The magic?'

'Yes. I remember perfectly,' I said.

'Do you think we might . . . ?'

'No, Thierry. Not now. It was all wonderful. You were wonderful, but you are you and I am me. You don't want to settle down . . .'

'But my chateau in the Garonne. It is still there . . .'

'So why aren't you in it?'

'Because I have no one to share it with.'

The look on his face was so beseeching I could have given in. I could have asked him to stay, thrown myself into his arms, and we could have rushed upstairs to my bedroom and picked up just where we left off ten years before – heaven knows I was lonely enough deep inside for that to be momentarily tempting – but I knew in my heart it could not last. I may write romantic novels but I have never been one to stretch credulity that far. Thierry was a born Gallic lover, destined to roam the earth in search of conquests, pleasing a woman and then, when custom began to stale her variety, moving on – nicely, politely, with that shrug and that winning smile, but he would move on. Thierry was never going to feature in a happy ending – at least, not for the woman who hoped to pin him down.

'*You should know,*' I heard myself saying, '*that I did love you . . . a little. I think I could have loved you more, but you moved on. It's what you do, Thierry. I really couldn't cope with that.*' I got up, anxious to bid him goodbye before I changed my mind and said something that would, in the long-term, only lead to heartbreak.

Thierry rose from his seat as I did and bowed gently before stepping forward and kissing me softly on the cheek. Just the one. Instantly I was back standing beside the plane and the aching void returned. But I stayed strong – I am still not sure how – and walked with him to the front door, avoiding the terrace and the consequent questions from Aunt Venetia.

'*Au revoir,*' I said as we reached the foot of the steps that led up to the villa.

'*Thank you for coming.*'

He smiled that smile one last time and made to leave. Then he turned and said, '*I almost forgot. I have a daughter now. The mother is no longer with me but I do see my little girl from time to time.*'

'*That's nice,*' I said, meaning it.

'*Her name is Christiane.*' And then he was gone.

Life is full of unforeseen ups and downs and I have learned the wisdom of the words carpe diem – seize the day. Aunt Venetia and I had begun our south of France adventure helped by the fact that my first novel was accepted for publication in 1949; it did so well that I was asked to write another one each year. The income was enough to support our modest lifestyle back in those days (modest except for Aunt Venetia's extravagant dinner parties which I did my best to restrain). Now I am lucky to have enough to afford me a very comfortable lifestyle.

As you know, Archie, Diana Molyneux married Billy Belgate

after the war – and that came as a surprise, I can tell you. As a result she was 'well set up', as Aunt Venetia put it. Their elder daughter – your mother – was my goddaughter.

Your great-grandfather Charles Belgate you will not remember, but he was the archetypal English gentleman who rather took a shine to me. It was he who christened me 'The Scarlet Nightingale' on account of my nom de guerre and my predilection for red ink. It was he who gave me the file containing this memoir after the war as a souvenir. If it had not been for your great-grandfather's intervention, I do not know what would have happened to me. He did his best to discourage Harry from returning to the fray, but I cannot blame him for failing on that front.

Harry was always going to fight for King and Country. He worked for the King on the royal stamp collection. Have I mentioned that? I cannot remember now. It was only a part of what he did, really, but he did enjoy it. And I do remember still the smell of that car of his – the Talbot. He was so proud of it, but I sold it after the war. It would have been too painful to hang on to it and, anyway, as you know, I never learned to drive.

I was only twenty-one when I was widowed, and you might assume that I was young enough to get over my bereavement and make a fresh start – certainly after what they used to call 'a respectable period of mourning' – but somehow I never did find anyone who quite measured up to Harry. Oh, there were dalliances with handsome Frenchmen whom I always rather foolishly compared to Thierry. But rather like Thierry himself, none of them seemed to quite match up to Harry. There is great good fortune in meeting the ones you love most when you are young, but incomparable misfortune if they are snatched from you without warning and you spend the rest of your life comparing them to others.

But I am not complaining. I have the happiest of memories and a good life here in a part of the world that I have come to love.

I think of Devonshire a lot, but I know I will never go back there. That countryside, rather like Harry and Thierry, is a part of my life long gone. Rosamund Hanbury is gone, too. When I married I became Rosamund Napier, and I took as my nom de plume *as a novelist the name that Harry bore during his time with the SOE – Rosamund Hawksmoor. By using both his names, I find I can feel more a part of him than if I were just* 'the Widow Napier'.

So there we are. I leave you with no advice about how to live your life, except to live it to the full and to make errors of commission rather than omission so that you never have to say 'what if?'

Grasp life by the scruff of the neck and love it. Love everybody and hang the consequences. You will risk feeling pain and loss and disappointment, but you will also find moments of deep joy which outshine and outlast all the sadness. But only if you take the risks. I took a few myself, and regret none of them.

My only sorrow is that Harry is not beside me as I write. But he remains steadfastly where he has always been – deep in my heart.

Find someone who can occupy that space in yours.

With much love,

Your honorary 'Aunt' Rosamund Hawksmoor.

Do you wish this wasn't the end?

Join us at www.hodder.co.uk, or follow us on
Twitter @hodderbooks to be a part of our community
of people who love the very best in books and reading.

Whether you want to discover more about a book
or an author, watch trailers and interviews, have the
chance to win early limited editions, or simply browse
our expert readers' selection of the very best books,
we think you'll find what you're looking for.

And if you don't,
that's the place to tell us what's missing.

We love what we do, and we'd love you to be part of it.

www.hodder.co.uk

 @hodderbooks

 HodderBooks

 HodderBooks